Praise for
The Kaiju Preservation Society

'Purely entertaining . . . An escapist delight'   *The Times*

'Sheer geeky pleasure from start to finish'   *Financial Times*

'Hugely enjoyable, intelligent and good-humoured fun'
The Guardian

'*Jurassic Park* meets the camaraderie of *Parks and Recreation* in this
wonderfully witty and refreshingly earnest adventure yarn . . . Sure
to delight'   *Publishers Weekly*, starred review

'Scalzi's latest is a wildly inventive take on the kaiju theme'
Booklist, starred review

'Bubbles with . . . banter and snarky humour'   *Kirkus Reviews*

'An inventive, light-hearted, sprightly romp . . . that slyly makes,
along the way, a few sharp points about ethics, friendship, capitalism,
pure scientific research and humanity's duty to other species. It's
guaranteed to go down smooth and leave you grinning and happier
than when you opened its covers'   *Locus Magazine*

'Funny and flippant, *The Kaiju Preservation Society* brings a welcome
dose of impish heart and humour to a story with grand scale and
grand scales'   *SciFiNow*

'Entertaining . . . A huge success'   *SFX*

THE KAIJU PRESERVATION SOCIETY

John Scalzi is one of the most popular and acclaimed SF authors to emerge in the last decade. His debut, *Old Man's War*, won him science fiction's John W. Campbell Award for Best New Writer. His *New York Times* bestsellers include *The Last Colony*, *Fuzzy Nation*, *The End of All Things* and *Redshirts*, which won 2013's Hugo Award for Best Novel. Material from his widely read blog *Whatever* has also earned him two other Hugo Awards. He lives in Ohio with his wife and daughter.

BY JOHN SCALZI

The Interdependency series

The Collapsing Empire
The Consuming Fire
The Last Emperox

The Old Man's War series

Old Man's War
The Ghost Brigades
The Last Colony
Zoe's Tale
The Human Division
The End of All Things

Other Novels

Agent to the Stars
The Android's Dream
The God Engines
Fuzzy Nation
Redshirts
Lock In
Head On
The Kaiju Preservation Society

JOHN SCALZI

THE KAIJU PRESERVATION SOCIETY

TOR

First published 2022 by Tom Doherty Associates

First published in the UK 2022 by Tor

This paperback edition first published 2023 by Tor
an imprint of Pan Macmillan
The Smithson, 6 Briset Street, London EC1M 5NR
EU representative: Macmillan Publishers Ireland Ltd, 1st Floor,
The Liffey Trust Centre, 117–126 Sheriff Street Upper,
Dublin 1, D01 YC43
Associated companies throughout the world
www.panmacmillan.com

ISBN 978-1-5098-3531-7

Copyright © John Scalzi 2022

The right of John Scalzi to be identified as the
author of this work has been asserted by him in accordance
with the Copyright, Designs and Patents Act 1988.

5 7 9 8 6 4

A CIP catalogue record for this book is available from the British Library.

Printed and bound by CPI Group (UK) Ltd, Croydon, CR0 4YY

Visit **www.panmacmillan.com** to read more about all our books
and to buy them. You will also find features, author interviews and
news of any author events, and you can sign up for e-newsletters
so that you're always first to hear about our new releases.

To Alexis Saarela,
my favorite publicist;
and to Matthew Ryan,
who writes the songs

"Jamie Gray!" Rob Sanders popped his head out of his office door and waved at me, grinning. "Come on down. Let's do this thing."

I got up from my workstation and grabbed the tablet with my notes, grinning as well. I glanced over to Qanisha Williams, who gave me a quick fist bump. "Knock him dead," she said.

"Stone dead," I said, and walked into the CEO's office. It was time for my performance review, and I'm not gonna lie, I was going to crush it.

Rob Sanders welcomed me in and motioned me over to his "conversation pit," as he liked to call it, which was four massive, primary-colored beanbags around a low table. The table was one of those ones that had a magnetic bead that dragged around blinding white sand under the glass, making geometric patterns as it did so. Currently the bead was making a swirly pattern. I picked the red beanbag and sank into it, only a little awkwardly. My tablet briefly flopped out of my hand, and I caught it before it skittered off the beanbag and onto the floor. I looked up at Sanders, who was still standing, and smiled. He smiled back, rolled over a standard desk chair and sat in backward, arms crossed over the back, looking down at me.

Oh, I see, CEO power move, very nice, I thought. I wasn't worried about it. I understood how CEO egos worked, and I was prepared to navigate my way through this one. I was here for my six-month performance evaluation from Rob, and I was going to, as previously stated, knock him dead.

"Comfortable?" Rob asked me.

"Supremely," I said. As discreetly as possible, I adjusted my center of gravity so I was no longer listing ever so slightly starboard.

"Good. How long have you been here at füdmüd, Jamie?"

"Six months."

"And how do you feel about your time here?"

"I'm glad you asked, Rob. I feel really good about it. And in fact"—I held up my tablet—"I'd like to spend some time in this session talking about how I think we can improve not just the füdmüd app, but our relationships with restaurants, delivery people, and users. It's 2020 now, and the food delivery app space has matured. We really need to go all out to distinguish ourselves if we want to genuinely compete with Grubhub and Uber Eats and all the others, here in NYC and beyond."

"So you think we can improve?"

"Yeah, I do." I attempted to lean forward in the beanbag and succeeded only in driving my ass farther into its recesses. I rolled with it and just pointed to my tablet. "So, you've heard about this COVID-19 thing."

"I have," Rob allowed.

"I think it's pretty clear we're heading for a lockdown. Here in the city that means people will be getting food deliveries even more than usual. But it also means that restaurants are going to be pinched because they won't be able to do table service. If füdmüd offered to lower our fees in exchange for exclusive listings and delivery service, we'd both make friends with restaurant owners *and* get a leg up on the other apps."

"You want us to lower fees."

"Yes."

"Decrease revenues during a possible pandemic."

"No! See, that's the thing. If we move quickly and lock down, pardon the pun, the popular restaurants, we'll see revenues go up because order traffic will go up. And not just our revenue. Our delivery people—"

"Deliverators."

I shifted in the beanbag. "What?"

"Deliverators. That's what we're calling them now. Clever, right? I thought up the term."

"I thought Neal Stephenson did."

"Who?"

"He's a writer. He wrote *Snow Crash*."

"And that's, what, a *Frozen* sequel?"

"It's a book, actually."

Rob waved his hand dismissively. "If it's not Disney, we won't get sued for it. You were saying?"

"Our, uh, *deliverators* could also see an uptick. We could pay a higher delivery fee to them—not too much." I saw Rob starting to frown here. "Just enough to differentiate ourselves from the other apps. In a gig economy, just a little boost goes a long way. We could actually build some loyalty, which would improve service, which would be another differentiator."

"You want to compete on quality, basically."

"Yes!" I made a pointing gesture, which sank me farther into the beanbag. "I mean, we're already better than the other apps. We just have to drive the point home."

"It'll cost us a little more, but it will be worth it, is where you're going with this."

"I think so. I know, wild, right? But that's the whole point. We'll be where everyone else in the food delivery app space isn't. And by the time they figure out what we're up to, we'll *own* New York City. For starters."

"You have bold ideas, Jamie," Rob said. "You're not afraid to take risks and move the conversation."

I beamed, and set down my tablet. "Thank you, Rob. I think you're right. I took a risk when I left my doctorate program to come work at füdmüd, you know? My friends at the University of Chicago thought I was nuts to pack up and move out to New York to work for a start-up. But it just felt right. I think I'm really making a difference in how people order food."

"I'm glad to hear you say that. Because the reason we're here is to talk about your future with füdmüd. Where best to place you, so you can utilize that passion you so clearly feel."

"Well, *I'm* glad to hear *you* say that, Rob." I tried to move forward again in the beanbag, failed, and decided to risk a small push-up. It realigned the beanbag so I was in a slightly less compacted position, but my tablet slid into the well my body had created. I was now sitting on my tablet. I decided to ignore it. "Tell me how I can serve the company."

"Deliverationing."

I blinked. "What?"

"Deliverationing," Rob repeated. "That's what our deliverators do. They deliverate. So, deliverationing."

"Is that manifestly different from *delivery*?"

"No, but we can't trademark *delivery*."

I changed the subject. "So you want me to head up füdmüd's deliver . . . ationing strategies?"

Rob shook his head. "I think that's too limiting for you, don't you think?"

"I don't understand."

"What I'm saying, Jamie, is that füdmüd needs someone like you on the ground. In the trenches. Giving us intel from the street." He waved out the window. "Real. Gritty. Unvarnished. As only *you* can."

I took a minute to let this sink in. "You want me to be a füdmüd delivery person."

"Deliverator."

"That's not actually a position in the company."

"That doesn't mean it's not important *to* the company, Jamie."

I tried to adjust again, failed again. "Wait—what's going on here, Rob?"

"What do you mean?"

"I thought this was my six-month performance review."

Rob nodded. "In a way, it is."

"But you're telling me you want me to be a delivery per—"

"Deliverator."

"—whatever the *fuck* you want to call it, it's not actually a position with the company. You're laying me off."

"I'm not laying you off," Rob assured me.

"Then what are you doing?"

"I'm presenting you with an exciting opportunity to enrich the füdmüd work experience in an entirely different way."

"A way that doesn't pay me benefits *or* give me health insurance *or* a salary."

Rob tutted at this. "You know that's not true. füdmüd has a reciprocal agreement with Duane Reade that gets our deliverators up to ten percent off selected health products."

"Yeah, all right, we're done," I said. I hefted myself up out of the beanbag, slipped, and fell back on my tablet, cracking the screen in the process. "Perfect."

"Don't worry about that," Rob said, pointing to the tablet as I finally hauled myself out of my seat. "It's company property. You can just leave it when you go."

I flung the tablet over to Rob, who grabbed it. "You're a real asshole," I said. "Just so you know."

"We're going to miss you as part of the füdmüd family, Jamie," Rob said. "But remember, there's always a slot open for you in delivering. That's a promise."

"I don't think so."

"Your choice." He pointed out the door. "Qanisha has your severance paperwork ready to go. If you're still here in fifteen minutes, building security will help you find the door." He got up out of his chair, walked to his desk, dropped the tablet into the trash can there, and pulled out his phone to make a call.

"You *knew*," I said accusingly to Qanisha as I walked up to her. "You knew and you wished me luck *anyway*."

"Sorry," she said.

"Put up your fist."

She did, confused. I punched it, lightly. "There," I said. "I'm taking back that previous solidarity fist bump."

"Fair." She handed me my severance paperwork. "I was also told to tell you that a *deliverator* account has been opened in your name." She said *deliverator* like it hurt her to say it. "You know, just in case."

"I think I'd rather die."

"Don't be hasty, Jamie," Qanisha warned. "That shutdown is coming. And our Duane Reade discount is now up to fifteen percent."

"So that was my day," I said to my roommate Brent. We were in the pathetically small fourth-floor walk-up on Henry Street that I shared with Brent, Brent's boyfriend, Laertes, and a convenient stranger named Reba, who we almost never saw and, if she didn't leave long strands of hair on the shower wall on the daily, might not believe actually existed.

"That's rough," Brent said.

"Firebomb the place," Laertes said, from the room he and Brent shared, where he was playing a video game.

"No one's firebombing anything," Brent yelled back to Laertes.

"Yet," Laertes replied.

"You can't firebomb your way out of every problem," Brent said.

"*You* can't," Laertes called back.

"Don't firebomb the place," Brent said to me, his voice lowered so Laertes wouldn't hear.

"I'm not going to," I promised. "But it's *tempting*."

"So you're looking for something else now?"

"I am, but it's not looking great," I said. "All of New York is in a state of emergency. Everything's closing up. No one's hiring for anything, and what jobs there are won't pay for *this*." I motioned to our crappy fourth-floor walk-up. "I mean, the good news, if you want to call it that, is that my severance payment from füdmüd will pay my share of the rent here for a few months. I might starve, but I won't be homeless at least until August."

Brent looked uncomfortable at that. "What?" I said.

He reached over to the pile of mail on the kitchen table we were sitting at, and picked up a plain envelope. "I assume you didn't see this, then."

I took it and opened it. Inside were ten one-hundred-dollar bills, and a note which read, in its entirety, *Fuck this plague town I am out—R.*

I looked over to where Reba's room was. "She's gone?"

"To the extent she was ever here, yes."

"She's a ghost with an ATM card," Laertes yelled, from the other room.

"Well, this is *great*," I said. "At least she left her last month's rent." I dropped the envelope, the note, and the money on the table, and put my head in my hands. "This is what I get for not putting any of the rest of you on the lease. Don't you two leave, okay?"

"So," Brent said. "About that."

I glanced at him through my fingers. "No."

"Look, Jai—"

"*No.*"

Brent held up his hands. "Look, here's the thing—"

"*Noooooooo,*" I whined, and dropped my head on the table, thunking it nice and hard as I did so.

"Drama won't help," Laertes said, from the bedroom.

"You want to *firebomb* everything," I yelled back at him.

"That's not drama, that's revolution," was his response.

I looked back over to Brent. "Please tell me you're not abandoning me," I said.

"We work in the theater," Brent said. "And it's like you said, everything's shutting down. I don't have any savings, and you know Laertes doesn't either."

"I am *hilariously* broke," Laertes confirmed.

Brent winced at that, then continued. "If things get bad, and they're going to get bad, we can't afford to stay."

"Where will you go?" I asked. As far as I knew, Brent had no family to speak of.

"We can stay with Laertes's parents in Boulder."

"My old room is just the way I left it," Laertes said. "Until I firebomb it."

"No firebombing," Brent said, but his heart wasn't in it. Laertes's parents were the sort of outwardly very nice conservative people who wouldn't miss an opportunity to call Laertes by his deadname, and that shit will wear you down over time.

"You're staying," I said.

"We're staying for now, yes," Brent agreed. "But if we run out of—"

"You're staying," I said, more firmly.

"Jamie, I can't ask you to do that," Brent said.

"I can," Laertes said, from the bedroom. "Fuck Boulder."

"It's settled, then." I got up from the table.

"Jamie—"

"We'll make it work." I smiled at Brent and then went to my room, which was the size of a postage stamp, but at least it was drafty and the floor creaked.

I sat on my shitty twin bed, sighed, then lay down and stared at the ceiling for a good hour. Then I sighed again, sat up, and pulled out my phone. I turned it on.

The füdmüd app was waiting for me on the screen.

I sighed a third time and opened it.

As promised, my deliverator account was signed in and ready to go.

CHAPTER 2

"Hello and thank you for ordering from füdmüd," I said to the dude who opened the door to the ridiculously nice condo in the brand-new building that the doorman let me into because he knew I was an expected delivery person and not, probably, a robber. "I am your deliverator, Jamie. It is my passion to bring you your"—and here I looked at my phone—"seven-spice chicken and vegan egg rolls." I thrust the bag forward for the dude to take.

"They make you say that?" he said, taking the bag.

"They really do," I confirmed.

"Delivering isn't actually your passion, is it?"

"It's really *not*."

"I understand. It will be our little secret."

"Thank you." I turned to go.

"Hope you find your samurai swords."

I stopped turning. "What?"

"Sorry, inside joke," the dude said. "You know 'deliverator' is from *Snow Crash*, right? The Neal Stephenson book? Anyway, the protagonist of the book is a delivery guy who has samurai swords. I forget the hero's name."

I turned back all the way. "*Thank you*," I said. "I've been delivering food for six months, and you're the first person to get the reference. At all."

"I mean, it's pretty obvious."

"You would *think*, right? It's only a modern classic of the genre. But *no one* gets it. First, no one *cares*"—I waved wildly to encompass all of the philistine Lower East Side, and possibly, all five boroughs of New York City—"and second of all, when anyone comments on it they think it's a play on *The Terminator*."

"To be fair, it *is* a play on *The Terminator*."

"Well, *yeah*," I said. "But I think it's come into its own."

"I'm pretty sure we've just found your passion," the dude said.

I was suddenly aware of my emphatic body language, perhaps made more emphatic by the fact that I, like the dude, was wearing a face mask, because New York City was a plague town in a plague country and any potential vaccine was still undergoing double-blind studies somewhere we were not. "Sorry," I said. "At one point in my life my dissertation was going to be on utopian and dystopian literature. As you might expect, *Snow Crash* was in there as one of the latter." I nodded, and turned again to go.

"Wait," the dude said. "Jamie . . . *Gray*?"

Oh my god, my brain said. *Just walk away. Walk away and never admit that someone knows your deliverationing shame.* But even as my brain was saying that, my body was turning back, because like puppies we are enculturated to turn when our name is called. "That's me," I said, the words popping out, with the last one sounding like my tongue was desperately trying to recall the whole sentence.

The dude smiled, set down his bag, took a step back to get out of the immediate breath zone, and unhooked his mask for a second so I could see his face. Then he put it back on. "It's Tom Stevens."

My brain raced around in the primordial LinkedIn of my memory, trying to figure out how I knew this dude. He wasn't helping; he clearly expected to be so memorable that he would pop up in my head instantly. He wasn't, and *yet*—

"Tom Stevens who dated Iris Banks who was best friends with my roommate Diego when I lived in that apartment on South Kimbark just above Fifty-third Street and used to come to our parties sometimes," I said.

"That's very exact," Tom said.

"You went to the business school."

"I did. Hope you don't mind. Not super academic."

"I mean"—I motioned to the very nice condo in the brand-new building—"it turned out okay for you."

He glanced at the condo as if noticing it for the first time, the bastard. "I guess it did. Anyway, I remember you talking about your dissertation at one of those parties once."

"Sorry," I said. "I did that a lot at parties back then."

"It's fine," Tom assured me. "I mean, it got me to read *Snow Crash*, right? You changed lives."

I smiled at that.

"So why did you leave your doctoral program?" Tom asked me, the next time I delivered food to him, which was an Ethiopian mixed meat combo with injera.

"I had a quarter-life crisis," I said. "Or a twenty-eight-year-old crisis, which is the same only slightly later."

"Got it."

"I saw all these people I knew of, people like *you*, no offense—"

Tom grinned through his mask; I saw it through the eye crinkles. "None taken."

"—going off and having lives and careers and taking vacations and meeting hot people, and I was sitting in Hyde Park with the same sixteen people, in a crappy apartment, reading books and arguing with undergrads that no, actually, they *did* have to turn in their papers on time."

"I thought you liked reading books."

"I do, but if you're only reading books because you *have* to, it becomes much less fun."

"But when you got your doctorate, you could become a professor."

I snorted at this. "You have a much more optimistic view of the academic landscape than I do. I was looking down the barrel of adjunct professorships for the rest of my life."

"Is that bad?"

I pointed at his food. "I'd make even less than I do delivering your injera."

"So you ditched it all to become a deliverator," Tom said as I delivered his Korean fried chicken.

"No," I said. "I actually got a job at füdmüd. A real one with benefits and stock options. Then I got fired by their dicknozzle CEO just as the pandemic ramped up."

"That sucks."

"You know what really sucks," I said. "After he punted me into the street, he took the ideas I had for locking up restaurants and paying deliverators more. Well, *some* of the deliverators anyway. You only get paid more if you get more than four stars. So remember to give me five stars, please, I'm right on that edge. Every star counts, my dear deliverationee."

"Deliverationee?"

I rolled my eyes. "Don't ask."

Tom smiled again; eye crinkles. "I take it you weren't the one to come up with the 'deliverator' name."

"Oh, hell, no."

"So, you worked there, you can tell me this," Tom said, when I delivered his Chicago-style deep-dish pizza, which honestly I was surprised was allowed within the borders of New York City at all, much less this close to Little Italy. "What's with the umlauts?"

"You mean, why is it füdmüd, and not the more logical Food-Mood?"

"Yes, that."

"Because FoodMood was already taken by a food delivery app in Bangladesh, and they wouldn't sell the name," I said. "So if you're ever in the Mymensingh area, be sure to use the app with the name that actually makes sense."

"I've been to Bangladesh," Tom said. "Well, sort of."

"Sort of?"

"For my job. It's complicated."

"Are you a spy?"

"No."

"A mercenary? That would explain this very nice condo in a brand-new building."

"I'm pretty sure mercenaries live in double-wides in the woods of North Carolina," Tom said.

"Of course you would say that," I said. "That's what they tell mercenaries to say."

"I work for an NGO, actually."

"*Definitely* a mercenary."

"I'm not a mercenary."

"I'm going to remember you said that when I see you on CNN as part of a Bangladeshi coup."

"This is the last time I'm going to get a delivery from you for a while, I'm afraid," Tom said to me, when I delivered his shawarma platter to him. "My job is taking me back out into the field and I'll be there for several months."

"Actually this is last time you'll ever get a delivery from me," I said.

"You're quitting?"

I laughed. "Not exactly."

"I don't understand."

"Oh, you haven't *heard,* then," I said. "füdmüd is being bought out by Uber for, like, four billion dollars, and rolled into Uber Eats. Apparently, we were so successful at locking up the best restaurants and the best deliverators that Uber decided it was just easier to buy us and all our exclusivity contracts."

"So the CEO who stole your ideas—"

"Rob Shitmonkey Sanders, yes."

"—is now becoming a billionaire."

"It's an eighty percent cash deal, so, yup, pretty much."

"And you don't want to deliver for Uber."

"See, that's the *best* part," I said. "Uber already has their delivery people, and they didn't want to have to roll over *all* the deliverators. That would make the delivery people they already have unhappy. So they're only taking the ones that had four-star and above ratings." I opened my füdmüd app and showed him my stats. "Three point nine seven five stars, baby."

"I always gave you five stars," Tom said.

"Well, I appreciate that, Tom, for what little good it does me now."

"What are you going to do?"

"Long term? I have no fucking idea. I was barely scraping by as it is. I'm the only one of my roommates who had anything approaching close to steady work, so I was paying the rent and the utilities and most of the food. We're in the middle of a plague, so no one's hiring for anything. I have no savings and nowhere else to go. So, yeah. No idea, long term. But"—I held up a finger—"short term? I'm gonna buy a bottle of shitty vodka and drink the whole damn thing in my shower. That way, when I make a mess of myself, it'll be easy for my roommates to clean up."

"I'm sorry, Jamie."

"It's not your fault," I said. "And anyway, I apologize for unloading on you."

"It's all right. I mean, we're friends."

I laughed again at this. "It's more like we have a workable service relationship with a tenuous personal history. But thank you, Tom. I actually did enjoy deliverating to you. Enjoy your shawarma." I started to go.

"Hold on," Tom said. He set down his shawarma and disappeared into the recesses of his very nice condo. A minute later, he came back and thrust his hand out at me. "Take this."

I stared at his hand. There was a business card in it. My face did a thing.

Tom noticed, even through the mask. "What is it?"

"Honestly?"

"Yeah."

"I thought you were going to give me a cash tip."

"This is better. This is a job."

I blinked at this. "What?"

Tom sighed. "The NGO I work for. It's an animal rights organization. Large animals. We spend a lot of time in the field. There's a team I'm a part of. We're supposed to ship out in the next week. One of my team members has COVID and is currently in a hospital in Houston, hooked up to a ventilator." Tom saw my face do another thing and held up a hand. "He's out of danger and is going to recover, or so they tell me. But he's not going to recover before my team ships out this week. We need someone to replace him. You could do it. This card is for our recruitment officer. Go see her. I'll tell her you're coming."

I stared at the card some more.

"What is it now?" Tom asked.

"I really did kind of think you were a mercenary."

It was his turn to laugh. "I'm not a mercenary. What I do is much, much cooler. And much more interesting."

"I, uh . . . I don't have any training. For whatever it is you do. That involves large animals."

"You'll do fine. Also, if you don't mind me being blunt, at this point what I really need is a warm body that can lift things." He pointed at his shawarma. "I know you can lift things."

"And the pay?" I asked, and immediately regretted it, because that seemed like kicking a gift horse in the mouth.

Tom motioned at the very nice condo, as if to say, *See?* Then he held out the card again.

I took it this time. "I'll let Gracia know you're coming," Tom said, and looked at his watch. "It's one p.m. now. You can see her today, probably. Or early tomorrow. But that's pushing it in terms of timing."

"You need an answer that quickly?"

Tom nodded. "Yeah, that's kind of the catch, actually. As long as Gracia signs off on it, the job is yours, but you sort of have to decide *now* whether you want it. I know that's not cool of me. But I'm in a bind, and if you can't take it, I have to find someone else, fast."

"Well, I'm *free*," I said. "You were literally my last deliverationee."

"Okay, good."

"Tom . . ."

"Yes?"

"Why? I mean, *thank you*, and I really, sincerely mean that. Thank you so much. You're saving my life right now. But, why?"

"One, because you need a job, and I have a job to hand out," Tom said. "Two, because from a totally self-interested point of view, you are saving *my* ass, because we can't go out into the field without a full team and I don't want us to be saddled with some random person we don't know. You're right, we're *not* friends. Not yet. But I *do* know you. And three . . ." Tom smiled again. "Let's just say you turning me on to *Snow Crash* a few years ago put me on the path I'm on now. So in a way I'm just returning the favor. Now—" He pointed to the card. "That address is in Midtown. I'll tell Gracia to expect you around two thirty. Get going."

CHAPTER 3

"Let's get right to it," Gracia Avella said to me. "What did Tom tell you about KPS?"

The offices for KPS—the name of the organization on the card Tom gave me—were on Thirty-seventh, in the same building as the Costa Rican consulate, on the fifth floor. The office apparently shared a waiting room with a small medical practice. I had been in the waiting room for less than a minute when Avella came to get me to take me to her personal office. There was no one else in the KPS office. I guess they, like most everyone else, were working from home.

"He told me that you were an animal rights organization," I said. "And that you do work in the field. And that you need people to lift heavy objects."

"We are, we do, and we do," Avella agreed. "Did he tell you what kind of animals?"

"Uh, large animals?"

"Is that a question?"

"No, I mean, he said large animals, but he wasn't specific."

Avella nodded. "When you think of large animals, what do you think of?"

"I guess, elephants? Hippos. Giraffes. Maybe rhinos."

"Anything else?"

"I suppose there are whales," I said. "But it didn't seem to me Tom was talking about those. He said 'in the field,' not 'out to sea.'"

"Technically, 'in the field' would indicate either," Avella said. "But yes, we do most of our work on land."

"I like land," I said. "I don't drown there."

"Jamie—may I call you by your first name?"

"Please."

"Jamie. Here's the good news. Tom was right: We need a body for this next field operation, and we need it now. Tom's recommended you, and between him calling me and you arriving, I did a background check on you. No arrests, no FBI or CIA or Interpol flags, no problematic social media posts. Even your credit score is good. Well, as good as it can be for anyone who has student loans."

"Thanks. I love forever paying off a master's I will never, ever use."

"On that topic, your master's thesis is pretty good."

I blinked. "You read my master's thesis?"

"I skimmed it."

"How did you *get* it?"

"I have friends in Chicago."

"Okay, *wow*."

"My point is, you're not an obvious danger or a potential problem for your other soon-to-be teammates. And for us, right now, that works. So, congratulations, you'll have the job if you want it."

"That's great," I said. "Okay." An immense boulder of stress I didn't even know was sitting between my shoulders was suddenly lifted. I wasn't going to be homeless and starving in the middle of a pandemic.

Avella held up a finger. "Don't thank me yet," she said. "The job is yours—but I need to make sure you understand what the job is so you can decide if you actually want it."

"All right."

"First, understand that when we say KPS is an animal rights organization, we are *actively engaged* with these animals—very large, very wild, very dangerous animals. We will train you on how to interact with them, and we maintain stringent safety protocols at all times. But you can get injured, severely, and if you're not careful, you can actually die. If you have *any* hesitation on this score, or if you have any problem following *to the letter* the directions and instructions you are given, then this is not the job for you. I need you to verbally acknowledge that you understand this."

"I understand," I said.

"Good. The second thing is that when we say we are away in the field, we mean that we are *away*. As in, away from civilization for months on end. As in, no internet. As in, very little communication with the outside world. Almost no news in or out. What you take with you is what you have. You live simply and rely on others and allow others to rely on you. If you can't live without Netflix and Spotify and Twitter, this is not the job for you. You will be in the field. Acknowledge this, please."

"Can I ask for a bit of clarification here?"

"Of course."

"When we say 'in the field,' how *in the field* is that?" I asked. "Is it, 'we are far away from the rest of the world but we still have walls' in the field, or is it 'we live in small tents and poop in holes we dig ourselves' in the field?"

"Do you have a problem with pooping in a hole that you've dug yourself?"

"I've never done it, but I'm willing to learn."

Avella smiled at this, I think; the mask made it more ambiguous than I'd like. "It's possible you may have to poop in a hole from time to time. That said, our field base does have freestanding structures. And plumbing."

"Okay," I said. "I understand and acknowledge this, then."

"The third thing is that what we do is confidential. Which means that you *cannot* speak to anyone outside of KPS about what you do or where you go. I need to *strongly* emphasize that security and secrecy are extremely important to what we do and how we operate, enough so that if you are discovered to have leaked *any* information to anyone—even loved ones—we can and *will* prosecute you to the fullest extent possible under the law. This is not an empty threat; we've done it before."

"Does this mean I have to sign a nondisclosure agreement?"

"This is the NDA right now."

"But I already know what you do."

"You know we're an animal rights organization."

"Right."

"It's a little like saying the CIA is a data services company."

"So you *are* spies! Or mercenaries."

Avella shook her head. "Neither. We operate the way we do for the safety of the animals we care for. Bad things would happen if we didn't."

I thought about the stories I'd read about poachers and hunters killing endangered animals by reading the geolocation data off of pictures tourists had put online. I got it.

"One question," I said. "I'm not going to be asked to break any laws, am I?"

"No," Avella said. "I can promise that."

"All right. I understand and accept, then."

"Very good." Avella got out a small sheet. "In that case, some very quick questions for you. First, do you have a valid passport?"

"Yes." I had intended to go to Iceland over the summer, before the plague hit, and I lost my job, and had to spend all my time delivering food to shut-in Manhattanites.

"No major physical disabilities?" Avella looked up. "I should be clear you're about to get a complete physical from Dr. Lee across the way, so this is just meant to cover things broadly."

"No disabilities, and I'm healthy."

"Any allergies?"

"None yet."

"How do you handle heat and humidity?"

"I interned one summer in Washington, D.C., and didn't die," I said.

Avella started to ask the next question and then paused. "This next question is on what you think about science fiction and fantasy, but I read your master's thesis, so we can skip this one. I assume you'd say you're pretty comfortable with the genre."

My master's thesis had been on bioengineering in science fiction from *Frankenstein* through the Murderbot novellas. "Yes, although that's kind of a random question."

"It's not," Avella assured me. "Do you have a will or have otherwise made any estate planning?"

"Uh, no."

She tutted at this and made a note. "Any dietary restrictions?"

"I tried being a vegan for a while, but I couldn't live without cheese."

"They have vegan cheese."

"No, they don't. They have shredded orange and white sadness that mocks cheese and everything it stands for."

"Reasonable," Avella said. "It would be difficult to be a vegan where you're going anyway. Final question. Do you mind needles?"

"I'm not a huge fan, but I don't have a phobia," I said. "Why?"

"Because you're about to meet a lot of them."

"Let's do this first and get it over with," Dr. Lee said, before shoving a cotton swab through my nostril all the way back to my brain. This was actually the last part of my physical, which I was informed I had passed, but the first part of my vaccine regimen.

"Well, that's fun," I said, when it was done.

"If you think that's fun, let's not ever meet socially," Dr. Lee said. She packed up the swab to be tested. "You don't look like you're infected, but of course no one ever looks infected at the beginning, so we'll just be sure. And in the meantime, let's get you shot up." She reached into a cabinet and pulled down a tray holding a series of syringes.

"What are those?" I asked.

"These are your basic vaccinations," she said. "Just the usual stuff, new and boosters. Measles, mumps, rubella, multispectral flu, chicken pox, smallpox."

"Smallpox?"

"Yes, why?"

"It's extinct."

"You'd think so, wouldn't you." She held up one of the syringes. "This is new. COVID vaccine."

"It's out?"

"Technically it's experimental. Don't tell your friends. They'll be jealous. Now. How much international travel have you done?"

"Not much. Canada for a conference last year. Mexico as an undergrad for spring break."

"Asia? Africa?"

I shook my head. Dr. Lee harrumphed and reached up for another tray of syringes. I started counting and got nervous.

Dr. Lee noticed. "I promise you want the shots more than you want what they're protecting you from," she said.

"I believe you," I said. "It's just a lot."

She patted my shoulder. "That's not a lot." She reached up again and pulled down a final tray, which had at least ten syringes on it. "There. *Now* it's a lot."

"Jesus *Christ*." I actually moved away from the tray table. "What the hell are those?"

"They told you you'd be working with big animals, right?"

"Yeah, and?"

"Okay, so . . ." Dr. Lee pointed to the closest syringes in the new tray. "Those are for the diseases the animals could give to you." She pointed farther down. "Those are for the diseases their *parasites* could give you." She pointed to the last of those. "And those are for the diseases you can catch just by existing in the open air."

"Holy shit."

"Look at it this way," she said. "We're not only protecting you from them. We're protecting them from you."

"Can't you just give them to me all at once in an IV drip or something?"

"Oh, no, that would be bad. Some of these vaccines don't react well to others."

"And yet you're going to put them all into my body."

"Well, we have a specific order they go in," she said. "So, your bloodstream will have diluted the first of them by then."

"You're fucking with me, aren't you," I said.

"Sure, let's go with that," Dr. Lee said. "Also, really quickly, let's talk side effects. For the next couple of days you might feel achy or sore, and you might run a slight fever. If that happens, don't panic, that's perfectly normal. It just means your body is learning about the diseases we want it to fight."

"All right."

"Also, at least a couple of these are going to make you feel ravenously hungry. Go ahead and eat all you want, but avoid excessively fatty foods, since one of these is going to tell your body to purge fats in a way that *absolutely* challenges normal sphincter control."

"That's . . . not great."

"It's a mess. Seriously, don't even think about trying to fart for the next eighteen hours. It's not a fart. You *will* regret it."

"I don't like you."

"I get that a lot. Also, you may find the color blue giving you a migraine for the next couple of days."

"Blue."

"Yeah. We don't know why it happens, we just know it does. When it does, just look at something not blue for a while."

"You know the *sky* is blue, right?"

"Yes. Stay indoors. Don't look up."

"Unbelievable."

"Look, I don't make it happen, I just give you the shots that make it happen. Finally, with this one"—Dr. Lee pointed to one of the last syringes in the longest tray—"in one in about two hundred fifty injections, the recipient feels the urge for, let's just say, intense and homicidal violence. Like, 'murder everyone in the building and build a pyre with their skulls' level of violence."

"I can understand that," I assured her.

"No, you can't," she assured me back. "Fortunately, there's a direct and accompanying side effect of extreme lassitude, which keeps most people from acting on the urge."

"So, like, 'I want to kill you but that would mean leaving the couch.'"

"Exactly," Dr. Lee said. "We call it *murder stoner syndrome*."

"That can't be real."

"It's *very* real, my friend. We've learned that certain foods help counteract the murderous urge. If it happens to you and you actually have enough energy to stand up and move around, fry up some bacon or eat a pint of ice cream, or have a couple of slices of bread with butter."

"So, fatty foods."

"Basically."

"You remember the part where you told me to *avoid* fatty foods, right?"

"I do."

"So, just to be clear, the choices here are 'homicidal maniac' or 'shit tornado.'"

"I wouldn't put it that way, and yes. But the chances are pretty good you won't experience either side effect, much less both at the same time."

"And if I do?"

"Angrily consume your bacon on the toilet, is my advice." Dr. Lee lifted the first syringe. "Ready?"

"Did your shots go well?" Avella asked, when I returned to her office.

"I didn't murder Dr. Lee," I said. "But that may be because I can barely move my arm right now."

"Thank you for not murdering our doctor," she said, then she removed her mask. "I was vaccinated weeks ago," she said, when she caught my look. "And now that you've had your shots, I don't have to pretend I haven't had mine. But I'll put it back on if it makes you uncomfortable."

"No, it's fine." I thought about taking mine off but didn't.

Avella tapped a folder on her desk. "We have some paperwork for you to fill out. We need information so we can direct deposit your salary and get you enrolled in our medical and benefits programs. We also have some optional paperwork here that gives us a limited power of attorney so we can deal with things like your rent and school loans."

"What?"

Avella smiled. "Tom didn't tell you about that, I see. In addition to your salary, KPS covers your monthly rent and any school loan payments you might have. If you have credit card or other commercial debt, you have to pay that, but we can either pay it for you and deduct it out of your salary, or help you set up an automatic payment for it if you haven't already done so."

"That's terrific," I said.

"We'll be asking a lot of you, Jamie. And we'll be taking you away from the world when we do it. The least we can do is make sure you have a place to come back to. Speaking of salary, I realize we haven't discussed numbers yet. If it's acceptable to you, we'll start you at a hundred twenty-five thousand dollars."

"I mean, that's fine," I said, dazed.

"That doesn't include the ten-thousand-dollar signing bonus to act as a bridge to your first paycheck."

"Of course it doesn't," I blithered, stupidly.

Avella reached into her desk and pulled out a manilla envelope and passed it over to me.

I stared at it. "Is that . . . ," I began.

"Two thousand in cash and a cashier's check for the rest," she said. "Although if you prefer we can Venmo the eight thousand."

"Can I . . ." I stopped.

Yes?" Avella asked.

"I was going to ask if I can transfer this to my roommates, to help them cover their expenses while I'm gone."

"It's a cash bonus, Jamie. You can do whatever you want with it. And if you're still worried about them, while you're away we can arrange to have some of your salary sent to them. We do that a lot. We're an international organization, and a lot of our employees send remittances home. This would be pretty much the same thing."

"This is *great*!" I exclaimed. It was stupidly perfect how all my problems were suddenly solved with the strategic application of money.

"We're glad you think so," Avella said, and then tapped the folder again. "There's an Amtrak ticket in here for two days from now. That should give you enough time to wrap up everything you need to here in New York City. Courier all the rest of the paperwork back to me before then, and then pack for a long trip. Don't worry about clothing except for travel clothes. But otherwise, take with you what you'd want to bring on a several-months-long trip. And don't forget your passport."

I took the folder. "Where am I going?" I asked.

"BWI airport, to start," Avella said. "As for the rest—you'll find out."

CHAPTER 4

Tom Stevens met me at the BWI rail station as I got off the train, and looked at my carry-on and backpack. "That's everything you're bringing?" he asked me.

"I was told I only needed to bring travel clothes," I said. "And other than that, I'm bringing a lot." I pointed to the carry-on. "Personal hygiene products and snacks." I turned to bring attention to my backpack. "All my electronics and several terabytes of movies, music, and books. Sunglasses and a baseball cap. I don't know, I figured I would need sunglasses and a baseball cap. Did I do it wrong?"

"No, you did it fine," Tom said. "We'll cover everything else. It's good to see you, Jamie. Thank you for taking the job. You're really saving our asses on this."

"Well, you really saved *my* ass, so we're even."

"I'll take that." He presented me with a ticket. "Your travel documents."

I took a look at the ticket. "Where the hell is Thule Air Base?" I asked.

"Greenland."

"We're going to *Greenland*?" I sputtered. "Are we hanging out with polar bears?"

I could see Tom grinning behind his mask, which I knew he was wearing as camouflage now, just as I was. "Come on, we have to take a shuttle to the airport. Let's get you checked in. Our flight doesn't leave until two in the morning. We've taken over a lounge."

* * *

"*Greenland?*" Brent said to me, over video, on my phone.

"Right?" I said. I was sitting in the Chesapeake Club Lounge, which in normal times, as I understood it, was the lounge British Airways passengers used before they boarded their flights to London. Today, however, it was populated by a few dozen KPS staffers, many of whom, like me, were chatting away on their phones, presumably to friends and loved ones, while they still could.

"I guess they have polar bears there," Brent said.

"And seals," I reminded him. "They can get pretty big."

"I suppose. I don't know. I just assumed that when they said you'd be working with big animals you'd be going to Africa. As far as I knew, that's where they kept all the big animals."

"That's your bigoted colonial cultural past showing," Laertes shouted, off-screen.

"No, it's *not*," Brent yelled back, and then turned back to me. "I mean, it probably is."

"I'm just worried that I've severely underpacked warm clothes," I said.

"Gut a polar bear and crawl inside," Laertes shouted, still off-screen. "Like a tauntaun."

"Stop helping," Brent shot back. "I'm pretty sure they won't let you freeze," he said to me.

"That's what Luke thought," Laertes shouted.

"Don't listen to him," Brent suggested.

I smiled and changed the subject. "Are you two going to be okay while I'm gone?" I asked.

"Are you kidding? Jamie, you've saved our asses. We don't have to move, and we're not going to starve. I could kiss you."

"Spicy!" Laertes shouted.

"Not that kind of kiss," Brent qualified.

"No, I get it," I said. "Apparently, I'm doing a lot of ass-saving today."

"Also spicy!" Laertes added.

"You're going to miss his interjections to our conversations," Brent promised. "And our conversations, come to think of it."

"I know it. I'll drop you updates when I can." *If I can* was more like it, but I didn't want to say that at the moment.

"Sounds good. Don't let them give you shit because you're the newbie. And if they do give you shit, let us know."

"We've got firebombs!" Laertes shouted.

"We don't have firebombs," Brent amended. "But you know we can get some."

I laughed and signed off, probably for the last time in a while. I glanced up and saw a young woman looking over to me.

"Sorry," I said. "I should have had earphones on for that conversation."

"No, it's fine," she said. "It's nice to hear people having lives outside of this"—she indicated the lounge and the KPS staff—"whatever *this* is going to turn out to be."

"Ah," I said, getting it. "This is your first day on the job, too."

"Yes," she admitted. "There are a couple of other of us new people, too, over there." She pointed to a pair of grad-school-looking sorts, animatedly chatting, and then turned back to me. "I'm Aparna Chowdhury. Biology."

"Jamie Gray. Lifting objects."

She smiled at that. "Would you like to come sit with us?"

I put my phone away. "I would," I said. We walked over, and the grad-school-looking pair looked up.

"I found another newbie," Aparna said, excitedly, and pointed. "Jamie lifts things!"

"That's me," I confessed.

"Well, at least one of us is useful, then," the one closest to me said, and waved. "Kahurangi." He pointed. "And this is Niamh. They do astronomy and physics, and I do organic chemistry and some geology. We're nerds."

"Hi," Niamh said, waving.

I waved back. "I mean, I was doing a dissertation on science fiction novels, so I think I qualify under 'nerd.'"

"Wow, you really do," Kahurangi said. "And here I thought you were just here for the meat hydraulics."

"Oh, I am," I said. "The failed doctoral dissertation is just a bonus."

"Tell Jamie what we were talking about earlier," Aparna said.

"Oh, right," Niamh said, and turned to me. "Greenland. What the actual fuck?"

I was going to respond, but someone started clapping their hands for attention. We all looked up to see a very authoritative-looking woman standing up. Everyone stopped talking, put their phones away, and gave her their attention. A couple of people started booing her, mockingly.

"Oh, shut up," she said, fake irritably, and there was laughter. "For those of you who are back, it's good to see you back. For those of you who are new—who is new here?"

The four of us raised our hands.

"Oh, clustered up already, very nice," she said, and there were laughs at that. "For those of you who are new, I'm Brynn MacDonald, commander of KPS Tanaka Base Gold Team, which is what this is." She motioned around to the room, which offered up slight cheers and applause. "Don't get too excited," she said, deadpan, and there was more laughter about that. "Now, I'm sure you new people have a lot of questions, including—" She motioned to the crowd.

"Why Greenland!" everyone shouted back, except the new people.

"—and we could tell you now, but we're not *going* to," MacDonald said. "Not because we're cruel—"

"Although we *are* cruel," someone interjected, to laughs.

"—but because it's a tradition to not spoil the surprise. Trust us, it will be worth it. In the meantime, just know none of us knew, either, until we saw it with our own eyes.

"With that out of the way: As usual, the flight to Thule Air Base departs at two a.m., it's a six-and-a-half-hour flight, and again as usual, we'll have a mix of civilian and military folks with us on the flight. This means that for the duration you're going to have to wear your masks"—there were groans—"and I *don't* want to hear whining about this. Just because you're vaccinated doesn't mean other people are or that you can't still transmit to the uninoculated, so don't be an asshole." More grumbling, but people settled down.

"Now, we're all supposed to be seated together, but some of you might still have non-KPS people strike up a conversation, so if anyone asks why you're going to Thule Air Base, use our usual backstory of being Department of the Interior employees doing a geophysical survey of Greenland's glaciation. For the new people, we use that story because it's so boring that in the entire history of KPS, no one has ever followed up on it." Laughter.

"Otherwise, the usual rules apply: Do not talk about KPS business on the flight, or once we land or to anyone who is not KPS. When we arrive, KPS intake personnel will be there to get us on our way, and so on and so forth, you know the drill, and you new folks, just keep an eye on everyone else and follow us. Do not get lost or you stay at Thule Air Base for the winter. You do *not* want that life for yourself." More laughter.

"Weather report for Thule is cloudy and overcast but above freezing"—a small bit of cheering here—"with light winds coming in from the east. Rest and relax, call anyone you need to call, get in those last emails and Facebook posts, because it's all going bye-bye soon. That's it!"

MacDonald sat back down. The general conversation noise started up again, and people started reaching for their phones.

Niamh was one of them. "Okay, so, having a base named 'Tanaka' is not helpful *at all*," they said, after a minute. "The first Google references are for a baseball player."

"I'm on Wikipedia," Kahurangi said. "It says 'Tanaka' is the fourth most common family name in Japan. There are a *bunch* of notable Japanese with the name."

"So we have no clue about anything other than we're going to Greenland," Aparna said.

"And that we're probably doing something with polar bears," I noted.

"Or seals," Aparna added.

"So, let me ask this," I said. "I know why *I'm* here. I was broke and desperate and needed a job or I was going to be homeless and starving. What about you all?"

The newbies all looked at each other. "Pretty much the same?" Kahurangi said.

"It's a fucking pandemic out there, mate," Niamh said.

"I'm here because of a bad breakup," Aparna said. "And, well. Money."

"It's like the foreign legion for nerds," I said, and laughed. "With polar bears."

"Or seals," Aparna added.

A few hours later, we newbies, along with every other KPS staffer, filed out of the Chesapeake Club and boarded a charter plane. As promised we were all seated together, but I was in a row with an unoccupied seat, which was taken by a young airman, who asked me why I was going to Thule. I gave him the line about being from the Department of the Interior. I have never seen someone's eyes go dead with disinterest that fast. He put on headphones; I went to sleep.

Six and a half hours later, we were at Thule Air Base. I wondered how long we would stay, and the answer was, as long as it took for us to get off the plane, get collected by KPS staff, and shoved into a pair of what I was later told were cold-modified Chinook helicopters, which took off immediately and started heading inland.

"Where are we going?" I asked Tom Stevens, who had waved me over to sit next to him as I got into the helicopter. We had to lean in to each other to talk. "I don't know much about Greenland, but I do know there's nothing in the middle of it but glaciers and cold."

"Okay, see, this is cool," Tom said. "There was a U.S. base called Camp Century that officially closed in the 1960s. It was a military research base. It had its own nuclear reactor for power that was shut down when the base closed. Right?"

"Okay."

"It's a lie," Tom said. "A cover-up. Camp Century never closed down. Neither did its nuclear reactor. KPS uses it now. That's where we're going."

"We're going to a secret nuclear base in Greenland?" I said.

"I told you it was cool."

"Okay, but how do you keep a nuclear base secret?" I asked. I pointed upward. "I don't know much about physics, but I know the Russians and the Chinese have spy satellites. I'm pretty sure they'd notice, I don't know, *neutrons* or whatever."

"You'll see," Tom said. I was suddenly very annoyed at the smug secrecy of KPS.

A bit over an hour later and we were on the ground at Camp Century, hustled from the helicopters to transport trucks to a garage-like area that sealed up behind us. A KPS staffer told us to put any carry-ons, backpacks, or personal effects on a baggage claim–like conveyor belt. I looked over to Tom at this.

"It's fine," he said. "Sterilization. You'll get everything back." I shrugged and put everything on a conveyor.

Then we queued up and checked in at tables. When I got to the front, I was given a bundle of plastic-sealed clothes and shoes and a bag, and pointed to a shower area.

"Old clothes and shoes in the bag, including everything in your pockets, and any removable jewelry, and put the bag in the collection bin," the KPS staffer said. "Shower thoroughly using the soap provided. Use it everywhere, including your hair and get down into the scalp. When you're done, do it again, just as thoroughly. If you wonder if you did it enough, do it again. Then put on the new clothes and head to the waiting area beyond the shower room."

I went in, stripped, and showered. The soap smelled like a combination of chlorine and raspberry, which was not a combination I ever really wanted to experience again. The new clothes were a jumpsuit of sorts, gray and with close elastics at the neck, wrists, and ankles, with shoes being a weird sort of light boot. Utilitarian underwear and socks were provided. I put it all on and then followed the signs to the waiting area. Eventually Aparna came in, followed by Niamh and Kahurangi.

"I don't have a mirror, so you tell me," Kahurangi said, and posed. "Flattering?"

"Sure," I said.

"That's funny, because it looks like shit on you."

I smiled at that.

I heard my name, turned, and saw Tom waving me over. I excused myself from the newbies and went over to him. "Stick with me," he said.

"Okay," I said. "Why?"

"Because I want to see your face when it happens."

I gave him a sour look. "This secrecy bullshit, I swear."

"I know, I know," he said. "Would you believe me if I told you it's worth it?"

"It better be."

On the far side of the room, a light came on, over a door. The door opened, rolling up like it was on a garage. "Come on," Tom said, and guided us inside this new room, maneuvering us close to the similarly garage-like door on the other side of the room. Others filled in behind us until the room was packed with people in goofy gray jumpsuits. The door behind us rolled shut.

"I feel like someone is about to pull a prank on me," I said to Tom.

"It's not a prank," he said.

The lights went out.

"You were saying?" I said back to him, in the darkness.

"You remember I told you about the nuclear reactor here?"

"What about it?"

"We're using it now."

"Using it for what?"

There was a huge, wrenching *thunk*. I instinctively hunched down in the darkness. Behind me, at least a couple of people screamed and yelled in surprise.

"For that," Tom said.

I was going to remark how I was going to punch him when the lights came back on, and the door in front of us started going up.

As it did, air rolled in from the outside, hot, heavy, humid, and so dense I could see light diffract in it as in poured in.

The door rolled up all the way.

Outside was a jungle.

I gaped.

"*That's* what I wanted to see," Tom said.

I ignored him and stepped out into a wide pavilion, obviously designed to accommodate arrivals. I went to its edge. The arrival area was ten or more meters up. Below was a base of some sort, shot through with green life that was obviously untamable; it might be cleared temporarily but it would come back faster and greener. That green built toward the perimeter of the base to an immense wall of vegetation that grew higher and bolder than any I had ever seen in my life, either personally or in documentaries. It made the Amazon rain forest look like a parking lot.

I took in a breath. It was like chewing on pure oxygen.

I looked to the left and saw the other newbies standing with me, mouths similarly agape.

"All right, where the fuck are we?" asked Niamh.

"Greenland," Tom said, from behind us.

Niamh turned. "Mate, this is *not* Greenland," they said. "It's . . . *green*."

"I promise you it is Greenland." Tom held up a hand to forestall objections. "Just not the one you're used to. I promise you there's a good explanation. We have an orientation session that goes into it."

"Or you could explain it now," I said.

"Fine. This is Greenland. It's just on a slightly different Earth."

Niamh motioned emphatically at all the green. "*Slightly* different?"

"Gotta go with Niamh's assessment at your use of 'slightly,'" Kahurangi said.

"All right, *very* different," Tom allowed.

"How different?" Aparna asked.

Tom pointed at the green. "Well, that's not the wildest part."

"What do you mean?" I asked, and then noticed a shadow cover me, the rest of the newbies, Tom, and the entrance pavilion.

I looked up, along with everyone else, to watch what looked like a 747 lazily flap its wings across the sky.

"Is that . . . a *dragon*?" Aparna asked, after a long minute.

"Technically not a dragon," Tom said.

"*Technically?*" Niamh exclaimed.

Kahurangi nodded and pointed. "Once again, Niamh speaks for me."

"If it's not a dragon, what is it?" I asked.

"It's a kaiju," Tom said.

"A *kaiju*."

"Yes."

"An actual fucking kaiju," I repeated. "Like the Japanese movie monsters."

"Almost exactly like that," Tom said. "Hey, I told you we worked with large animals."

"Dude, I thought you were talking about *polar bears*."

Tom laughed and shook his head. "Nope. Actual fucking kaiju, as you put it. It's in the name, after all."

"What?" I said.

"KPS," Tom said. "It stands for Kaiju Preservation Society. That's who we are, Jamie. That's why we're here. That's what we do."

From the distance a low, rumbling roar rolled over us. I turned and watched as a small mountain on the horizon stood up and looked in our direction.

CHAPTER 5

"So this is Tanaka Base," I said to Tom, after I had managed to pick my jaw up from the pavilion sidewalk.

He shook his head. "This is Honda Base," he said. He caught my look. "It's not named after the car company, I promise you. It's named for Ishiro Honda. He directed the original *Godzilla* movie in 1954. All the North American bases are named for the people who made the movie. Tanaka Base, Chuko-Kita Base, Nakajima Base, and so on. Tanaka is named for the movie's producer. There were other Tanakas involved with the movie, though. It's a common name."

"The fourth most common in Japan," Kahurangi said.

"Someone was looking at Wikipedia before we left," Tom observed.

"Naming your bases for *Godzilla* filmmakers is a little on the nose," Niamh said to Tom.

"It is," Tom admitted. "We sort of lean in to that here. You have to, because how could you not, right? You can't pretend you don't *know*. And not just with kaiju movies. You have no idea how difficult it was for me to *not* say, 'Welcome to Jurassic Park!' to all of you just now."

"*Jurassic Park* didn't end well for anyone in it," I pointed out. "Book *or* movie."

"Well, they were sloppy," Tom said. "We're not sloppy. And, they were fictional. *This* is real."

"But *how* is this real?" I asked. "How do we walk into a room in an icy Greenland and walk out in one that's a jungle?"

"And has dragons," Aparna added.

"Technically not dragons," Tom said to her, and then looked at all of us, taking the newbies in as a group. "Come on. Let's get lunch and I'll explain there."

The Honda Base commissary was the size of a small-town market, and offered a salad bar and buffet. All of us newbies looked at it, uncertainly.

"What is it?" Tom asked, his plate ready. "You're holding up the line."

"We just came from a world where salad bars and buffets are no longer a thing," I reminded him.

"It's fine. Look." He went around me and started digging in.

"All of this produce looks very . . . boring," Niamh said. "You could get it in any developed country."

"You're wondering where the native produce is," Tom said.

"Yeah."

"You wouldn't like most of it."

"Why not?"

"Because our produce has been designed by us for centuries to be things we want to eat," Aparna said to Niamh. "Nothing here has been cultivated with us in mind." Aparna looked at Tom. "Right?"

Tom nodded. "We grow the produce here, in greenhouses. It's just not *of* here. But if you're feeling adventurous, you can try some of those." He pointed down to the end of the salad bar.

We all looked. "Mate, those look like fossilized turds," Kahurangi said.

"That's why we call them *poopfruit*, yes," Tom said.

"You need to talk to your marketing people," I suggested.

"They taste better than they look."

"They would have to, wouldn't they?"

A couple of minutes later we were all seated at a wooden picnic table inside the commissary, because even a few minutes out in Jungle Greenland was a wilting experience. The plan, Tom told us, was to have lunch, and then we and every other member of Gold Team would be on our way to Tanaka Base.

But first, some explanations.

"I'm not a scientist," Tom said to us as we ate. None of us braved the poopfruit. "And I know *you* are—well, most of you"—he nodded at me—"and the one of you who isn't is an expert in science fiction. So I'm going to leave the scientific details to other people. I'm just going to tell you what they told me when I was in your shoes."

"Like how this place exists at all," I said.

"Right. So to start, and, well, *clearly.*" Tom waved around, taking in the whole planet. "Alternate Earths exist. I'm told in theory that there are an infinite number of them, but this is the only one we can get to. So far anyway."

"And it's the same as ours?" I asked.

"Well, I think you've noticed there are differences."

"You said 'North American bases' earlier. This implies a North America."

"Oh, okay, I see where you're going. Yes, in a very broad sense. This Earth has the same basic continents as ours, but there are some significant differences because this version is much warmer. There are no ice caps here, so there's also no Florida here, or a lot of what we think of as the Eastern Seaboard of the United States. Everything from Boston to Savannah is under water. Or would be, if they existed here, which they don't. Also, we know that this Earth exists roughly in the same time-space moment as ours."

"How do you know that?" Kahurangi asked.

Tom pointed to Niamh. "I bet you would know," he said.

"The stars are the same, I'll bet," Niamh said to him, and then looked at the rest of us. "If we look up in the sky and see the same constellations that we see at home, and they're not distorted, we're in the same place in the universe. In *this* universe anyway." They turned back to Tom. "And you say they look like what you expect them to."

"I mean, I know the Big Dipper and Orion and that's it," Tom said. "But they're up there, where I expect to find them. Other astronomers we've had here confirm the rest of it."

"So, what explains the difference in climate, then?" Aparna asked Tom.

"Lots of different theories, with part of the leading being that we don't think there was a Chicxulub impactor on this Earth. You know, the meteor that took out the dinosaurs."

We all looked at him impatiently.

"Aaaand of course all of *you* know what the Chicxulub impactor was, and *I'm* the one who looks like an uneducated dork for not knowing what it was called by name when I first got here," Tom said, only a little bitterly.

"But you just said that we're in the same place in space-time," Aparna said to Niamh. "Why wouldn't the asteroid have hit here?"

"Just because the stars are in the right place doesn't mean every single interaction in space has been exactly the same," Niamh said. "Our solar system has eight major planets, dozens of minor planets and moons, and about a hundred thousand objects larger than a kilometer. All of them interact with each other. And that's not even factoring in the Oort cloud."

"Never forget to factor in the Oort cloud," I said, with mock seriousness.

"There's too much chaos in the system for things to act perfectly predictably at the scale of asteroids or planets," Niamh said, ignoring me. "So it's entirely possible that the asteroid that hit our Earth sixty-five million years ago missed this Earth completely—or possibly never even existed."

"And also that things that missed us in our universe hit this Earth here," Kahurangi said. He turned to Tom. "What do the rocks say? Where are the dividing lines?"

"You'll have to check with the actual scientists," Tom said. "But yeah, that's the thinking. We missed some extinction events here and may have gotten other ones."

"So you think these monsters evolved from dinosaurs?" Aparna asked. She had a frown on her face that I suspected was what happened when she as a biologist was told something she was going to disagree with on a visceral level.

Tom pointed. "No," he said. "That I know. The kaiju have a whole other biology entirely. Technically they're not even animals."

"So, they're what?" I asked. "Very angry plants? Vengeful fungi?"

"None of those things," Tom said. "Their biology is different from anything we have back home. Very different. Don't think of them in terms of kingdoms of life. Think of them as biological systems. Kind of ecosystems in themselves." He turned to Aparna. "I can't tell you more than that, I'm sad to say. It's not what I do here." Aparna looked very dissatisfied with this answer.

"What *do* you do here?" Kahurangi asked.

"My official title is base operations executive," Tom said. "My unofficial title is 'that guy who keeps schedules and has to fix shit when it goes wrong.'" He pointed to me. "Jamie here is going to be doing all my grunt work."

"I lift things," I confirmed.

"How long as this been going on?" Niamh asked.

"I started with KPS three years ago."

"No, not *you*," Niamh said, and gestured. "*This.*"

"Right, sorry. Well, if you want to go all the way back, it started when Godzilla showed up on our Earth."

"*What?*" Aparna got to the "what" first, but we were all getting there.

"So, again, no scientist," Tom warned.

"We've established that," I said, impatiently.

"Nuclear fission and fusion do more than make energy. They also thin the barrier between universes." All the scientists immediately drew up at this to raise objections. Tom raised his hand. "I *know.* Feels like bullshit, even to me. There *is* science behind it, I just don't carry it around in my head. Point is, we started setting off nuclear bombs on our planet, and the kaiju on *this* planet sensed the detonations from here and started homing in on them."

"Why would they do that?" asked Aparna.

"It looks like food to them."

"What—" Aparna caught herself, when she remembered Tom wasn't a scientist. "Go on," she said, grimly.

Tom nodded. "In May 1951, the U.S. set off a prototype of a hydrogen bomb at a place called Enewetak Atoll. It's in the Marshall Islands. Two days later, one of the kaiju crossed over at the detonation site."

"The actual fucking Godzilla," Kahurangi said.

"Which to be clear looked and acted nothing like the Godzilla of the movies," Tom said. "It was just huge and hungry and stomped around for a bit looking for something to eat before the U.S. Navy spooked it and it took off into the ocean."

"Then what happened?"

"It swam away from the navy for three days and then died and sank in the Japanese shipping lanes. That's why we have Godzilla. Japanese sailors saw the U.S. Navy chasing something big, talked about it when they got back to Japan, and the story found its way to the filmmakers."

"I'm officially skeptical about this Godzilla origin story," I said.

"That's fine," Tom said. "The thing was, it kept happening. The U.S. had it happen four more times, once in the Nevada desert. The Soviets had it happen at least three times. The French and the United Kingdom at least once each. It was enough of a problem that in 1955 there was a secret meeting of the nuclear powers to try to figure out how to keep it from happening. Their solution was to fund a project that crossed over to *here* to keep the creatures from trying to come over to our world."

"The Kaiju Preservation Society," I said.

"Our predecessor organization, yes. Less concerned about preserving the kaiju than just keeping them on this side of the universal fence until the holes we tore through it with our bombs closed up again."

"And how would they do that?" Kahurangi asked.

"Lots and lots of daisy cutters, is my understanding," Tom said.

"We don't do nuclear testing anymore, though," I pointed out.

"No, we don't," Tom agreed. "And one reason—obviously not in any treaty—is that keeping the kaiju out was more of a hassle than the nuclear powers wanted to deal with. There was also the consideration that the aftermath of a nuclear exchange would include fifty-story monsters coming through a multidimensional tear to wreak havoc on any survivors of the ICBMs."

"That's nice," Niamh said. "It's okay if *we* turned entire cities full of people into nuclear ash, but the idea of monsters having a nibble afterward was *just too much*."

"My point is, there's no threat of the kaiju crossing over today," I said, and then motioned around. "So why *this*?"

"Why are we still here, you mean?" Tom said.

"Yes."

"Well, there's the science of it, of course." Tom waved to the rest of the newbies. "Your new friends here are going to be doing work that has never been done before. It's literally a whole new world, and we've just scratched the surface of it. We're doing things here that no one else gets to do—will never get to do. That's awesome."

"But we won't get to share what we do," Aparna said. "We'll be doing science in a vacuum."

"You get to share it," Tom said. "Just with a very small number of fellow scientists for now. In the future, that might change. In which case each of you is going to become a rock star in your respective fields. That won't suck." He turned back to me. "This is where lots of our funding comes these days, by the way. Governments still fund us, but less so than they used to. But the same billionaires who are racing each other to get to Mars are bankrolling us in the hopes that something we learn here will be applicable back home, in a general this-doesn't-look-like-it-came-from-another-planet way."

"Or they're funding us to have somewhere to go if things go to shit back home," Niamh suggested.

"I'm sure some of them might have thought about that," Tom said. "I'm not sure it's going to work out for them the way they'd planned. They'd be better off with Mars."

"Why's that?"

"It has a lot fewer predators, for one."

"It's not just the science, though, is it?" I said, bringing the topic back round.

"No," Tom said. "We're not called the Kaiju Preservation Society just because it's a catchy name. It turns out the kaiju really could use some help."

"What does a creature the size of a small mountain need with humans?" Kahurangi asked.

"I promise you that you will find out," Tom said. "But what we do is more than keep the kaiju on this side of the fence. We also keep others *out*."

"What do you mean?" I asked.

"It's like I said, nuclear energy thins the dimensional barrier." Tom motioned to show off Honda Base. "We keep Camp Century humming along because it's nicely positioned, for various reasons I don't understand, to make it easy to open the door between our worlds, and then to close it back up again, each time in a predictable fashion. It and a couple of other sites on the globe, run by the other signatories to the Kaiju Defense and Protection Treaty, are the only official ways in and out of Kaiju Earth. They are tightly controlled and secured. There's a reason we've managed to keep this all a secret for so long.

"But nothing is *that* secret anymore," Tom continued. "Governments and companies know Kaiju Earth exists. They *have* to, in order for us to do our work and get our funding. We control the doors to this world. But if you're ambitious, you can slip past the guards. Or, if you're ambitious enough, you can blow a hole in the fence if you want to. You just have to know *how*. And when that happens, and it *has* happened before, both our worlds are in danger. Kaiju are a danger to humans, sure. But it works the other way, too."

"They could step on us and not even notice," Kahurangi said.

"Mosquitoes kill more humans every year than every other type of animal combined," Tom said to him, "including other humans. And to flip that around, humans have wiped our version of Earth clean of almost every single animal much larger than we are. We hunt them to extinction, and we put ourselves into their environments. Size isn't the issue. It never was."

"So we're the monster police, too," I said to Tom.

"Correct," he replied. "The only real question is, who are the monsters?"

"They ask that question in every monster movie, you know. It's an actual trope."

"I know," Tom said. "What does it say about us that it's relevant every single time they ask it?"

CHAPTER 6

We newbies were all thinking it, but this time it was Niamh who got to it first. "We're flying in *that?*"

That in this case was an immense dirigible that looked like it was prototyped by a kaiju-size Leonardo da Vinci in the fifteenth century, and minimally maintained since then. Everyone else on the Tanaka Base Gold Team was going up the gangways like it was no big thing.

"What were you expecting?" Tom, who had directed us to the airfield, asked Niamh.

"Something far less rickety."

"It's a solid craft."

"Mate, that looks like an advertisement for alternate-world tetanus."

"We did get our shots," Kahurangi said.

"There are no shots for *that,*" Niamh countered.

"The *Shobijin* is totally safe," Tom said. "In fact, it's the safest airship you'll ever be in."

"*Convince* me," Niamh said. "It looks like it will go up *Hindenburg*-style if I stare at it too hard."

"One, it uses helium, not hydrogen," Tom said. "A hydrogen airship would be a bad idea here. So it won't *explode*. Two"—he pointed to the frame of airship—"it's mostly made of two local elements that we have in abundance here, bell wood and kaiju hide. Bell wood grows fast like bamboo, is both incredibly light and strong, and is fire-resistant."

"How fire-resistant?"

"If you put a log of it on a fire, the fire would die. And as for the kaiju hide—well, not much gets through that. Keeps helium in.

Keeps things on the outside out. So, yeah. The *Shobijin* looks like bad handicrafts. But around here, if you're going long distances, that's what you want to be in."

"Still not convinced," Niamh said, then started walking toward the airship anyway.

"How do you get the helium?" Kahurangi asked Tom, as we walked. "Are you getting it from natural gas?"

"We mostly use an air distillation process."

"That's not very efficient."

Tom waved at the thick air. "It's more efficient here. There's more atmosphere, and helium occurs here more than back home."

"And the kaiju hide?" Aparna said. "How do you get *that*?"

"Are you asking if we hunt the kaiju?"

"I was wondering that, yes."

"Hunting a kaiju would be a very ambitious undertaking," Tom said, "to use the mildest euphemisms possible. So, no. Kaiju die like anything else does. When they do, we scavenge the body."

"How does that happen?"

"*Very* carefully." We walked up the gangplank into the passenger area of the airship.

For all that the outside of the *Shobijin* looked like rotted steampunk, the passenger cabin was nicely appointed. Modern lounger-style airline seats were placed in wide rows facing each other, with enough space between to move around and look out through broad windows. There were small lounge areas fore and aft, with bathroom facilities and snacks, not in the same place. I glanced at Niamh, who seemed slightly more reassured at the interior than the exterior. We found ourselves seats and plopped our stuff down, and stored our carry-ons in cubbyholes in the baseboard.

"Welcome back, fellow Tanaka Base Gold Team members," said the voice over the *Shobijin*'s speakers. "This is your pilot, Roderigo Perez-Schmidt, and with me as always is my copilot, Mattias Perez-Schmidt. We're not related, we're just married." This got a low groan of familiarity; I had a feeling Roderigo used this line with every announcement. "Today is a lovely day to travel, and we are delighted to travel with you. Our destination is the delightful Tanaka Base, located in the scenic and lovely Labrador Peninsula, almost straight south from us, a mere two thousand six hundred fifty kilometers' distant. For you Americans, that's about one thousand six hundred fifty miles, and also, this is the last time you will hear imperial measures used because like the rest of the civilized universe, Kaiju Earth uses measurements that make logical sense."

Another low groan, but very low, as the number of Americans appeared relatively small, and also, they were scientists, so they used metric anyway.

"Once aloft and barring any bad weather or kaiju attack"—we newbies looked at each other with some concern, but no one else seemed to break what they were doing—"we will be cruising at a comfortable one hundred twenty klicks per hour. Honda Base tells me Betsy is to the northeast, so we'll cruise at between two hundred and three hundred meters until we reach the sea. For you new members, welcome, and also, the majority of our voyage will be over Baffin Bay and the Labrador Sea, so it will not be as scenic as you would like. Nevertheless I hope you will enjoy your time on the *Shobijin*. We will be at Tanaka Base in roughly twenty-two hours." Perez-Schmidt made some comments to the *Shobijin* crew and then signed off.

"Betsy?" Kahurangi asked Tom, who sat with us.

"That's the local kaiju," Tom said. "You saw her when you got here. She was the one that looked like a small mountain."

"You named the kaiju *Betsy*?" I asked.

"I didn't, someone else did. You have a problem with *Betsy*?"

"I don't know, I was expecting something Japanese, or a name like 'Hammer Fist' or something."

"Formally, the adult ones have numbers. But the ones that live near bases get informal names. And they get named something easy to remember. Like Betsy."

"'Hammer Fist' is easy to remember," Niamh said.

"When it's your turn to name a local kaiju, you can name it that if you like."

"What if someone goes by that name?" Kahurangi asked.

"Hammer Fist?"

"Sure, but I meant Betsy in this case."

"It's the twenty-first century; no one goes by Betsy anymore," Tom said. "But even if they did, there's usually context. If you're saying, 'Betsy has the results from the lab,' it's probably the human. If it's 'Betsy just got pissed off and burned down twenty thousand acres of jungle,' it's probably the kaiju."

"I thought we weren't using imperial measures anymore," Niamh said.

"I don't know what twenty thousand acres is in metric."

"About eight thousand hectares," Aparna said.

Tom stared at her. "Really, *that* fast?"

Aparna shrugged. "It's just math."

Tom turned to me. "Did you know that?"

"I did not," I assured him.

"Thank you."

"I lift things."

"Hey, where does that road go?" Niamh, who had a seat close to a window, pointed to a wide and meandering path that became visible as we gently and quietly took to the air.

"It's not a road," Tom said. "It's a kaiju trail. They make them when they walk."

We all craned to look.

"Jesus, that's wide," Kahurangi said.

"Do they keep to their trails?" Aparna asked.

"Mostly," Tom said. "For the same reason we walk on sidewalks and not in the bushes. And here's something interesting. In places here that correspond to where humans live back home, the kaiju paths often mirror the paths of our major roads."

"They're following the topographic path of least resistance," Kahurangi said.

"Bingo."

"So where do they go?" I asked. "The paths?"

"The adult kaiju have their own home territories. They clear out space in places that they like."

"And do those correspond to our cities?"

Tom smiled. "They do, sometimes." He pointed to the path. "In Betsy's case, though, this path more or less makes a loop around Honda Base. She seems curious about what we do here. That or she's trying to find the nuclear reactor. She mostly doesn't bother us, though."

"Mostly?" Niamh said.

"She's been known to chase the airships."

"*What.*"

"Relax, she hasn't caught one yet." Tom reconsidered. "Well, not one with people on it. She's gotten a couple of drones."

Niamh stared at Tom, and then buckled up in their seat, emphatically.

We had crossed onto the Labrador Peninsula, and were not too far off from Tanaka Base, when a noise reverberated in the *Shobijin* cabin. Everyone fell silent.

The noise came again, much closer.

"Tell me that's not what I think it is," Niamh said.

Roderigo Perez-Schmidt came on the speakers.

"Attention, Gold Team. We have a kaiju out of place. Kaiju out of place. Stand by."

Everyone continued their silence. Then Perez-Schmidt came back on the speakers.

"Attention, Gold Team. Correction, two kaiju out of place. Preparing to climb."

The cabin erupted with noise, and everyone rushed the windows.

"What does that mean?" I asked Tom, and then noticed him looking out the window with a not-at-all-reassuring expression on his face. I turned to look out the window.

There was a very large creature staring up into the airship. It was too close, and our path was bringing us closer.

"Oh, *shit*," I said. I actually backed out of my chair.

"There's another one," Kahurangi called out, from a window on the other side of the cabin. I went over to him and looked where he was looking.

This other kaiju was just as brain-defyingly large. It looked at us briefly, then turned its attention back to the first kaiju. It was also too close, and we were also getting closer.

In fact, our path was taking us directly between them. Into the middle of whatever they were doing, or were about to do to us.

"Well, this seems *bad*," I said to Kahurangi. I turned back and yelled at Tom. "I thought we were supposed to be climbing!"

"We are climbing!" he said.

Not fast enough, I was about to say, when one of the kaiju screamed like a thousand jet engines suddenly ignited, and drowned out the possibility of hearing anything else, ever.

That is, until the kaiju on the other side of the airship answered, just as loudly. I wasn't aware it was possible to go completely deaf in stereo.

The screaming stopped, or at least I thought it stopped; it was possible my eardrums had simply melted. Then came another rumbling, again in stereo. Someone screamed from inside the cabin. I looked back out the window and saw the kaiju on this side lumbering toward the airship, slowly but then picking up speed in a way that should be impossible given how large it actually was.

I turned to warn the folks on the other side of the cabin, and noticed through those windows the second kaiju running up on us just as quickly.

Ridiculously, I ducked.

There was a thundering sound and a jolt, and I was sure the cabin would soon tear itself apart, but it didn't. The noise was from below us; the sound of two kaiju colliding. We had actually climbed enough for them to miss us.

It took me a couple of seconds to realize they weren't trying to kill us. They were trying to kill each other.

The *Shobijin* turned slightly to the southwest, and the starboard side of the airship was treated to the spectacle of two creatures the size of skyscrapers trying to beat the crap out of each other. Kahurangi and I watched, joined by the other newbies and Tom.

"What the hell just happened?" I asked Tom. I waved at the kaiju fight. "How did the pilots miss *this*?"

"We have trackers on the adult kaiju," Tom said. "Sometimes we lose the signal. Which means sometimes they show up where we don't expect them."

"Yeah, like alongside our *fucking airship*," Niamh said.

"They look like terrain, until they don't." Tom pointed to one of them. "That's Kevin."

"Really?" Niamh said. "Fucking *Kevin*?"

"He's a local. I don't know who the other one is. It might be a new adult, looking to claim territory."

"So, this is a turf war," Kahurangi said.

Tom gave the tensest shrug I think I've ever seen someone give. "Maybe. Could be a mating thing."

A massive chunk of kaiju flew into the air, trailing viscera as it did. Deafening screaming flooded the cabin.

"Maybe not," Tom amended, when we could all hear again.

The kaiju who was not Kevin was stumbling away from Kevin now, crashing through trees in the general direction of the *Shobijin*.

"Oh, no, no, no, run *the other way*, you dim-witted pile of rock," Niamh said.

"It's all right," Tom said. "Kevin's not going after the other one."

"Okay, but what about *that*?" Aparna said, and pointed.

We all looked. Kevin had gouged up a clot of ground the size of a small park in his massive clawed fist and had cocked back a gargantuan arm.

"Tool user," Aparna whispered, almost to herself. I stared at her, half-impressed she could be thinking about science at a time like this.

The speakers popped on. "Uhhhhhh, I would recommend seat belts right about now," Roderigo Perez-Schmidt said.

We dived for our seats.

As I clicked in, I saw Kevin pitch the small park in the direction of the other kaiju, which meant in our direction as well. The massive clod flew apart, and one sizable chunk sailed right toward us.

That has trees in it, my brain said, and then the entire cabin violently rocked and swayed as the spray of earth and rock and trees pelted the *Shobijin* at an oblique angle, pummeling the airship before falling prey to gravity.

We did not fall prey to gravity. We stayed afloat. And kept going.

"How are we even alive?" Niamh asked, again speaking for all of us. "We were hit by *trees.*"

"I told you this thing was tough," Tom said.

I looked around the cabin. Windows were shattered but had stayed in their frames. Carry-ons had dislodged from their cubbyholes. One woman didn't make it to her seat on time and was now holding the side of her head with a small trickle of blood oozing out, but otherwise, everyone seemed safe. Tom was right. The *Shobijin* looked ramshackle, but it survived the attack.

Well, survived two kaiju attacking each other and being collateral damage. Which I think was as close as I wanted to get to actually being attacked by a kaiju.

"Tell me it isn't always like this," I said to Tom. "Trees being chucked at us by a kaiju, I mean."

"First time it's ever happened to me," Tom promised.

The speakers clicked on again. "Gold Team, just reported into Tanaka Base. You'll be happy to know Kevin's tracker is safe and sound and reporting in from eighty klicks away," Perez-Schmidt said. "Best thinking is one of his parasites dislodged it somehow. Anyway, now some of us will have a new mission on the schedule, getting him another tracker. Sorry about the surprise. If we'd known, we'd have taken her up before we hit land. The good news is we're still on schedule and we don't anticipate any more surprises between here and base." He clicked off.

"No one anticipates surprises," Kahurangi said. "That's what makes them surprises."

In the distance now, there was a mournful cry of a mountain in pain.

CHAPTER 7

About fifteen minutes before arrival, a Gold Team member walked through the cabin, distributing hats and gloves. Everyone took them, and so did we. The gloves looked suspiciously small, as did the hat, which looked like a cap with a veil that went all the way around.

"This looks like a jellyfish," I said. "A small one."

"It stretches," Tom said. "So do the gloves. Put them on. The veil attaches to your suit like Velcro. Get a good seal." He nodded to Aparna and Kahurangi, both of whom had long hair. "You'll want to tuck your hair into your cap."

"Well, this is a fashion statement," Niamh said, when we had all put on our accessories.

"I'm guessing insects," Aparna said. "Bitey ones."

"You're not wrong," Tom said.

"How bad are they?"

Tom smiled. "The good news is, it's only until we get to the base proper. The bad news is, that's two hundred meters."

"Look." Niamh pointed out the window. "I think we're here."

Out of the trees was a clearing, either a natural or man-made meadow. On one side of it, on pylons, was an immense wooden hangar, accompanied by smaller hangars on each side. I assumed the large one was for the *Shobijin,* and the smaller ones for things like helicopters or tinier airships. This suspicion was confirmed as I saw what looked like a two-person helicopter being towed out onto an adjoining pad. A small distance away was another platform that looked like it held, of all things, a refinery. Farther out, another platform, holding an array of solar panels and three lazily turning vertical wind turbines.

Some distance away from all of that was the *Shobijin*'s mooring station, alongside which were mobile gangways that led to a platform raised off the meadow floor. From the platform, a walkway stretched up and over into a gathering of sequoia-size trees. Among the trees were wooden platforms and walkways and buildings, the whole affair swaddled in what looked like fine nettings and coverings.

"That's Tanaka Base?" I asked.

"It is."

"Did you mean to make it look like an Ewok village, or was that just an accident?"

"Well, technically speaking, Tanaka predates the Ewok village by a couple of decades. So it looks like *us*."

"Does George Lucas know that?"

"He might."

The *Shobijin* was maneuvered into her moorings and the gangways extended. We had officially landed. People got up and grabbed their things.

"Ready?" Tom said.

The doors opened. We shuffled out, stepped through the doorway onto the gangplank, and were immediately swarmed by apparently all the small flying insects that ever existed in the history of the universe.

"Jesus," Kahurangi said, swatting.

"Don't swat," Tom said to him. "It just encourages them."

"They're very excited to eat me."

"It's not personal, they want to eat everyone. Just keep walking."

"Is this usual?" I asked.

"This is light," Tom said. He pointed to Tanaka Base, which everyone was moving speedily toward. "Now you know why the whole place is screened in."

"You could have warned me about the danger of being exsanguinated in my first five minutes here," I said.

"It gets better," he said. "Watch." He pointed to the long walkway into the base, which was covered and screened. As we got closer, I heard the sound of fans blowing air forcefully away from the entrance of the covered walkway, blowing away the swarm as they did so. Ten steps into the covered walkway and the number of flying insects had dropped from dangerous to merely annoying. Twenty-five steps in and they were mostly gone.

I admired the lack of bloodthirsty creatures. "Nice."

"The big blowers go on when sensors notice someone approaching," Tom said. "But the fans are always blowing a light breeze through the walkway, away from Tanaka. It's a determined bloodsucker that makes it all the way in."

"And if they do?"

"Well, that's why we keep frogs, of course."

"What?"

Tom ignored the question and pointed to my cap-and-veil ensemble. "Out in the world this will keep most of the small ones away from you. The bigger ones, the ones near water, are the ones you want to look out for. They smell your breath, they come right for your face."

"How big are they?" Aparna asked.

"The bigger ones you don't swat. You *punch*."

"I can't tell if you're joking," Aparna said after a minute.

"The air here is thicker and has more oxygen in it than it did on Earth when we had insects with a meter-long wingspan," Tom said. "You're the biologist, you tell me."

Aparna sighed. "Punchable insects, okay, got it."

From ahead of us, the first of Gold Team had made it into Tanaka, and cheering had started going up. We all looked at Tom.

"That's Red Team," he said. "The people we're replacing. They are very happy to see us."

We cleared the walkway and were immediately confronted by several dozen people cheering us, wearing festive shirts over their jumpsuits, straw hats of various sorts, playing ukuleles and guitars, and holding up drinks. Presumably, Red Team.

When all of Gold Team had made it up the walkway and stripped off their insect caps, there was a dramatic shushing, and then Brynn MacDonald stepped forward to a man in a particularly loud shirt, wearing a particularly ratty straw hat, holding a particularly large drink.

"Brynn MacDonald, commander of KPS Tanaka Base Gold Team, here with my team to formally relieve KPS Tanaka Base Red Team," she said.

"Joao Silva, commander of KPS Tanaka Base Red Team," the man in the loud shirt and terrible hat said. "I am formally relieved you are here!"

Silva reached up and put his ratty-ass hat on MacDonald. A wild cheer went up from both camps. Silva and MacDonald hugged, and then Silva took off the terrible shirt and presented it to MacDonald, who put it on, apparently signaling the transfer of authority.

With that, members of Red Team surged forward and welcomed their counterparts, handing over hats and shirts and musical instruments, but not drinks. I was personally accosted by a friendly chap who gave me a ukulele, a straw boater, and a polyester shirt with parrots on it. "It is you," he assured me, gave me a hug, and wandered off.

"You know how to play that thing?" Kahurangi asked me. He was clad in an orange shirt with white bucking broncos on it, and a straw trilby.

"Not a clue," I assured him.

"May I?"

I handed the ukulele to him. He started playing it like he'd been playing all his life, which maybe he had. He smiled when he saw me looking at him play. "I debated about whether to bring mine. I decided against it, and I regretted it almost as soon as we left."

"I'm glad they had one here."

"More than one, it looks like. I can teach you how to play, if you want. In our I'm sure voluminous free time."

"I'd like that," I said. Kahurangi grinned and then wandered off, playing as he went.

I turned back to Tom, who had been festooned with a sombrero and a loud shirt with kittens. "So, there's two teams at Tanaka Base, and we rotate?"

Tom shook his head. "Three teams. Each team has a six-month stay, offset three months with the other teams." He pointed at the now de-hatted Red Team. "Red Team has been here for six months, and they're about to get three months off back home." He waved farther into the base, where I could see other KPS personnel. "Blue Team arrived three months ago to relieve us so we could have a three-month break, and will be here for another three months. Then they will be relieved by Red Team, who will be returning. Every team works with every other team for three months. That way Tanaka is always fully staffed and there's always continuity."

I pointed at Tom's kitten shirt. "And this? We do this every three months?"

"You have something against loud shirts and ugly hats?"

"Yours are loud and ugly. Mine, on the other hand, are quite fetching."

"We just do it when we arrive and leave. The middle transfer, we keep things running while the other two teams do their transfer. Like Blue Team is doing right now."

I fingered my shirt. "And, uhhhh, do we keep the shirts and hats?"

Tom smiled. "You can if you want. But they usually go back into the storeroom. The musical instruments are community property, too. We usually sign them out. We're big on the community sharing here. Which reminds me, you said you brought books and movies on hard drives. You should let our IT people know, they'll add them to the community Plex server."

"Okay."

"You have licenses for all that stuff, right?"

"Er."

"That's a joke. The treaty we work under creates a special carve-out for us in terms of copyright."

"Really."

"Yeah, apparently, they thought if we were being sent to an alternate Earth ruled by one-hundred-fifty-meter-tall creatures who could step on us at any moment, we should be able to borrow each other's ebooks and watch *Stranger Things*."

"Seems fair."

"Helps keep us sane, anyway. More than just ukuleles." Someone called Tom's name; he looked around, saw the person, and waved.

"You don't have to babysit me," I said to him. "If you have people to say goodbye to, go do that."

"All right, thanks," he said. "Also, in a little bit, Brynn MacDonald is probably going to collect you and your friends to help get you situated. Then tomorrow she's going to start you on your actual orientation. You know, starting on your actual job."

"I lift things," I confirmed.

"You will indeed lift things," Tom agreed. "But there's going to be more to it than that."

"Dun dun *dunnnnnnn*," I said, mimicking dramatic music.

Tom laughed and left, and I turned and watched two groups of friends, one arriving and one departing, try to catch up on three months' worth of life in a couple of all-too-short hours.

"Let me start by informing you that I'm a little drunk right now, so I'm going to keep this very short," Brynn MacDonald said. She was holding a glass of something, presumably alcoholic.

We newbies, whom she had gathered on Tanaka Base's main thoroughfare, waited politely. Some of us may also have been a little drunk; the Red Team goodbye party had been a little more intense than we expected.

"First, welcome, I'm Brynn, but you knew that. I know who each of you are because I have your files, but I'm also, you recall, a little drunk right now, so I'm not going to pretend to remember which of you is which. I will have it down tomorrow, I promise. And speaking of tomorrow"—she pointed to a modest wooden structure, a bit down the path—"I'll see all of you in the administration building at nine a.m., after breakfast, to start your orientation. I'll try to make it quick so you can get to your work as quickly as possible. I know you're all scientists"—she stopped and looked at me—"except you, you're our new grunt."

I grunted.

"Anyway you all have jobs, and you're all smart, so we'll rush you through it. As for tonight . . ." She pointed down the other way. "You've all been assigned the same barracks suite, which is that way, don't worry, your last names are on the door, keys inside, along with a fresh set of jumpsuits, you'll be fine, you're smart, you'll figure it out, but if you can't just ask literally *anyone,* they'll help you, because we're not assholes here. Well, some of us *are,* but even they will help you. If they don't we'll feed them to the tiny bloodsucking insects. You saw those earlier today. Hey, did you see the frogs?"

We nodded. We had seen the frogs, which lived in little decorative ponds peppered around the base. Aside from being the closest things to pets that there were at Tanaka Base, they also served the purpose of eating any flying insects that managed to get inside the netting. The insects would sense the water, go in for a drink, and then frogs would get them. Natural insecticide. Also cute. Aparna, our biologist, wondered if they were from here or if they were imported from our Earth, but it was a party, so that question remained unanswered for now, and Aparna may also have now been slightly drunker than the rest of us and not in a state of mind to receive an answer.

"We love the frogs," MacDonald said. "I know you know where the community center's at, because it is literally *right there*"—she pointed to the building right by the walkway to the airfield—"and you should come back tonight after you get yourself situated because it's a Gold Team tradition to watch movies together the first night. Tonight we're watching—wait for it—*Godzilla,* and then *Pacific Rim.* Because, you know"—we waved, to signal the world. "And that's the original, uncut Japanese version of *Godzilla,* not the bullshit American recut with Aaron Burr."

"Raymond Burr," I said.

"Oh, jeez, *right.*" MacDonald tapped her head, lightly. "Sorry. Got a whole lot of *Hamilton* going on up here. Also I'm a little drunk. Any questions?"

We had none. MacDonald dismissed us, by which I mean she waved goodbye vaguely with her drink and then wandered off.

"I really don't know what to make of this place," Aparna said, watching her go.

"I like it," Kahurangi said. He still had the uke and was plucking one of the strings absentmindedly.

"Let's go find our *barracks suite,*" Niamh said. "I can't wait to see what it looks like. And whatever it looks like, I get the top bunk."

There was no top bunk. The barracks suite with our names on it was a tiny freestanding cottage in a row of tiny freestanding cottages that stretched well down a wooden path that was clearly meant to be the residential area of the base. The suite consisted of a small common room with a couch, table with chairs, and bookshelves. A monitor was placed between the bookshelves and was currently showing a screen saver. On the bookshelves were individually labeled packages—presumably our additional jumpsuits.

Two short, narrow hallways on either side of the common room revealed the individual bedrooms, each already with our names on their doors, which were wide enough for a twin bed and a small path to a wardrobe and a tiny desk with a chair. A small shelf was above the desk. A small window was above the bed. The bed included a mattress, a pillow, two sets of sheets and pillowcases. The desk had a folder on it, which said Tanaka Base Guide and Directory. On the shelf was an envelope, which read New Occupant, and a small plant in a tiny pot. I went into my room and walked over to the desk and picked up the envelope.

"Where's the kitchen?" I heard Aparna say.

"Forget the kitchen, where's the damn *loo*?" Niamh responded.

"Check the base guide," I yelled back.

"The what?"

"It's in your room," I said, and then opened the envelope. There was a letter inside.

Dear new occupant,

It's tradition here when we swap out our lodgings that we leave a note and a small gift for the new occupant, to welcome them and to wish them luck with their tour. This time, it's bitter-

sweet for me because I've decided this will be my last tour. No one else knows this yet; you're the first person I've told besides myself.

I paused at this, and then kept reading.

It's also bittersweet because when we leave this world behind we leave everything about it behind. We can take nothing from it and tell no one of it. Three years of my life—four tours!—and all I have is the memory. It's one of the reasons I have to leave it. As wonderful as it has been, it feels like too much of my life has been unreal. Imaginary. Maybe I'm the only one who feels this way, but even if it's just me it's enough. It's time for me to go back to the real world, and have a real life.

I did a foolish thing this last tour: I decided my room would be nicer with some green in it, and brought a cutting home and put it in a pot on my windowsill. When it came to go, I realized I couldn't take it with me. So I am leaving it to you, as a gift. I hope you will care for it like I did, and that it gives you joy as it did for me. And perhaps when you leave again in six months you will give it to the next occupant of this room, who might even be the person who replaces me.

Good luck and best wishes to you. Think of me from time to time, I who am back in our other world. I will think of you, too, whoever you are, and fondly.

> *Yours,*
> *Sylvia Braithwhite*

I set the letter down, picked up the small pot with the plant, and put it back on the windowsill.

"Whoever had my room last left a big pile of poopfruit on my desk," Niamh yelled, from their room. "Seriously, what the actual fuck?"

CHAPTER 8

Brynn MacDonald pointed at Aparna. "Okay," she said. "You're the new biologist. Say it."

"Say what?" Aparna asked.

"The thing that's been bothering you since the moment you saw a kaiju."

We were all in a (very) small conference room at the administrative building, and it was just after nine in the morning, and we were having, as promised, our orientation session. Brynn MacDonald, who we last saw a little bit drunk, was emphatically not so now, and as promised she remembered all our names and what we were at the base to do. We all sat at the (very) small wooden table, in (normal-size) wooden chairs, and I wondered if they had been made at the base. MacDonald stood, next to a bookcase. Right at the moment she was staring at Aparna in particular, waiting on an answer.

"All right, fine," Aparna said. "These kaiju are too big. They shouldn't exist."

"Because of the square-cube law," MacDonald prompted.

"For starters."

"Everyone up on the square-cube law?" MacDonald asked. Nods all around; Niamh and Kahurangi were scientists and I was a nerd, we all knew that as things got bigger, their volume increased as a cube of the multiplier while the surface area increased as a square. MacDonald turned her attention back to Aparna. "So, the kaiju have far too much volume, their muscles would snap, their lungs couldn't give them enough oxygen, they couldn't feed themselves enough energy, their nervous systems would run too slowly to move them around, their bones would tear out of their bodies, and by all known physical laws, they would lie groaning in their own pile of meat until they died."

"They wouldn't groan because there's no way they could inflate their lungs, but yes, I think that otherwise covers it," Aparna said.

MacDonald nodded, turned, pulled a massive binder from the bookshelf, and dropped it in front of Aparna with a thud.

"What's this?" Aparna asked.

"Your homework," MacDonald said. "It's a precis on all the biology of the kaiju that we understand so far."

Aparna goggled at the massive binder. "This is a *precis*?"

"The short version, yes," MacDonald said, and then looked at us other three. "You don't have to read this, but you should, it's fascinating. If you don't look at it, all I ask for you to remember is that the kaiju have a biology that is utterly unlike anything we have back home. There is literally no analogue. The kaiju don't break physics because you can't break physics. The square-cube law applies to them just like it does to any creature. But their unique biology allows for their size and movement. Unique to us, I mean. Relatively common biology here."

"Tom Stevens said yesterday we shouldn't think of them as animals. That they're systems or environments," I said to MacDonald.

MacDonald pointed to the binder. "He's quoting that," she said. "And good for him, I thought he just skimmed it when I gave it to him. But even that is too limiting." She pointed at me. "*You* are a system and an environment, after all—in terms of sheer numbers, there are as many nonhuman cells in and on your body than there are human cells. Bacteria, fungi, protists, even tiny parasitic mites that live in your face."

"I could be happy never talking about tiny skin mites ever again," I said.

"They come out when you sleep, you know."

"I do now, thanks for that."

"Wait until you see the kaiju parasites, they're a trip," MacDonald said. "My point here is that any of the metaphors that we use to understand animals or any creature back home don't quite convey what we deal with when we talk about what kaiju are."

"Give us an example," Niamh said.

MacDonald squinted at Niamh. "Physics, right?"

"Physics and astronomy, yeah."

MacDonald hefted another binder out of the bookshelf and thudded it down in front of Niamh. "Kaiju get their energy from nuclear reactors."

Niamh stared at the massive binder, and then back up at MacDonald. "Excuse me, what?"

"Nuclear reactors," MacDonald said.

"Where . . . do they get a nuclear reactor?"

"They grow them."

"The actual fuck do they do *that*?"

Aparna pushed her biology binder over to Niamh. "You're going to want this one," she said.

MacDonald pushed the binder back to Aparna and then turned her attention back to Niamh. "How do *you* grow a brain? Or, if you're someone of the uterus-bearing persuasion, an entire other human being?"

"There's a *difference*," Niamh said.

"Is there?"

"You're saying they *evolved* to grow nuclear reactors," Kahurangi said to MacDonald.

"We think so, yes."

"Not to repeat what Niamh said, but how does that even make sense? What's the fossil record on that? Do we have any evidence of proto-kaiju with intermediary structures that somehow lead to fully functioning nuclear reactors?"

"Ah, the geologist." MacDonald turned back to the bookshelf.

"Oh, shit," Kahurangi said, anticipating another thuddingly large binder, but the one MacDonald pulled out this time was thin enough that she was able to simply hand it to him. Kahurangi took it and appeared almost disappointed in its size. "That's it?" he said. "Really?"

MacDonald nodded. "Unlike these two"—she motioned at Aparna and Niamh—"you have less prior work on the geology and paleontology fronts because as a practical matter, it's more difficult to do site work."

"Ah," Kahurangi said. "And why is that?"

"A proportionally higher chance of being killed and eaten."

"Yes, I can see how that would put a damper on research."

"The last Gold Team geologist decided to retire after we basically had to reattach a limb. For a second time."

"Oh."

"Well, that's not completely accurate. It wasn't the same limb twice. They were different limbs."

"I . . . had not been informed of this," Kahurangi said.

"There's a reason Tanaka Base is in the trees," MacDonald said. "The jungle floor is not very friendly. Which reminds me, which of you have had weapons training?"

We all stared blankly.

"Hmmmm," MacDonald said, and appeared to make a mental note. She turned her attention back to Kahurangi. "To answer your question briefly, we don't have much evidence of intermediary structures because we've been limited in what we can do and how we can research. You have a lot of ground you can break here, literally."

"As long as I don't get eaten, got it," Kahurangi said.

"We can say that in general the evolution of life here is wildly different, because of differing factors that are represented in the geological samples we do have. Because some initial conditions were different, life here evolved very differently."

"How differently?" Aparna asked.

"We're the only mammals on this planet, for one thing," MacDonald said. "They otherwise didn't evolve at all. Same with birds. There are reptiles here but they're not as successful as a biological class as they are back home. We have analogues here for each, of course. Life evolves to fill niches. But they're not the same biologically."

"You have frogs, though," I pointed out.

"Yes. Not the same species of frogs as back home, but frogs and other amphibians. Lots of fish, insects, and invertebrates."

"So whatever happened differently here happened around the time amphibians and reptiles branched off."

MacDonald pointed to the thin binder. "Well, you tell us," she said. "But it's worth noting that it's not that simple. We have flowering plants here, for example. As far as we can tell they evolved almost exactly like they do at home. It's complicated."

"It always is," Kahurangi said.

"Which reminds me, you're chemistry, too," MacDonald said, and heaved a huge binder toward Kahurangi before he could react. "There's a lot more there."

"Evidently." Kahurangi stared at the new binder.

"One big difference here is that there is a relatively higher percentage of actinides present on this version of Earth than ours. Which includes uranium and thorium. They are taken up and used by the life-forms here in a way they're not back home."

Something clicked in my brain. "So everything here refines uranium. And the kaiju evolved to use it."

"That's nuts," Niamh said.

"That's evolution," Aparna corrected.

"Maybe," Kahurangi amended.

MacDonald squinted at me. "You're our new grunt."

"I lift things," I agreed.

MacDonald nodded, turned, and got out the biggest binder of all.

"Starting with that, apparently," I said.

"Tanaka Base systems and operations," MacDonald said. "No fair you not getting homework, too."

"This is actually kind of fascinating," I said to the rest of the newbies, at lunch, as I flipped through my binder.

"You really *are* a nerd," Kahurangi said.

We sat together in the base dining hall. It was formally serving lunch, one of the four meals that were put together by staff, but it also featured an area open for grazing at all times, and a couple of kitchenettes that anyone who wanted to could use.

"Don't listen to him," Niamh said. "Live your truth. Go on, tell us something fascinating about this place."

"We make fuel and plastic out of thin air," I said.

"How do we do that?" Aparna asked.

"You all saw that refinery-looking thing by the airfield?" They nodded. "That's where they do it. They suck carbon dioxide and water vapor out of the air and then catalyze it. Depending on the process, you get plastics or fuel."

"Great, we're polluting a second Earth," Niamh said.

"If we're pulling it out of the air, it's carbon neutral," Kahurangi pointed out.

"I'll remember you said that the next time you're sucking on exhaust fumes."

"What uses fuel or plastic here anyway?" Aparna asked. She held up her wooden chopsticks and then tapped them on her wooden bowl. "I don't see much of it. And I was told this base runs mostly on solar and wind."

"The airships use the fuel, mostly. The plastic gets used to repair things we bring over, like laptops and tablets, and for some other things." I pointed to the netting that encased the whole of the base. "That stuff." I picked at our suits. "This stuff, too."

"Yeah, what's the deal with the jumpsuits?" Kahurangi said. "I feel like we're being dressed by someone who watched way too many science fiction movies from the seventies."

I flipped through the binder. "So, they keep the critters out, for one. They're also designed to encourage evaporation of body sweat in hot and humid conditions, like this planet, all the damn time."

"That's not a joke," Aparna said. "I feel like I'm swimming."

"You feel like you're swimming, I feel like I'm stinking," Niamh said, slapping their jumpsuit. "These things make me want to take a shower every fifteen minutes. Which reminds me, why do they make us walk to a common lavatory to shower and shit? Why don't we have those in our cottages?"

I flipped to the section about the showers. "Ease of plumbing, mostly," I said.

"That's bullshit. I protest."

"Please don't poop in our cottage," Aparna said.

"I will not," Niamh said. "But you know I'm right."

"Ease of plumbing and also to help with collection of human waste," I continued, "which when sterilized and treated is used for various light manufacturing purposes, and to fertilize the crops we eat."

We all stopped and looked at our food. "Well, that's just *great*," Niamh said.

"Everything gets recycled here," I said. "And everything we can't recycle gets shipped back to human Earth. We're meant to have zero ecological impact."

"What about meat?" Kahurangi said, spearing something that looked meaty on his plate. "Is this, like, actually beef?"

"Probably," I said a minute later, after checking. "We have some aquaculture tanks for various arthropods and fish stocks, and we bring in some foods we can't easily grow here. Anything meat-, dairy-, or grain-based. Sugar and some spices. Coffee and tea. Most of the runs that the *Shobijin* makes are for supplies. Food, medical supplies, technology."

"That sounds expensive," Kahurangi said, swallowing his (probably) meat.

"From what I can see, everything here is expensive," I said. "Or would be, if we had to consider what everything cost, which, apparently, we don't have to, much."

"It's a socialist paradise!" Niamh crowed.

"It might be easier just to bring along a few chickens, is my point," Kahurangi said.

Aparna shook her head at this. "They don't want to run the risk of introducing foreign species here any more than they have to."

Kahurangi smirked at this. "I think if a chicken tried to escape here, it wouldn't last very long."

"It's not just the chicken, it's everything that comes with the chicken," Aparna said. "Microbes. Parasites. Viruses. Life here is different, but it's probably not all *that* different. Well, not on the smaller end of things. And the creatures here don't have any defenses against anything a chicken might carry. A bird flu could wipe them all out." She turned to me. "I'm guessing the greenhouses are the most biologically secure buildings on the base."

I flipped to the greenhouse section. "You would be correct," I said. "Airlocks and heavy air and water filtration and hand pollination."

"Someone's job here is to swab flowers," Niamh said.

"Actually," I said, and flipped to another page, and held it up. "It's *most* people's job at some point. Everyone here has one or two primary roles that they do, but there are only a hundred fifty of us at the base, and a lot of jobs that need doing. So in addition to your full-time job, every day everyone gets chores that have to be completed and reported in as done." I pulled out my phone, which was connected to the local Wi-Fi. "There's an app."

"Enjoy your swabbing," Aparna said to Niamh, who threw a crouton at her.

"What about the kaiju?" Kahurangi asked.

"What about them?"

"I mean, look," Kahurangi said. "We're in a place where monsters roam free and things that humans have never experienced wait for us, and so far, all we're doing is wearing plastic pants, catching up on required reading"—he tapped his two binders—"and being told we'll be doing menial tasks."

"So, you're asking when you get to play with the kaiju," I said.

"I wouldn't put it that way, but yes."

"Your predecessor played with the kaiju and had a limb ripped off twice," Niamh reminded him.

"Two limbs, ripped off once," Aparna amended.

"Either way, not exactly a *fun* time on Planet Kaiju."

"I'm not saying I want to walk up to one and announce that I'm on the buffet," Kahurangi said. "But the name of the organization is the Kaiju Preservation Society. When do we get to preserve some kaiju?"

As it turned out, the answer to that was: the very next day.

CHAPTER 9

"Oh, there you are," Tom said to me as I came into the dining hall. I had stopped by the dining hall to get something cold to drink, he was coming out with a mug of something hot, most likely coffee.

"Here I am," I agreed. I motioned to his coffee. "How can you drink that?"

"It's . . . coffee?" he said. "And it's ten a.m. and yet my brain still needs to wake up?"

"It's like ninety degrees."

"Thirty degrees," Tom corrected. "We're metric here."

"It's *hot,* is my point."

"You get used to it after the first couple of tours. I hardly notice it anymore."

I stood there sweating in my jumpsuit, overloading its ability to wick away my sweat. "That must be nice."

"It'll happen to you," Tom promised. "How's the first workday?"

"I'm lifting things," I said. I had woken up and checked the base app and discovered that I was a very, very popular person: My task queue had fifteen items on it, mostly involving moving things, lifting things, and couriering things from one place to the next. Tanaka Base was not as vast as the Lower East Side, but I was getting a workout regardless. "I'm vaguely resentful that füdmüd gave me more relevant experience for this world than a full decade of higher education did."

"It's funny about that. Listen, I just put a priority task in your queue. Chem lab has some canisters it needs to get down to the helipad, which means you will meet Martin, our copter pilot. That should be fun, he's a kick." There was a light notification ping on my phone as Tom said this. "That's probably the notification right now."

"Is it such a priority that I can't get something to drink?"

"Not at all. Always hydrate. Then go to the chem lab. Enjoy your beverage." He tipped his mug full of queasily hot liquid at me and headed off.

I went into the dining hall and perused my choices. There was water, tea, coffee, juice that looked like orange juice but, I don't know, could have been poopfruit or something. There was also a soda fountain, but our in-room base guides had warned us to be moderate with its use, because otherwise the syrups would run out fast. The guide suggested no more than one eight-ounce glass of the colored sugar water a day. I decided to do without. There was no need to import my crippling diet cola addiction to a brand-new world, and besides, the fountain was Pepsi products anyway. New planet, new life.

I downed two large glasses of water and checked the base app. Tom's priority task was indeed there, along with a long list of other tasks I was requested for, which was being added to by the minute. To be fair, I wasn't the only one working the queue; there was also my Blue Team counterpart, Val, who looked like she could bench-press me and not break a sweat. I met her earlier in the day because hauling a compost canister from Sewage and Recycling to Greenhouse C was a two-person job, unless you wanted compost to break loose and roll all the way through the base, which we emphatically did not.

I checked off Tom's task in my queue, signaling to Val that I was taking that task, and alerting the chem lab that I was on my way. Then I bussed my glass and walked across the base to my destination, picking up a transport cart at Maintenance along the way.

Kahurangi was there with his Blue Team counterpart, Dr. Pham Bian. "I found out what we use chemistry for on Kaiju Earth," he said.

"Meth," I said.

"Even better."

"What could possibly be better than meth?" I asked, amazed.

"Pheromones," Dr. Pham said, and rapped a large, pressurized canister, which I suspected I was there to retrieve.

"Not just any pheromones," Kahurangi added. "*Kaiju* pheromones."

"Wow," I said. "Okay. Cool. And we do this *why?*"

"To get them to do what we want them to," Dr. Pham said. "You can't just talk to one. So we make these to get our point across. Like, 'Danger here' or 'This is claimed territory.'"

"And they listen?"

"Sometimes."

"I'd be worried about that qualification."

"You work with what you have," Dr. Pham said.

"I suppose you do." I pointed to the canister. "And what do these pheromones say?"

"These say, 'Let's get it on,'" Kahurangi said.

I considered this. "Kaiju booty call in a canister."

Kahurangi grinned. "Cool, right?"

"It's nice to see you've been keeping busy on your first day of work."

"Nah, Dr. Pham has had these brewing for a while. I get to work on the next set, though."

"You must be very excited."

"You mock me, but I *am,*" Kahurangi said.

"Dr. Lautagata has been very enthusiastic about our work this morning," Dr. Pham said. It took me a moment to realize that she was referring to Kahurangi; in the three days that I had known him, I never learned his surname. Or, apparently, that he had a doctorate.

"I mean, who wouldn't be," I replied. "So, how many canisters am I picking up?"

Dr. Pham pointed. "These four," she said. "And you'll have some others to pick up from Martin, but there's no rush on those, we won't need them immediately. Dr. Lautagata will accompany you."

"Good," I said. "Then maybe Dr. Lautagata will help me get the canisters on the cart, too."

Kahurangi grinned again and started lifting.

"These the baby-makers?" Martin Satie asked, pointing to the canisters. He sounded like he might be originally from Québec, which meant that strictly speaking, he was closer to home than any of us.

"They are," Kahurangi said. He swatted at the tiny flies trying valiantly to eat his face, only to be frustrated by the netting. The three of us were standing on one of Tanaka Base's helipads, on which a helicopter appeared at the ready.

Satie grunted at this and headed to the hangar by the helipad, then stopped and looked at the two of us. "Well, come on," he said. "Let's get this put together."

We both looked at the helicopter, confused. "Pardon?" Kahurangi said.

"Do you think I'm gonna fly up to a kaiju, roll down a window, and throw a canister at it?" Satie said. "No, I am not. Come help me set up the scaffold." He started walking again. Kahurangi and I looked at each other, shrugged, and followed Satie into the hangar.

The scaffold in question was a carbon-fiber structure that passed through the helicopter's cargo hold, behind its main cabin. We put it on the helicopter while Satie secured it and then showed us how to attach the canisters, first to the scaffolding and then to an apparatus that would release the contents of the canisters. The helicopter now looked like a crop duster.

"You want to stand back now," Satie said to us. We did as he said and stood back. Satie went into the main cabin and quickly flipped a toggle switch, and just as quickly flipped it back. The tiniest bit of the kaiju pheromone spritzed out.

"Oh, holy Jesus," I said.

Kahurangi groaned and turned away, covering his face.

Satie laughed. "Like it?"

"Not really."

"Describe the smell to me."

"Are you serious right now?"

"Yes, I want to know."

"It's like a family of raccoons hotboxed themselves to death in a dumpster, and someone distilled their fermented remains."

"Huh," Satie said. "I usually just say it smells like Malört, but I like your version, too." He motioned to us. "Okay, then. Get in."

"What?" I said.

Satie stared at us. "Which one of you is Dr. Lautagata?" Kahurangi raised his hand. "So, you need to come observe and report back to Dr. Pham."

"Report back what?"

"How well your perfume works," Satie said. "And you." He pointed at me. "You have to spray the stuff when I tell you."

"You can't do it yourself?" I asked. "It's just a toggle."

"You ever fly a helicopter around an aroused and amorous kaiju?"

"I have not," I admitted.

"Okay, then." He looked at the two of us. "Either of you been in a helicopter before?"

"I have," Kahurangi said.

"How did it go?"

"I threw up."

Satie motioned to the rear of the main cabin. "You sit in the back."

"I realize I should have asked this before I got into the helicopter," I said, over the headset Satie gave me, "but . . . *why* are we doing this?"

"You mean why are we traveling a hundred klicks to spray a monster with horny juice?" he said.

"Yes, that."

"Well, you know how back in the other place, we have pandas?"

"I've heard of them, yes," I said, and reflected on how quickly the place I had lived all of my life up to three days ago was now "the other place."

"Pandas are cute, but they're not what you would call rocket scientists, and sometimes they forget how to breed, you know? So humans have to help them make a love connection. Well, kaiju are the biggest, stupidest pandas you will ever meet."

"Kaiju forget how to have *sex*?" Kahurangi said.

"They forget a lot of things, I'm gonna tell you," Satie said. "They're the top of the evolutionary ladder here, but evolution definitely didn't select for brains on this planet. Everything here is dim as a rock. The gentleman we're calling on today is even less smart than your average kaiju. There's a lady of his species one valley over from him, has been trying to make his acquaintance for the last year. Every time she comes over, he tries to fight her. So, we're here to change his mind."

"Okay, but why do we care?" I asked.

"Why do we care about pandas?"

"Because they're cute," Kahurangi said. "Literally that's why."

"You're not wrong, but the answer I was thinking about is that they're endangered. Well, so are Edward and Bella."

"Edward and Bella?" I said. "You named these kaiju after friggin' *Twilight*?"

"*I* didn't," Satie said. "If it were up to me, I would have named them Sid and Nancy. Fits their personalities better. But no one asked me. One of you millennials did it."

"Millennials ruining kaiju naming," I said to Kahurangi.

"We're just the worst," he confirmed.

"Ed and Bel are the only two of their species on this part of the continent. We don't usually see them north of forty degrees latitude, and we don't see too many of them below that as it is. So we want to see if we can get them to make more of each other. We're the Kaiju Preservation Society. We're gonna try to preserve some kaiju."

"And how is that going so far?" Kahurangi asked.

"Not great! This is try number five." Satie jerked his head back toward the canisters. "Dr. Pham's been tweaking the formula as we've gone along. That's why you're here, Dr. Lautagata. You get to tell her how Ed reacts to this version."

"How did he react the first four times?"

"Various sorts of pissed off, mostly."

"That's not good."

"It's not, but I'm a good pilot. The helicopter usually doesn't take any damage."

"Usually," Kahurangi said, looking at me deadpan as he did so.

"The last version was almost there. Doc said she definitely saw evidence of a tumescent cloaca."

I laughed.

"What's got you chuckling?" Satie said.

"I was just thinking that *Edward's Tumescent Cloaca* would have been an excellent band name."

"Emo, obviously," Kahurangi said.

"Their first album glistened with promise, but their follow-up was a little flaccid."

"Their third album was really shitty."

"To be fair, the competition was stiff that year."

"I just thought that they should have showed more spunk."

I was going to add more to this terrible, disgraceful conversation, but then we crested a hill and I got my first look at Edward.

"Holy shit," I said.

Satie grinned. "Cute like a panda, right?"

Kahurangi made a noise at this. "Mate, if you think that's cute, you've been on this planet too long."

"Seconded," I said. "That thing looks like H. P. Lovecraft's panic attack."

Satie nodded. "Wait 'til you see his cloaca."

"We're not *actually* going to see his cloaca, are we?" Kahurangi asked.

"Dr. Lautagata, by the time we're done, there's not much of Edward we *won't* see."

"How close are we going to get?" I asked.

"Pretty close."

"Is that absolutely necessary?" Kahurangi asked.

"Did you put missiles on my helicopter?" Satie asked him. "Filled with pheromones?"

"No."

"Then it's absolutely necessary. Don't worry, Doctor. Getting up close to him is the easy part. It's the getting away that's going to be the trick."

CHAPTER 10

"Why isn't he eating us?" I asked. We were now close enough to Edward that this was not an entirely irrelevant question.

"He's asleep," Satie said.

I glanced over at him. "Asleep?"

"They sleep, yup."

"How can you tell when he's asleep?"

"He's not eating us, for one," Satie said. "You can't see his eyes, for another."

I looked out at Edward. "He has *eyes*?"

"We call them eyes. I'm sure by now someone explained to you how it's all more complicated than that. Trust me, you'll know them when you see them."

"No real eyes, but an actual *cloaca*," Kahurangi said, from the back.

"I don't design them, I just fly to them," Satie replied.

"Well, let's douse this thing with pheromones and go," I said. I kept looking at Edward not being awake and was reasonably certain *awake* would be a bowel-loosening state.

Satie shook his head. "Not how it works. We spray now, he'll just sleep through them. Then Dr. Lautagata will have nothing to report, and Dr. Pham will be angry with you."

"I'm willing to lie," Kahurangi said.

"Today's your first day on the job, so I'll tell you something you don't know, which is you don't cross Dr. Pham," Satie said. "She will come for you in the night, son. This is a tip I am giving you for free."

"She seems pretty nice."

"She is nice. Wonderful person. And also if you lie to her about these pheromones, she will gut you and leave you for the tree crabs."

"There are *tree crabs*?" Kahurangi asked.

Satie ignored this. "We have to wake him up," he said to me.

"And how do we do that?" I asked.

Satie moved the helicopter closer to Edward. Much closer.

"Whoa, whoa, *whoa*," Kahurangi said.

"I'm with him," I added.

"Getting this close is usually enough to get his attention," Satie said.

"You've done this before."

"Sure."

"And you think this is *wise*." I gestured to us being mere meters away from a fleshy wall of kaiju.

Satie snorted. "If we were wise, we wouldn't be on this planet."

"Hey, what are those?" Kahurangi pointed at the wall of kaiju flesh. I followed his finger to a spot on Edward where things were, for lack of a better word, squirming.

"Parasites," Satie said.

"The size of *rottweilers*."

"If we stick around, you'll see larger."

"I think I've already cast my vote on sticking around."

"It doesn't look like he's waking up," I said to Satie. Edward's parasites might be moving about, but he was not.

Satie grimaced. "Okay, well. I have one more trick up the sleeve." He took us vertically up the wall that was Edward, until we were hovering over the top of him. There was enough room on the top to land, if we wanted to. I hoped that we did not want to.

"You ready with that switch?" Satie asked me.

I grabbed it. "Ready."

"Okay. I'm going to do a thing, and then I'm going to count to three. When I get to three, you flip it on and count to five, then switch it off."

"We're not going to just let it run?"

"Why would we do that?"

"Look, Martin," I said. "I don't know why I need to remind you of this, but this is literally my first time doing this and *I know nothing*."

"A five count is gonna work just fine," Satie said. "We'll cover the rest after. Ready?"

"For what?" I asked.

"This," he said, and brought the copter down hard on top of Edward. Edward squished like a pudding with a hard crust on it. Satie hovered the copter a couple of meters above where he just poked Edward.

The area that Satie had just bounced off started to glow.

"One," Satie said.

The glow suddenly focused itself into an intensely bright three-meter circle.

"Uhhhh, I think I found the eye," I said.

"Two," Satie said, and then jammed the copter back down into the heavily illuminated surface.

Edward roared.

"Three!" Satie said, and drove us straight up. I flipped the switch and started to count, watching the eye as I did so. It took until four before we started gaining altitude relative to it. Edward had been chasing us up the whole way.

"Off!" I yelled at Satie. He yanked us over and away from Edward, who narrowly missed swatting us with, well, whatever it was you wanted to call what he was swatting us with, since *tentacle* seemed too limited at the moment.

"Can you still see him?" Satie asked. Both I and Kahurangi said yes. "Watch his eyes!"

"What are we looking for?" Kahurangi said.

Edward stopped roaring. There were four wide disks of light we took for his eyes. We stared at them.

They suddenly contracted. The new sunlike pinpoints focused on us.

"Oh, shit," Kahurangi said.

And then, equally suddenly, there were wings.

"Oh, *shit*," Kahurangi repeated.

"There are fucking *wings* on this thing?" I yelled, incredulously.

"There sure are," Satie said.

"There were no wings a minute ago!"

"They were there," Satie said. "You were just looking for eyes."

Edward heaved into the air.

"Oh shit oh shit oh shit oh shit," Kahurangi said.

"We should *go*," I said to Satie.

Satie wheeled the helicopter around and started to fly away from Edward.

"Okay, so, right now, there's good news and some potentially not-great news," Satie said. He reached over with his left hand and clicked a button, which turned on a monitor showing us the view from the rear camera. It was, at the moment, mostly filled with Edward. "That head bounce pissed him off, and he was probably going to kill us, but then he got a whiff of those pheromones and now he doesn't want to kill us anymore."

"Are you sure?" Kahurangi said.

"Eyes dilated, right?"

We nodded.

"That's your sign."

"If he doesn't want to kill us now, why is he chasing us?"

"Because he wants to do something else to us instead."

"We're gonna get *fucked by a kaiju*?!?" Kahurangi yelled, processing the implication.

"That's the good news."

"How is this *good news*?"

"It's good news because as long as he wants to mate with us, he doesn't want to kill us," Satie said. He dipped the helicopter down, flying it dangerously close to the canopy of trees below. Edward was momentarily confused but then trimmed to match. "Which means he'll *chase* us but won't *attack* us. We want him to chase us because we're leading him to Bella."

"And when he sees Bella, he'll go for her instead of us," I said.

"We'll see. That's the plan."

"What's the less-great news?"

"The pheromones wear off. Quickly. We have to keep dosing him until we get him to Bella."

I considered this. "So we have to keep close enough to him to hit him with more pheromones."

"Yes."

"Because if we don't, he'll want to kill us, in which case we're dead."

"Yes."

"But if we do, and we're sloppy, then he'll grab us and try to fuck the helicopter. In which case we're dead."

"Yes."

"And you do this *all the time*."

"Yes," Satie said. "Sort of. This is as far as we've ever gotten."

"Wow, he's close," Kahurangi said, pointing at the monitor.

"Dose him again," Satie said to me. "Count of five."

I flipped the toggle switch and did a five count. Edward took the spray straight in the maw, seemed to choke and sputter in the monitor, and then disappeared.

"The hell?" Kahurangi said.

"Uhhhhh," I said, looking around through the helicopter windows.

"He does that," Satie observed.

"Disappear?"

"Yeah."

"He's a one-hundred-fifty-meter-tall nightmare. How the fuck does he disappear?" Kahurangi yelled.

"Well," Satie said, and then Edward dive-bombed us from above, setting himself directly in our path, appendages grasping toward us.

We all screamed and Satie did a thing and our helicopter did another thing and somehow we got past Edward, but not before I saw an image I would take to my grave.

Edward's tumescent cloaca.

After I gathered myself, I looked back at Kahurangi, who was mouth agape, eyes unblinking.

"You saw it, too," I said.

Kahurangi nodded. "I'm going to need to get seriously shit-faced when we get back."

"I'll be joining you."

"Jesus, Jamie. What is *wrong* with this planet?"

"He's back on our tail," Satie said to me. "Hit him again."

"You sure about that?" I asked.

"If he wasn't hopped up on that stuff, we'd already be a debris field on the jungle floor," Satie said. "So, yeah. I'm sure. Make it six seconds this time."

We hit Edward with three more blasts before we got to the Valley of Bella. She was awake, had her wings out, and, if possible, was even more objectively terrifying than Edward.

"It's like she knew we were coming," I said.

"She did," Satie said. "She has ears. Sort of."

"We can go now, right?" Kahurangi said.

Satie shook his head. "One more thing to do."

I looked at Bella. "Let me guess," I said.

"If he's following the pheromones, they have to lead to her," Satie said.

"And how does *she* feel about us?"

"She's been hot for Edward for a while now. Let's hope she keeps her eyes on the prize." Satie goosed the helicopter forward.

We went at Bella straight on, Edward right behind us. Bella stood her ground.

"This could be a *very bad* sandwich scenario," Kahurangi said.

"Let the canisters run," Satie said to me. "Just make sure they're off the instant we clear her."

I nodded and flipped the canisters on. I could see what he planned to do.

"Very bad," Kahurangi said. "Very, very, very, very, very bad."

Edward started screaming. Bella started screaming back. We joined in, for what good it would do, and Satie wrenched us over what passed for Bella's shoulder. I flipped off the canisters as we passed over her, and then there was an explosion of Earth and kaiju as Edward smashed into Bella and the two of them rolled into the ground, snapping trees like Popsicle sticks as they did so. We dodged clods of earth the size of MINI Coopers and climbed into the sky.

When we were high and far enough away, Satie turned us so we could get a look at the aftermath of our mission.

"So, uh, *that's* a sight," Kahurangi said. "I'm going to have a hell of a time trying to describe that to Dr. Pham."

"Don't worry, I had cameras running the whole time," Satie said.

"What?" Kahurangi stared at Satie. "I thought you said you needed me to report back."

"I never said I wasn't running video."

"I could have stayed at Tanaka!"

Satie motioned at the copulating kaiju. "You would have missed this."

"We almost *died*."

"Nah," Satie said. "I'm good at my job."

Kahurangi stared some more and then took off his headset, signaling he was done speaking to Satie for at least a while.

"He'll get over it," Satie said to me.

"Do we need to be here for this?" I asked.

"Are you kidding? This is pure science."

"It feels like kaiju Pornhub."

"This is the first time we're seeing this species mate," Satie said. "If I weren't getting footage of this, every biologist in the KPS would hunt me down. No, we'll stay for a while longer, if that's all right with you."

"I mean, I feel like we should flee while the fleeing is good," I said. "When they're done, they might both want a snack."

Satie considered this for a moment. "You know what, I think we've had enough science for one day," he said, and started to wheel us around to home.

As he did so, the radio sparked to life. "Tanaka Chopper Two, come in," someone said, from base. It sounded to me like it could be MacDonald, but I couldn't be sure.

"This is Tanaka Chopper Two, go ahead," Satie said.

"Chopper Two, we need you to check out an untagged kaiju forty klicks southwest of your location," base said.

Satie glanced at his instruments. Apparently, being chased by a kaiju will take a lot out of a helicopter. "Base, what's the nature of the issue?" he asked. "Is this a spot and identify?"

"Negative, Chopper Two. We think we have a venting issue."

Satie paused. "Say again, base."

"We think we have a venting issue, Chopper Two. Request visual confirmation and estimate of severity. Acknowledge."

"Acknowledged. Heading out, over." He turned to me. "Well, shit," he said.

"Is this a problem?" I asked.

"Let's hope not," Satie said, turned to Kahurangi, and motioned for him to put his headset back on.

"What is it?" Kahurangi asked.

"We just got another mission. Emergency. We have to head southwest forty klicks."

Kahurangi frowned at this. "Are we likely to get killed on this one, too?"

"Maybe."

"Maybe?"

"I could let you out here if you want," Satie said. "You could walk back."

Kahurangi rolled his eyes and took off his headset again.

Satie looked at me and smiled. "He'll get over it," he said, and set us on our way.

11

We spotted the smoke before we spotted the kaiju itself; the smoke curled into the sky and hung in thick and listless air. There was more than one area offering up smoke. Dark smudges traced a path toward the creature, and we followed it.

"Do they usually set things on fire?" I asked. Satie shook his head. "Then why is this one doing it?"

"It can't help it," he said.

"There it is," Kahurangi said as we came around a hill. He'd put his headset back on as we traveled. He was pointing to the edge of a largish lake. The creature stood there, motionless, looking for all the world like it was trying to catch its breath. Behind it, things burned.

Satie maneuvered the copter out of the path of the smoke, and we hung motionless in the sky about a kilometer away from the kaiju.

"We're not getting closer?" I asked.

"Not if we can help it, no," Satie said.

Kahurangi snorted. "*That's* new."

"That *is* new," I agreed. "Why are we holding back this time?"

"We're here to see if it's venting," Satie said. "If it's venting, we don't want to be anywhere near it."

"What's 'venting'?" Kahurangi asked.

Satie didn't answer directly. Instead he looked down at my wrist, which had a smartwatch on it. "That thing have a stopwatch on it?"

"Sure." My smartwatch had multiple functions, about 90 percent of which I, like most people, never ever used. The stopwatch was one of them.

"Get it ready." Satie looked back at Kahurangi and motioned with his head to a console in between my seat and his. "There's a small set of field glasses in there. Get them out and use them."

Kahurangi nodded.

"Stopwatch is up," I said. "What am I using it for?"

Satie motioned with his head to the kaiju. "The next time that thing vents, start the timer as soon as it stops, until the next time it vents again."

"And this venting will be obvious?"

The kaiju split its head open, and a blinding stream of light came out of it and hit the surface of the lake, vaporizing it instantly.

"Pretty obvious, yeah," Satie said.

The stream of light stopped and I started the timer. "That thing has fire breath," I said.

Satie shook his head. "It's weirder than that. It's an ionized stream of particles. A plasma. It's several thousand degrees Celsius."

"I can see why you didn't want to get close to it." If a stream of plasma interacted with the helicopter, it would be a bad day for it and for us.

"How does the kaiju survive that sort of heat?" Kahurangi asked. He had the field glasses out, and was training them on the kaiju.

"If they keep it up, they don't," Satie said.

"Hey, I know this kaiju," Kahurangi said. "I remember this thing. It's the one that fought Kevin."

"You sure?" I asked.

He handed me the field glasses. "Check for yourself."

I took the glasses and trained them on the kaiju. I didn't remember the face, but I did remember a chunk of kaiju flying into the air during the fight. This kaiju had an impressive chunk of it missing in its midsection. "That's the one, all right," I said, and handed the glasses back to Kahurangi. "It covered a lot of ground between then and now."

"It got its ass kicked and hasn't stopped running since." Kahurangi put the glasses back up to his face.

"You saw this thing get in a fight?" Satie asked us.

"Yeah," Kahurangi said. "We were almost in the middle of it. We had trees flung at us."

"And this one was injured?"

"We saw chunks come off. Big ones. Why?"

"Because—" Satie stopped because the kaiju let out another stream of plasma. This one traced up the edge of the lake, making trees burst as it did so. I stopped the timer. Satie looked at me. "How much time?"

I glanced down. "Two minutes, eight point three eight seconds," I said.

"Okay, this is weird and gross," Kahurangi said. "Things are dropping off the kaiju."

"Like what?" Satie asked.

"I don't know. It looks like dandruff the size of small animals." Kahurangi looked around the glasses at Satie. "Are those its parasites?"

"Most likely," Satie said.

"So why are they falling off the kaiju?"

"For the same reason rats leave a sinking ship." Satie opened up a line back to base. "Base, this is Chopper Two."

"Chopper Two, go ahead."

"Spotted untagged kaiju, can visually confirm venting. Kaiju is currently at a two-minute interval and parasites are abandoning, over."

"Acknowledged, Chopper Two. Recommend RLH protocol."

"Acknowledged, base. Initiating RLH protocol." Satie switched off. He glanced at Kahurangi. "You can put those glasses away now."

"What's the RLH protocol?" I asked.

"It means *run like hell*," Satie said, turning the helicopter.

"And we're running like hell because—"

"Because the kaiju is probably about to go up."

"Define 'go up,'" Kahurangi said.

"You two were told about how kaiju are nuclear, yes?"

"Yeah. I'm still not sure how that's supposed to work or if I really believe it."

"Believe it. They're nuclear, and it's not a problem, until it is. A kaiju hits puberty and its bioreactor formed badly, or it gets into a fight and the integrity of the reactor is compromised. And then it goes very, very bad, very, very quickly."

A light went on in my head. "Venting," I said. "That plasma beam isn't something it's doing on purpose."

Satie shook his head. "No. It's something it's doing to try to get its reactor back under control."

"Does it work?"

"Sometimes. You can tell how bad it is by how much the kaiju vents. Once every couple of hours, it might survive."

"That one was two minutes between vents," I said.

Satie shrugged. "That's not so survivable."

"How do the parasites know that?" Kahurangi asked. "They're not leaving because they're counting the intervals."

"No," Satie agreed. "They're leaving because they're starting to burn."

Kahurangi opened his mouth to say something, closed it, and opened it again. "I'm going to ask a really stupid question here—"

"Yes, the kaiju is a walking nuclear bomb," Satie said. "That was your question, yes?"

"Actually I was going to ask something else about the parasites, but, uh, I guess, never mind that now. A *fucking nuclear bomb*?"

"How are you surprised?" Satie said. "What did you think we were talking about?"

"We were told these things had reactors!"

"Yes, and?"

"A nuclear reactor is not the same as a nuclear bomb! There are actual, like, *safeguards* in a nuclear reactor!"

"He has a point," I said.

"No, he doesn't," Satie said. "These things weren't *built*. They *evolved*. Evolution doesn't overengineer. The kaiju nuclear bioreactors work well enough. Until they don't."

"And then they wipe out all life over a hundred square kilometers," Kahurangi sneered.

"They don't go up that big," Satie said.

Kahurangi started to say something, but I held up a hand. "How big *do* they go up?"

"Your average kaiju will go off like a ten- or fifteen-kiloton bomb," Satie said.

"I don't have any sense of that," I said.

Satie checked his instruments. "It means that if that kaiju went up *right now,* we'd be just beyond the light blast damage radius." He glanced back briefly at Kahurangi. "Which means we'll survive. This helicopter has shielded electronics and instrumentation so it's resistant to being fried by an electromagnetic pulse. This is not the first time we've had a venting kaiju. Every minute we fly takes us farther away from it."

"Unless it decides to chase us," Kahurangi said.

Satie shook his head. "It's not chasing anything anymore. It went to that place to die."

"How do you know that?"

"When kaiju know they're dying, they try to head to water. The ocean if they can get to one, but any large body of water will do. Don't ask me why; I'm a pilot. But it's definitely a thing. The KPS learned that the hard way."

"What do you mean?" Kahurangi asked.

"This Tanaka Base isn't the first Tanaka Base," Satie said. "The first one was about forty klicks east, on a peninsula on the inlet there. This was in the sixties. Juvenile kaiju with a bad reactor came through, walked right up to the base and went off. Eighty people dead before they knew it."

"Why'd it come into the base at all?" I asked.

"I'm not a kaiju, I don't know why they do things. But now we keep bases away from large bodies of water, and"—he motioned with his head to Kahurangi—"Dr. Pham and now Dr. Lautagata here make the 'stay away' pheromones to mark our territory around the base."

"And that works," I said.

"It's like everything about the kaiju," Satie said. "It works until it doesn't."

The world in front of us got very bright, which meant the world behind had gotten even brighter. The kaiju had gone off.

"It's about to get very bumpy," Satie warned us. "Dr. Lautagata, if you want to throw up now, you go right ahead."

"I did not throw up," Kahurangi said, at dinner that night, as he recounted the day's events to Aparna and Niamh. He and I had just gotten out of an hours-long meeting with Brynn MacDonald, her Blue Team counterpart, Jeneba Danso, Tom Stevens, and the leads of the biology and physics labs, going over everything from our helicopter ride. Martin Satie had been excused to tend to his helicopter. Apparently, he would be going out again soon.

"No, you just got enough radiation passing through your body to spontaneously turn into a tumor," Niamh said.

"I'm pretty sure it doesn't work like that," Kahurangi replied.

"That's just what a person who has spontaneously turned into a tumor would say."

Kahurangi turned to Aparna. "You're the biologist here. Help me."

"I'm not saying you are a sentient tumor," Aparna said. "But I would have to run some tests to be sure."

Kahurangi pointed at me. "Jamie was in the same helicopter! Where are the tumor accusations there?"

"I am definitely mostly tumor at this point," I admitted.

"I thought we were friends," Kahurangi said, narrowing his eyes at me.

"Tumors have no friends," I replied. "In other news, I found out today that Kahurangi has a doctorate."

"I mean, we all have doctorates." Aparna pointed to herself. "Dr. Chowdhury." She pointed to Niamh. "Dr. Healy."

"Fun fact, *Healy* means 'scientific' in Gaelic," Niamh said. "I am Dr. Scientific. You may bow to me now."

"I think I *won't*," I said.

"Look at that, the tumor is jealous it only has a master's."

"I am not. Okay, maybe a little."

"We still like you," Aparna said.

"And by *like,* we mean 'pity,'" Niamh added.

"If it makes you feel better, you have added a whole bunch of stuff to our workload," Aparna said.

"Well, good," I said. "How did I do that?"

"Technically, you didn't, the poor exploding kaiju did," said Niamh. "And not just us, everyone. Turns out exploding kaiju within traveling distance don't happen that often."

"They do for *us,*" Aparna noted.

"Yes, strictly going by numerical averages it happens to us four far more often than most people here," Niamh agreed. "Today has been all about looking at the data you two tumors have brought back, plus the material we got from the aerostats."

I nodded at this. Aerostats were what we had instead of satellites— Balloons with instruments, up where the kaiju won't try to fight them or eat them. It's how we knew about that kaiju in the first place. An aerostat picked up the radiation from the kaiju venting.

"See." Kahurangi pointed with a fork. "They definitely did *not* need us there. They could have covered it all with an aerostat."

Aparna shook her head. "No. Your video of the kaiju was useful. A much better angle. We got a better look at the parasites running away."

"Not that it did them any good," I said. "It's hard to outrun a nuclear blast."

"You did," Niamh pointed out.

"We didn't outrun it, we outflew it."

"Barely," Kahurangi added.

"Oh, come *on,*" Niamh said. "Stop with your whining already. Today you outran a horny kaiju *and* a mushroom cloud. If you can't enjoy that, there is a problem with you."

"Thank you for the horny kaiju footage, by the way," Aparna said. "That was . . . interesting to see."

"You should have caught the live show," I said.

Aparna nodded. "I'll bet it was something. Unfortunately, it's on the back burner for a while because of the exploding kaiju. It's a huge disruption to the ecosystem."

"A nuclear explosion will do that," Kahurangi said.

Aparna shook her head. "It's not that. Well, it *is* that, just not the way you think it is. The creatures here have a different relationship to radiation than we do, or life back home does. It scrambles our DNA and is lethal to us in high doses."

"Turns us into tumors," Niamh said, toggling fingers between me and Kahurangi.

"Here they *use* it," Aparna continued. "It's not a danger to them like it is to us. A nuclear event happens, anything that isn't immediately killed by the blast starts heading to the blast site."

"To do what?" Kahurangi asked.

"To feed, basically. A kaiju going up like that is just part of the life cycle here."

"So, you're saying there's a migration of life *to* the blast crater."

"There is. From small insects all the way up to other kaiju. They're all on the move."

"Which is the other thing," Niamh said. "You remember how they said something as powerful as a nuclear explosion thins the wall between this reality and ours?" Kahurangi and I nodded. "Well, we just had a big damn nuclear explosion, and right now the barrier between our world and this one is tissue thin at that location."

"What's there on our side?" I asked.

"Apparently, nothing," Niamh said. "It's part of a Canadian provincial park or something. No people and nothing larger than a moose, and I'm sorry for any moose who wanders over here. But on this side, we've got kaiju. Lots of them. Fucking Kevin and Bella and Edward, and some others, too, all starting to head in that direction. They can accidentally push through to our side. So our job until the breach seals enough to block them is to keep them away. Which means you"—she pointed at Kahurangi again—"will be making lots of your time brewing avoidance pheromone to keep them out, and *you*"—they pointed to me this time—"will be spending lots of time taking helicopter rides to spray it into their faces."

So here is what happens when a kaiju explodes with the force of a nuclear bomb.

First, there's the actual explosion and what comes immediately after.

To start, there's a nuclear fireball about 250 meters in diameter vaporizing anything inside of it, including the kaiju in question. This made an impressive crater on the shore of that unnamed lake, which because it was on the shore, was now filled in by the lake itself.

After that, a kilometer-wide zone of heavy damage: trees shredded and on fire, animals turned into charcoal, everything literally a smoking ruin.

Beyond that, four kilometers of trees knocked down and everything in the zone receiving what on our Earth would be a decidedly fatal dose of ionized radiation. Kaiju Earth creatures were hardier, as Aparna noted, but it's not to say that those in this area were *happy*, because there was still thermal radiation to consider. Everything alive in that zone got burned, fatally or otherwise.

The kaiju exploded near the surface, and the mushroom cloud sucked up a vast amount of dust and debris, launching it thousands of meters into the air to be distributed by the prevailing winds— fallout. That fallout would eventually spread itself over more than a thousand square kilometers of the Labrador Peninsula.

The Kaiju Earth atmosphere was thicker and more oxygenated than the air back home, which offered special considerations concerning the damage of the blast—the initial shock wave from the blast had more pressure behind it, creating a wider radius of destruction, and the extra oxygen gave fires more fuel to burn. This was counteracted by the fact that the place the kaiju went up at was effectively a swamp jungle, and the trees on Kaiju Earth have evolved rather better fire resistance than the ones back home. Which meant the firestorm resulting from the blast was relatively brief and limited. A storm that came up from the west in the evening dampened it further.

At no time was the Tanaka Base threatened by the blast or its aftereffects. All the action happened almost a hundred kilometers southeast of the base, and the prevailing winds in the area blow generally toward the east, driving the fallout away from the base in any event. We were fine. It was fine.

This felt . . . *weird*.

"Of course it feels weird," Niamh said to me the day after the explosion, after dinner, when I confessed my feelings about it to them. "Back home, a nuclear explosion is an existential threat. Here, it's just Tuesday."

"It's Monday," Aparna said, from the couch, where she was reading a report on the day's events.

"It's just Monday," Niamh amended, then turned back to Aparna. "You sure it's a Monday?"

"Pretty sure."

"It feels like a Tuesday."

"I think every day feels like a Tuesday here."

Niamh snapped their fingers. "That's it exactly. And my point to *you*"—coming back to me—"is that you've drunk up decades of cultural angst about nuclear explosions and nuclear power. It's a big bad back home." She pointed at Kahurangi, who was also catching up on his reading. "This one's whole damn country is a nuclear-free zone."

"Go, Aotearoa," Kahurangi said, absentmindedly, pumping a fist. He didn't look up from his reading.

"Now you come here," Niamh continued, "and not only is it *not* a big bad, it's part of the actual ecological setup. A kaiju going up here is like a whale fall back home."

"A what?" I asked.

"A whale fall," Aparna said from the couch. "When a whale dies its body sinks to the bottom of the ocean, where it feeds an entire ecosystem for months or even years." She looked up at Niamh. "Not a perfect one-to-one metaphor, but okay."

"Thank you for your qualified approval," Niamh said, and returned to me. "It feels weird because not only are you being forced to look at this terrible event in a whole new way, and in a way that's positive for the world it exists in, but you're also not allowed to have it completely rewrite your opinion of the event in *our* world. Because back home it's still a terrible thing."

"'One nuclear bomb can ruin your whole day,'" quoted Kahurangi.

"Yes, that. You're feeling cognitive dissonance, Jamie. Two contradictory-yet-entirely-valid-within-their-contexts thoughts about the same subject. And humans *hate* that shit. We hate it *so much*. The worst answer for us for anything is, 'It depends.'"

"You've thought about this a lot," I said, after a moment.

"Mate, my entire professional life deals with nuclear energy in one way or another," Niamh said. "You're damn right I've thought about it. And now *all* of our professional lives deal with it. The cognitive dissonance you're feeling right now? It's just the start."

So that was the first thing. The second thing is that everyone at Tanaka Base gets very, very busy.

As Niamh noted, exploding kaiju don't happen every day, and exploding kaiju near enough to a base to do useful science on happens even less. Schedules get thrown into the air, projects are shuffled, and resources are reassigned in order to take advantage of the opportunity. I knew this because I spent a lot of time hauling materials and equipment to and from storage for the bio, chem, and physics labs; at one point I picked up lab materials Val had just dropped off because the chem lab changed its mind about which projects to prioritize. Kahurangi looked a little sheepish when I came through the door just as Val was heading out.

Martin Satie and Yeneva Blaylock, the pilot who flew Chopper One, were inundated with flight requests for observation and experiments. There was general outrage that the *Shobijin* had not yet returned from dropping off Red Team and would additionally need at least a few days for maintenance when it returned. Administration had to step in and take over assigning flight time to keep various science divisions from knifing each other to get priority. They also ended up re-tasking an aerostat to float over the explosion site as a stopgap, to have constant aerial observation, and to allow Satie and Blaylock to sleep and maintain their vehicles.

It was reassigning the aerostat, in fact, that revealed the thing that upset some proposed missions and created others.

"Bella is nesting at the explosion site," Ion Ardeleanu, a Blue Team biologist, told a meeting of the Tanaka Base scientists and administrators, four days after the explosion. I was there because I was catering for the meeting, which meant I had wheeled in platters of rolls and cookies and jugs of water and tea, along with plates and napkins, and was expected to wheel them out again at the end.

Ardeleanu projected images from his laptop, taken from the aerostat. The image up right now was of Bella wandering through the shattered landscape of the lakeshore and then plopping herself down right at the edge of the small inlet of the lake created by the blast crater.

"That's not good," said Angel Ford, a Blue Team physicist.

"Well, that depends," Ardeleanu said.

"We have a flying kaiju that has decided to make a new home in the one spot where the dimensional barrier between our planets is the thinnest right now," Ford replied. "This is exactly how we've had incursions before. Tell me how this is a *good* thing."

"Because she doesn't want to go over," Aparna said. She was sitting next to Ardeleanu and was clearly his support team for the meeting.

Ford gave Aparna a once-over. "You're new," she said.

"I am new," Aparna agreed. "We were all new here, once."

"My point is that maybe you don't understand how easy it is for this kaiju to breach into our world, and how bad it would be if she did."

"I do understand it," Aparna said. "I mean, it's just physics." This got a chuckle; it took some nerve for Aparna, who was new, to dunk on Ford like this. She pointed to the screen, which had been looping the video of Bella sitting and making herself comfortable. "*This* is biology, and there are some things going on here that aren't obvious." She paused and looked over to Ardeleanu. "May I?"

Ardeleanu looked tolerantly amused. "By all means," he said.

"Yes, I'm new, but I can read, and I can research," Aparna said. "When the mission to get Edward and Bella to mate was a success, I checked the KPS database to find out what we know about their particular species after mating. It turns out that for them, once mating is over, the male of the species is done. He has no additional part. The female, however, immediately selects a nest site. And because this species does some nurturing of their young, which other kaiju will see as snacks, the female becomes intensely territorial. More than they already are, I mean."

She pointed again. "It makes sense why she picks the explosion site. One, the radiation there won't hurt her or her offspring. Two, every living thing within a hundred kilometers sensed the explosion and is on its way there to feed on it and the fallout. Any kaiju that come around she'll fight off, including Edward. She's over him now." Chuckles again. "The smaller creatures she'll want for food, for herself and her brood." She looked up at Ardeleanu. "Show them the parasite video."

"This is pretty nasty," Ardeleanu warned everyone, and pulled up another video. On it, Bella stood motionless like a statue while a swarm of creatures squirmed off her and another swarm squirmed on.

"She's feeding," Aparna said.

"I thought kaiju were atomic powered," I said, before I remembered I was just there for craft services.

"They are, but they have biological components, too," Aparna said. "They're too big to hunt most creatures themselves, so their parasites do it for them. They detach, go out and hunt and scavenge, kill and eat their prey, come back and reattach and share nutrients, which Bella is using to create her eggs. They get safety, she gets food for her babies." She turned her attention back to Ford. "Which is why she's not going to cross over. She has everything she needs *here*. She's staying put, and while she does, she's not going to let any other kaiju come close to the dimensional barrier."

Ford was not going to give up that easy. "But the blast—"

"Happened on *this* side," Aparna said.

"That doesn't *matter*."

"You're right, it doesn't matter," Aparna said, "*if* you're a human physicist. From a physicist's point of view, the thinning happens between our worlds and the dimensional barrier is the thing you focus on. But if you're a kaiju, you're not attracted to the barrier, you're attracted to the blast. The blast means power. It means food. That's *why* they cross over. To get at the blast." Aparna pointed a final time. "Bella's already got it. She's not going to let anyone else have it. And she's not going to leave her children unattended. By the time they're grown enough that she'll leave them, the dimensional barrier will be healed."

Ford thinned her lips at Aparna, then looked to Ardeleanu. "And you agree with this?"

"I do," Ardeleanu said. "Although I might have been nicer about it."

"Oh my god, you two, Aparna stuffed her so hard," I said later that night, back at the cottage, as I recounted the encounter. "It was a thing of beauty."

"Was it?" Niamh asked Aparna. "Was it indeed a thing of beauty?"

"It was fine," Aparna said. "I didn't mean to get snippy. But then she was all 'You're new,' and I knew if I didn't put a stop to that right then, I wouldn't hear the end of it for as long as we're here."

"You have a nemesis now," Kahurangi said. "I'm officially jealous. I've always wanted to have a nemesis."

"I'll be your nemesis," I volunteered.

"Thanks, Jamie, I appreciate the offer. But you have to win your nemesis on the field of battle."

"I could punch you if that helps."

"Tempting, but no."

"The offer stands."

"Stop it, you two," Niamh said, then turned back to Aparna.

"He's not wrong, though. She's probably going to hate your guts for the rest of the tour. Well, the rest of her tour anyway."

"It'll be fine," Aparna said. "I'll bake her some cookies. All will be forgiven."

"Those will have to be some damn fine cookies," I said. "I was there. That was some heavy-duty stuffage."

"They've worked before."

"You've done this before?"

"Enough times that I've gotten very good at making cookies."

"Damn, Aparna," Niamh said, impressed. "You are now officially my new role model."

"Shut up, I know it," Aparna said, mildly.

"Now I want cookies," Kahurangi said.

"You know the price," I said.

"It'll be worth it. Although I should probably be baking Aparna cookies. After your meeting, I was told I didn't have to brew up a new vat of 'go away' pheromones because Bella would be taking care of that problem for us. I appreciated that, because those things are rank."

"Worse than the 'come hither' pheromones?" I asked.

"You have *no* idea. But now I don't have to make them, or as much of them anyway, and *you*"—he pointed at me—"don't have to go spray them."

"Imagine my disappointment," I said.

"I'm sure you'll find some other way to get yourself on a helicopter," Kahurangi said.

He was right about that. Because it turned out there was a third consequence of having a kaiju explode:

Tourists.

CHAPTER 13

"Excuse me, *what*?" I said.

"Tourists," Tom said.

"We have *tourists*?"

The two of us were back in the dining hall, having lunch the day after Aparna stuffed Angel Ford in the meeting. In fact, Aparna was in the dining hall *with* Angel Ford; they were sitting at a table farther inside the dining hall, laughing. Both of them were eating cookies. Aparna caught me looking over and crooked her eyebrow, then waggled her cookie at me before returning her attention to Ford. Those were some cookies.

"Maybe *tourist* is dismissive," Tom amended. "Maybe the better way to say it is that there are certain people and organizations to whom KPS is beholden, and to whom we occasionally have to show our appreciation in various ways. One of those ways is to let them visit the world."

"That's pretty much the exact definition of *tourist*, Tom," I said.

Tom sighed. "Fine. They're tourists."

"Who are they?"

"Pretty much who you think they are. Politicians, scientists, the billionaires who fund us. Certain notable dignitaries. A few others."

"I see you trying to skip past some embarrassments there with the phrase *a few others*."

"You should let me."

"Not a chance. Spill."

"Last year, a certain president's large adult sons came over."

My eyes narrowed at Tom. "They. Did. *Not*."

"They *did*," Tom confirmed. "We kind of had no choice on that."

"And?"

"They wanted to hunt a kaiju."

"You should have let them."

"It was tempting," Tom said. "To be fair, they're not the only ones who have ever asked. One time, a member of the Joint Chiefs of Staff wanted to bring over an M1 Abrams to do it." I stared. "That's a tank," Tom added.

"I know what it is," I said. "I'm wondering why he thought that would *work*."

"Once he got here he figured out why it wasn't a great idea. Which is one reason why we *do* bring them here. So they get it, and get what we're doing here."

"How many tourists does this place get?"

"Globally or in North America?"

"Either?"

"For North America we get a few dozen a year. I think other continents do similar numbers."

"So, conservatively, a couple of hundred non-KPS people a year visit Kaiju Earth."

"That sounds about right. A lot of them are repeat visitors, but yeah."

I made a face. "How . . . how is all of this still *secret*?"

"Nearly everyone who visits has a security clearance. They know how it works."

I looked at Tom blankly. "Large. Adult. Sons," I said.

"And for everyone else, I mean, what are they going to say? That they've been to an alternate dimension where Godzilla-size creatures are real? No one's going to believe that."

"They might if they take selfies and video."

"We take their phones before they cross over," Tom said. "And even if they did sneak something through, you've seen the pictures and video we take. *Screamingly* low-production value. It looks like what some high schooler can do with Photoshop and After Effects."

"You have a lot riding on shitty video quality, Tom."

"No, we have a lot riding on improbability. We're like Area 51 that way."

I blinked. "Wait. Area 51 is real?"

Tom looked annoyed. "*I* don't know. I'm saying that even if it *was,* the idea of it is already so deep into our common culture that the reality of it is completely swamped by the Hollywood version of it. Remember when you interviewed, and you were asked what you thought about science fiction?"

"Sure."

"We ask that question because the people who watch *Godzilla* movies and *Jurassic Park* movies are fundamentally better prepared for the reality of this place. Our brains already have a model for it so we don't blow a fuse when we come over. Well, it works the other way, too. If we're so used to a fictional version of something, it makes it easier to deny the existence of the real version."

"That's some next-level-conspiracy thinking there, Tom."

Tom nodded. "Granted. Human brains are bullshit. But it's also how we've been able to hide this place more or less in plain sight. There are other things we have to do, of course. We can't send everything we need through Thule Air Base because eventually it becomes obvious there's too much traffic to a supposedly dead camp in the interior of Greenland, even if there's an official sanction and a treaty with various nations. As one example. But by and large, we keep it under wraps. It's too ridiculous to believe."

"It's a reverse lampshade," I said.

"I don't know what 'lampshade' means here, much less its reverse."

"It's a literary term. It means calling attention to something improbable, acknowledging its improbability in the text, and then moving on."

"And that works?"

"More than you might think."

"I suppose it might," Tom said. "Anyway. Yes, we have tourists. Yes, it would be better in many ways if we didn't. But inasmuch as we *do* have them, it makes sense to work them to our advantage. Which is why I'm talking to you, Jamie."

"Oh, boy," I said.

"When I was thinking about you for this gig I checked your

LinkedIn. Your official title at füdmüd was something like 'director of marketing,' was it not?"

"Assistant director of marketing and customer retention," I said. "It mostly meant I went into meetings and listened to other people talk. When I finally presented my own ideas, I got axed."

"It's not your fault," Tom said. "I checked out füdmüd's CEO after we talked. Turns out I know him."

"You know Rob Sanders?"

"I mostly knew *of* him, to be fair. He was a couple of years ahead of me at Dartmouth as an undergrad. Even then, he had a reputation for smarmy backstabbing. He was a legacy kid. Fourth generation or something. Family mostly makes money in defense contracts. I believe most of the füdmüd angel investing came out of the family venture capital fund."

"Must be nice."

Tom nodded. "There's something to be said for being a Large Adult Son. So I believe you didn't get fired for lack of competence. Which is good, because marketing and customer retention is just about perfect—"

"Don't you say it," I warned.

"—for babysitting our tourists while they're here."

"I lift things," I protested.

Tom raised his hands placatingly. "I know. And you're very good at that, from what I've been hearing. Even Val likes you, and she's number one on the base betting pool for Most Likely to Throw Someone Out of the Trees."

"Come on, she's great."

"She *is* great. She will also throw you out of the trees if you cross her."

"Is there something about this place that everyone is great, except that they will murder you if you cross them?"

"There is a certain personality type that thrives here, yes," Tom said.

"But if Val likes me, then I should just *keep* lifting things," I said. "Don't you have someone else you can bother with this?"

"We did, but she's Red Team, and she left KPS this year anyway."

"Sylvia Braithwhite?" I asked.

Tom looked at me funny. "You know her?"

"She had my room before I did," I said. "Left me a very nice welcome note. Asked me to watch after her potted plant."

"We don't usually get tourists at Tanaka Base," Tom said. "Honda Base is larger and better suited for visitors anyway. Many fewer bloodsucking flies, for one. But every now and again, some would come here and she would chaperone them around. Keep them busy. Make sure they weren't eaten. That sort of thing. We'd like you to take up the gig."

"This strongly implies tourists are imminent."

"We just had a kaiju go up. News got back to Earth. We were swamped by requests. And by 'requests,' I mean demands. The Pentagon. Department of Energy. NASA. Several senators. Pretty much all the billionaires. And that's just the U.S. people."

"How do you choose?"

"We don't. The people back home do. They were clever about it, at least. They said they could accommodate three small groups here, once a week, starting two weeks from now. Then they have to shut down the Honda Base gate for maintenance for a couple of weeks."

"Is that something they usually do? Shut down the gate, I mean."

"Yeah. They usually do it a few weeks later into every team rotation than this, but this isn't completely out of line. And it has the advantage that a couple of weeks down will give them an excuse for thinning out the requests. Three straight weeks of guests isn't great for our work. Time and resources we spend on them are time and resources we can't spend on our things. But this is what we get for being an NGO and being officially off the books."

I sighed. "So you need me to be cruise director for three weeks."

"Yes. More accurately, for two days each of those three weeks. A group of six tourists each time. They come in on the *Shobijin*, we plop three of them into Chopper Two to the site while the others settle in, rotate the groups, the next day we do lab presentations and you take them on a field trip. Then they go home. Which reminds me, you need ground training." Tom pulled out his phone.

"Why? What's ground training?"

"It just means you're rated to work on the jungle floor. You and the rest of the new people were going to get the training anyway, but not for a few weeks. I'll just get Riddu to give you an early tutorial." Tom typed in something, paused, and then started typing again. "Probably weapons training, too."

"Weapons training is not usually part of cruise directing," I said.

"It's fine," Tom said. "So, you'll do it?"

"I mean, do I have a choice?"

Tom put down his phone. "Actually, yes, you do have a choice, Jamie. I'm asking you to do something outside of the scope of your employment, mostly because I suspect you'll be good at it. But also because, if you don't mind me being blunt about it, everyone else who I'd pick for this is doing actual science at the moment. If I have *them* do it, we potentially lose knowledge. If I have *you* do it, then Val lifts a few more things for a couple of days each of the next three weeks."

"You could do it," I said.

"I could, but I'm an asshole," Tom said. I smiled at this. "Also, I'll be busy enough coordinating the lab presentations and other things. Don't worry, I'll have your back."

"All right," I said. "I'll do it."

"Thank you."

"Think nothing of it. Just promise me Val won't toss me over the side because I'm adding to her workload."

"She'll understand," Tom said. "And if she doesn't, I'll just tell her if you turned down the gig, I was going to ask her next."

"Do you trust that I will allow no harm to come to you?" Riddu Tagaq asked me, in the foyer of the jungle floor elevator. Both the foyer and the elevator were open air but screened. The elevator and the adjoining, zigzagging staircase that was part of its support structure were the only direct ways down to the jungle floor from the base proper; another such elevator existed out on the airfield. Both elevators were large enough to accommodate vehicles and operated through hydraulics I couldn't even fathom. "Do you trust?"

"Uhhhh, sure?" I said.

Tagaq nodded and pointed to what looked like a thick, quilted beekeeper suit. "Then put that on. Over your clothes is fine."

I hesitated. "That's going to get hot pretty fast," I said.

"You won't be in it long," Tagaq said.

"Define *long*."

"Only as long as it takes to make a point." Tagaq waited, silent. I shrugged and put on the beekeeper's uniform.

As I suspected, I immediately began to sweat. "This thing is gonna kill me," I said to Tagaq.

"Just the opposite," she said, and motioned me into the elevator. I got in. She followed and pressed the button to take us down.

Riddu Tagaq's position at Tanaka Base was base facility and security manager; it was the latter of these hats that she was wearing with me now. "You know the reason our base is in the trees," she said, in a tone that indicated she did not expect it to be a question.

"Yes," I said. "The jungle floor is dangerous."

"It is dangerous," Tagaq agreed. "But it's one thing to know it in your head and another to know it in your heart. I know you know it here." She pointed to my head. Then she pointed to my heart. "Now it's time to know it here."

"I mean, I believe it," I promised.

Tagaq shook her head. "Not yet you don't."

The elevator came to a stop; we had made it to the jungle floor.

"What now?" I asked.

Tagaq pointed. "Get out. Take a walk."

"Are you coming with me?"

"In a minute. Go on."

I looked at her through the impermeable plastic visor of my suit doubtfully; she stared back with an expression that suggested she was ready to wait until the mountains wore down for me to do what she told me to do. I sighed and got out of the elevator.

I was immediately swarmed by all manner of small insects. That was just par for the course. I kept walking, looking down at my boots as I did so. They sank down slightly with every step; the jungle floor was damp to the point of wetness. With every step, creatures skittered up from the jungle floor, some flying away in alarm, others hopping over or onto my boots. A few of these decided that I would make for good aerobic exercise and started climbing up my suit, heading straight, or so it seemed, for my eyeballs.

"Oookay, so this is terrible in every possible way," I yelled back to Tagaq, who said nothing. Something big landed on my plastic visor, blocking my view. I cursed and swiped away, nearly tripping as I did so. I reached out to the nearest tree to stabilize myself.

Something large and pale skittered around the tree toward my hand.

I pulled my hand back like it had landed on something hot.

The skittering thing stopped and started waving a series of antennae around. I looked at the thing, and some part of my brain was trying to place it. After a second I knew what it reminded me of: a coconut crab, those big Pacific Island monsters that could grow a meter long and were smart enough to crack open coconuts by dropping them from trees.

Except you're uglier, I thought to the thing. *By a lot.*

The thing swiveled all its antennae to me like it could hear my thoughts.

"Fuck," I said, out loud.

It chittered, making a sound like a dove being strangled mid-coo.

"*Fuck,*" I said again.

From around the tree, several other of the things skittered into view.

"Fuck!" It was time to go back to the elevator. I turned just as the first of the things leapt to me, hooking onto my suit.

I tried to brush it off and failed, looked up, and saw that nearly every tree was now festooned with the things, all of them looking at me run, or so it seemed.

I tripped, because of course I did. I was immediately swarmed, because of course I was. I looked up into my plastic visor and saw one of the creatures opening an orifice and something both serrated and spiky shoot out, hitting the visor. Where it hit, some sort of liquid spattered out. I was reasonably sure it was a venom. I heard but did not feel other similar attacks as the spiky tongues made *zzzzip* sounds across the fabric of my suit. It seemed inevitable that sooner or later one of those would get through.

I tried to get up, but couldn't see to look where to run. The creatures were swarming around me now, making it hard to find a place to put my hand to prop myself up. I began to hyperventilate. I was definitely going to be dying now.

Someone reached down and yanked me up off the jungle floor, and started grabbing the creatures off of me and hurling them away. It was Tagaq, obviously.

"Hold still," she said, snatching the creatures and hurling them away as if they were nothing. Most of the creatures ran off at this point; a few tried a second attack, launching at me. Tagaq kicked away most of them and caught one mid-leap, punching it in the air, which I would have thought very cool, were I not presently wetting myself, and had she not been the one who had put me out there to be attacked in the first place.

In a few minutes, we were all alone, standing on the jungle floor.

"You are fine," Tagaq said to me.

I screamed at her.

"You are fine," she repeated. She poked my suit. "Quilted carbon fiber. They would have poked at it for years and never gotten through it."

"You could have told me that!"

"I could have," she agreed. "But I needed you to feel *this* in your heart. What you're feeling now."

I was about to yell at her again, but stopped. "Okay, one, *fuck you*," I said. "This is a super-shitty way to do this." Tagaq said nothing to this, waiting. "Two, fuck you, you're right, I get it now."

"Good," Tagaq said. "Because here is another thing. The tree crabs that attacked you just now are the least dangerous things you're going to find here on the jungle floor. Much worse will be things that feed on the tree crabs, of which there are many. Much worse than them are the things that feed on them. And worst of all are the kaiju parasites."

"Not the kaiju?"

Tagaq shook her head. "We are beneath their consideration. Their parasites, however, are very interested in us."

I started to ask something and stopped. I looked at Tagaq and looked around. "Why aren't we being attacked?"

Tagaq pulled something out of the pocket of her jumpsuit and showed it to me. "Ultrasonic," she said. "The tree crabs hate it."

"And the things that eat the tree crabs? And the things that eat *them*?"

"We have other things for them. I'll show you." Tagaq looked around. "I know you've been told to chaperone tourists. They always want to see the jungle up close. They want to feel they've seen the true world here. If we showed them the true world here, they would all be dead. And do you know why?"

"Because they don't feel it in their hearts," I said.

"And we don't have the time to make them feel it." Tagaq motioned to where we are. "So, we bring them here, to this spot, and we lie to them that this is the true face of this world. They should be glad we do it, and that we make them believe it." She pointed to me. "But don't you believe it. Ever. Because you'll walk other places in this world. And it will take you before you can scream. Understand?"

"Yes," I said, meaning it.

"How are you?"

"Honestly? I'm pretty sure I pissed myself."

Tagaq nodded. "Let's go back and get you out of this and changed, and we'll start again." We started walking back to the elevator.

"Did you do this?" I asked her as we walked. "The first time you were on the jungle floor."

"I did."

"How did you do?"

She looked at me. "I shit myself running."

"That . . . makes me feel better."

She grunted. "It's the ones who don't you have to worry about."

CHAPTER 14

"Exciting day in maternal kaiju observation," Aparna said to the group as she entered the cottage after her shift in the lab. She was the last of us to be done with her work for the day; we were waiting on her to go to dinner.

"So exciting you're making us late for food?" I asked. I was on my second day of ground training with Riddu Tagaq, so I was very ready to eat.

"You tell me." Aparna opened up her laptop, which had been in sleep mode; it woke up and displayed the last thing that had been on her screen, which was a picture of Bella from on high, care of the aerostat stationed above her. We all peered at the photo.

"Bella shit herself," Niamh said, after a second.

"She did *not*," Aparna replied, annoyed.

"Are you sure?" I asked. "Because Niamh is not wrong. That looks like shit to me."

"Bird shit specifically," Kahurangi said. "Like the most mighty seagull shit that has ever been taken."

"'The Mighty Seagull Shits' is a good band name," I observed.

"It is *not*," Aparna said. "And it's not shit. Bella just laid her eggs."

"By shitting herself," Niamh said. "Not how I would do it, but okay."

Aparna made an exasperated noise. "*It's not shit*, okay? It's kaiju natal jelly. It's a nutrient-dense medium for her fertilized eggs, and it's *fascinating*." She pointed to the spatter that was allegedly not the largest seagull dump ever taken. "That jelly contains everything the embryos developing in it need to survive their development inside their ovum. There's a transfer of nutrients and waste. It's almost placental. But that's not all it does."

"It's also a dessert topping," I joked.

"Actually you're not wrong," Aparna said. "I mean, actually you *are* wrong, horribly wrong, and you should be ashamed of yourself. But *also,* you are correct that it's something other creatures here will find irresistible as a food source. It's designed to draw them in."

Kahurangi looked confused. "Why would Bella want that? Her eggs will get eaten."

"Some of them will, sure. But there are thousands of them in that. Tens of thousands. They were never all expected to survive anyway. And while creatures are coming in to feast on them and their medium, Bella's parasites are swooping down and feeding on them. And she uses what she gets from the parasites to make more eggs."

"She's going to mate with Edward again?" I asked. I remembered the last time and was not looking forward to repeating as Cupid.

Aparna shook her head. "She's stored his sperm inside her."

Niamh made a face at this. "Gross."

"It's more common than you think, biologically speaking."

"Biology is gross. All of it. But especially storing sperm in your body like you're a thermos for jizz."

"'Jizz Thermos' is a good band name," Kahurangi said. I gave him a high five for his efforts.

Aparna rolled her eyes at all of us. "The point is that she'll repeat this maybe three or four more times over the course of the next several weeks. We've seen this before with her species." She pointed to the gooey egg mess. "But this will be the first time we ever get to see her species' early development up close. And that's exciting." She snapped her laptop closed. "But clearly you jerks can't appreciate that. You're all terrible and I hate you."

"We are the worst," I agreed. "Can we go to dinner now?"

"Wait, I can top egg goo," Niamh said, and reached over for their own laptop.

"Dinner? Anyone?"

"Jesus, Jamie, you're not starving."

"I kind of am."

"Chew on Kahurangi."

"I'd rather not."

"Thank you," Kahurangi said.

"But I might if we don't eat soon."

"I'll be quick." Niamh pulled up a silent night vision video of a forest; a drone or helicopter was slowly circling a portion of it. There was nothing particularly remarkable about it, and then there was a tiny glitch. "There!"

"That's it?" I asked.

"What do you mean, 'that's it'?"

"It's trees."

"It's not the trees, you dense argumentative *spoon*." Niamh scrubbed the video back. "It's the flash."

"What flash?" Aparna asked.

"This one!" Niamh pointed when the tiny glitch happened again.

"That's it?"

Niamh narrowed their eyes at Aparna.

"I know we're supposed to be torturing Niamh right now, but I would actually like to know, what's so fascinating about that flash?" Kahurangi asked.

"*Thank* you," Niamh said. "This video was taken by a Canadian drone back home. What it's flying over is our world's counterpart to where Bella has her enormous kaiju ass. And this *flash*"—Niamh paused the video at the glitch—"is us."

Kahurangi nodded. "Excellent likeness."

Niamh smacked him, lightly. "Not *us* us, 'us' as in *this planet* us."

I looked over at Aparna. "I thought you said Bella wasn't going through."

"She's not," Aparna said, then looked at Niamh. "Is she?"

Niamh grinned in triumph. "See, I told you I could beat egg goo. And no, she's not going through. But"—they pointed at the flash again—"that doesn't mean a connection between our worlds isn't open. The kaiju going up thinned the barrier between our worlds. That started healing up immediately since the barrier thinning correlates with active nuclear energy generation. But then Bella took a seat right where the barrier thinned—"

"And she has her own nuclear reactor on her," I said.

"Right." Niamh nodded. "Normally, the kaiju are moving around too much to thin out the barrier by themselves. To thin it, you either need to have a big burst, like a bomb, or a gradual residual buildup in one place, like Camp Century. They can get through if it's already thin, but once the barrier closes up, they're stuck. That's what happened to the ones who came through. They couldn't get back, and they're not adapted to our world, and they died."

"But Bella's *not* coming through," Aparna said. "She's just sitting there."

"Because she has no reason to come through, like you said," Niamh agreed. "She's got everything she needs here. She's just sitting there, radiating nuclear energy into the barrier, so it's staying thin. And every once in a while"—they pointed to the glitch—"we see *this*."

"What causes the flash?" Kahurangi asked.

"I have no idea," Niamh said. "It's something we've never seen before, because we've never had *this* happen before—a nuclear explosion followed by a reactor showing up and keeping the barrier thin. At least, we haven't seen it happen before. I suppose the chances of one kaiju getting knocked up and another kaiju exploding on the same day, both in proximity to each other, are pretty low."

"Are they as low as us actually getting to the dining hall before they finish serving dinner?" I asked.

Niamh looked at me and then smiled at Kahurangi, sweetly. "And you? What amazing science did *you* do today, Dr. Lautagata?"

Kahurangi grinned at this new attempt to make me starve further. "Alas, nothing as groundbreaking as the two of you," he said. "All I've been doing is making smelly things for us to use to make kaiju do things, or *not* do them, depending. I do it enough that I'm beginning to be able to identify kaiju pheromones by scent. This is both useful and appalling."

"*Useful and Appalling* is my next band name," Aparna said.

We all looked at her.

"What? I can't get in on the band name thing?"

"Can we go now?" I asked. "I really am going to die of not eating soon."

"Poor Jamie," Niamh mocked. "Tromping around the jungle floor really takes it out of you."

"It'll happen to you, too," I promised. "It'll happen to *all* of you. The good news is that tomorrow I get weapons training. No more tromping, just shooting."

"How is that good news?" Kahurangi asked. "The idea of you with a weapon is objectively terrifying."

"If you think that's terrifying," I said, "wait until you see me with low blood sugar."

"Have you ever used a weapon before?" asked Riddu Tagaq.

"In video games," I said. "Is that bad?"

"Did you ever have a reason to use a weapon, outside a video game?"

"No."

"Do you feel your life would have been improved by using a weapon?"

"No."

"Then it's not bad," Tagaq said. "There is a certain type of person who feels like they must be armed at every moment of the day or else the world will come for them in some way. Back home, this is very much not a good way to live. Here, however, outside of the base, it is the only way you are going to survive."

We were at the Tanaka Base screened-in shooting range on the jungle floor, standing at a table, on which an array of weapons rested, their various magazines and cartridges and whatnot beside them. Some of them I recognized. A rather large number I did not.

I pointed to one of them I did recognize, a handgun. "Am I going to have one of these?"

"Do you think it would work for you?"

"I've never used one."

Tagaq nodded, picked up the handgun, checked it, loaded it,

disengaged the safeties. "This is a Glock 19," she said, and fired at a man-shaped target ten yards down the range. I jumped at the noise and immediately heard ringing in my ears.

"How do you feel about it now?" she asked me a minute later.

"Weren't we supposed to be wearing ear protection for this?" I yelled.

"Wear ear protection in the jungle and you won't hear what's coming to eat you. Answer my question."

"I don't think I'm ready for that," I said.

"You're not," Tagaq agreed. She reset the safeties and cleared the Glock and set it back down on the table. "It's just as well. A handgun is not a very good weapon for this planet, or for most of the people who come to this base. It requires training and constant practice to maintain skill and accuracy. It's a short-range weapon, and here the range is shorter because the atmosphere is so thick. Bullets tumble fast here. Creatures move fast here. Most people are not very good at aiming at something close to them, moving fast." She pointed to the Glock. "If something on this planet is close enough to you that this is the weapon to use, you are likely already dead."

"If this is such a terrible weapon here, why did you show it to me?" I asked.

"Because it's what you think of as a weapon," Tagaq said. "Not just you. Everyone. You don't use weapons but you see them used all the time, in movies and TV and video games. Handguns and rifles, mostly." She pointed to an assault rifle of some sort down the table. "These are what you expect. These are what you think you *want*, even if you don't know it. You've been trained to think of these as the best weapons available. I need you to believe that there are better ones here."

I cocked my head at Tagaq. "You do this a lot," I said. "The whole 'I need you to believe this' thing."

"I could just tell you," Tagaq said. "And at the end of me telling you, you would still want the handgun or the rifle. It's not just you. I have to break everyone of this. This world is not our world. I need you to believe that."

"The head and the heart thing again."

"Yes. You believe it or you die."

"Has that happened? People dying?"

"Of course it has. And it's hard. Hard on the people here. Especially hard on the people back home."

"Why?"

"Because usually there is nothing left to ship back."

I considered this. "I don't mean to be disrespectful here, but you're not a lot of fun at parties, are you?"

"I'm a fucking delight at parties," Tagaq said. "Especially if there is karaoke involved. But this isn't a party. It's me trying to save your life, and maybe help you save someone else's life. Now, are you ready to see what weapons I think you should use?"

"Yes. Please," I said.

"Good." She reached over and organized several objects on the table into a group. One I recognized as a shotgun. The rest were new to me. "There are two basic definitions of a weapon. The first, and the one everyone uses, is an object that causes or inflicts pain or damage. The second, which is more relevant here, is an object one uses to defend one's self or gain an advantage. What do we know about the creatures here?"

"They're horrible and want to eat every human they meet?"

Tagaq shook her head. "No. They're horrible and they want to eat *everything*. Not just us, and not us first. They'll kill and eat us if we make ourselves convenient. But if we make something else more convenient, they're happy to eat them instead. So we do two things: make ourselves less attractive to attack, and make it worth their while to attack other things."

She pulled an object out of her pocket. "You remember this."

"The ultrasonic thingy," I said.

"We call it the *screamer*," Tagaq said. "Works on the tree crabs and a few other things. You'll be getting your own." She pointed to a canister. "This makes you smell like a particularly nasty kaiju parasite."

"And that's good, somehow?"

"Since most things think you smell like a thing that will absolutely start to eat them while they're still alive, yes. It means they will run in the other direction when they smell you coming."

"And what do the particularly nasty parasites I'll smell like think of me?"

"They might leave you alone. They might see whether you want to mate. They might try to eat you."

"They eat their own?"

"Everything here eats their own, including kaiju."

"That's not reassuring."

Tagaq nodded, and reached for another object. "That's why we have this. This launches canisters of actinides and stress pheromones that mimic those of injured prey creatures. It opens up on impact. If you see something coming for you, shoot this."

"At them?"

"If you want."

"It's *optional*?"

"It's not meant to kill them, it's meant to get their attention. It says, 'I'm good to eat,' in every native language here. They will forget you and go after it, wherever it lands. So will everything else in the area."

"And then they'll all try to eat each other instead of me."

"You or anyone else in your party, yes."

"If I shoot it *at* them, then everything around will go *after* them, right?"

"Do you think you're going to be that good of a shot?"

"I see your point."

"Thank you."

"Okay, so." I pointed. "Screamer, parasite pheromones, Eat Me launcher. All good, but what if they still keep coming?"

Tagaq lifted a baton.

"You want me to hit them with a stick."

She clicked a button on the stick. "The stick comes with fifty thousand volts."

"Okay, better."

"The charge doesn't last. If you can just beat them with the stick instead, do that. Things here feel pain just fine. Save the voltage for when you need it."

"And what about when a stick won't do?"

Tagaq grimaced and picked up the shotgun. It had a short barrel. "This is your last resort. Wide spread right out of the barrel, to compensate for your complete lack of aiming ability. It *will* kill almost anything at a short range, and at a longer range, the pheromone-dipped depleted-uranium pellets in the shotgun shells will make anything hit but not killed smell like food to everything else. That and the blood. Don't even think about pointing it within ninety degrees of any human. This is the thing I will train you the hardest on."

"Fair enough," I said. "And if this doesn't work?"

"Then you're dead."

"Oh. I was kind of hoping there was something else."

"No. Dead. Dragged into the jungle. Eaten and scavenged down to the bones, which will then also be eaten. Nothing will remain of you. At all."

"This is what I mean when I say I think you're no fun at parties."

"When you finish your training and survive your first mission on the jungle floor, you and I can sing 'Total Eclipse of the Heart' as a duet at karaoke," Tagaq said. "Until then, you learn." She handed the shotgun to me. "Let's start with this."

The elevator finished rising, and I was surprised to find Aparna and Niamh there.

"You need me for something?" I asked.

"Not in the least, you egocentric monster," Niamh said. They motioned at Tagaq. "We're here to see her."

"Niamh and I were told to get ground training," Aparna said. "We're going to help set cameras at the birthing site this next week."

"Is that so," I said. Then I turned back to Tagaq, who was looking at both of them, impassively. "Be as thorough with them as you were with me," I said. The tone came out jokingly, but it wasn't joking at all.

"Yes," Tagaq said. Then she looked at Aparna and Niamh. "We need to get you suits."

CHAPTER 15

"Here's the deal," Martin Satie said to us as we neared Bella's nest. "I'll drop you off, you have ten minutes to plant your instruments and do anything else you need to do. At ten minutes, be back at the landing zone. I'll come down and pick you up."

"You're not landing?" Aparna asked. She and Niamh were in the passenger area of the helicopter, along with Ion Ardeleanu. I was in the copilot seat. Nominally, Ardeleanu was in charge of the mission, but in reality, he and I were along to be armed security for Aparna and Niamh while they planted cameras and instrument packages. They were armed as well—Riddu Tagaq gave them the same very basic weapons training I got a couple of days ahead of them—but not as heavily as Ardeleanu and I were. They had cameras and instruments to set up.

"Dr. Chowdhury, I never land on the jungle floor if I can help it," Satie said. "It's a very good way to get those critters in your back seat. Now"—he tapped his headset—"I'll keep a channel open, and I'm ready to come get you if you need an emergency extract. Please do not need an emergency extract. They're messy and dangerous. Come back to the landing zone instead. Ten minutes, that's all."

"How do these things usually go?" Niamh asked Satie. "Do you have to do a lot of emergency extractions?"

"Not when people are smart," Satie said. "Every one of these is different. This is the first time I'm landing near a nuclear explosion site. This is the first time I'm landing near a nesting kaiju. Maybe those things don't make a difference. Maybe they change everything. I don't know, you don't know, Dr. Healy, Drs. Chowdhury and Ardeleanu don't know, and even this one"—he pointed at me—"is in the dark. When we get back, we get to write it up so everyone else can learn about it. Until then, however, we choose to be smart and not have an emergency extraction."

"Mate, if that's your idea of a reassuring speech, you have work to do," Niamh said.

"It wasn't supposed to be reassuring, so that's all right." Satie nodded. "And here we are."

We all looked out to see the mountain of Bella, roosting at the edge of the water-filled explosion crater. Around her was the mass of her natal jelly, and around that was a carpet of green, leading up and through the downed trees. A mat of moss and algae had grown aggressively on the previously scorched ground, a reminder that life here treated radiation much differently from back home.

South and east of Bella, about eighty meters from her, was a small, flattish area, just big enough for Satie to drop us off. I looked at Bella as we came in. She appeared not to notice us.

"Is she asleep, like Edward was?" I asked Satie.

"Ask the experts," he said.

"She's nesting and conserving her strength to make more eggs," Ardeleanu said. "Staying in one place makes it easy for her parasites to go feed and come back to her. Based on the behavior of other nesting kaiju over the years, unless we directly disturb her or she's otherwise in physical distress, she's not going to rouse herself, or bother us or the helicopter."

"If she does you'll be walking home," Satie said.

"It'll be fine," Ardeleanu assured us. He looked over to Aparna and Niamh. "We just do it liked we practiced yesterday, we'll be in and out and back home looking at the data."

The two of them nodded at this. Our practice session the day before had been on the jungle floor directly below the base, with spots corresponding to where the aerostat pictures had suggested would be optimal places to put the cameras and instruments. Niamh and Aparna got good at pounding in the stakes that the instruments would attach to, and then popping on the clear domes of the camera and instrument packages themselves. I got better at moving around with both a shotgun and the canister launcher, either of which was literally a handful in itself. This on top of the electrified baton and a bandolier that held shotgun shells, pheromone canisters, and various sprays. Niamh had taken one look at the bandolier during practice and informed me that Chewbacca had called and wanted his clothes back.

"Bringing us down," Satie said. We started our descent.

"Remember, Jamie and I get out first," Ardeleanu said. "Then I'll signal you two, and you get the instrument packs out of the cargo hold. Jamie will signal Satie to lift off when you two have gotten everything and secured the hold." Aparna and Niamh nodded at this. "It'll be fine," Ardeleanu repeated.

The earth rose to meet us, and then Satie hovered, inches above the ground. "This is it," he said. And nodded to me. "Watch your step."

I nodded, took off my headset and attached a much smaller headset, opened the door to jump out, exited, and slid hard on my ass. The moss and algae had made the ground slippery. I cracked my knee on the way down and cursed at the pain. I could hear Satie saying something to me through my new headset, but the racket of the rotors made it difficult to hear. I decided to ignore it and instead got up (carefully), retrieved my canister launcher and shotgun, switched over the safeties, then hobbled over to the passenger door. I pounded on it; Ardeleanu opened it up and got out. He'd seen me tumble and was more careful about putting his feet down before retrieving his own weapons.

The two of us did a quick look-see and didn't see anything bounding up toward us; the copter was probably scaring the hell out of everything in a hundred-meter radius. Ardeleanu motioned to Aparna and Niamh, who got out—carefully—and then went to the small cargo hold directly behind the passenger area, getting out the two large, soft-walled instrument bags that carried inside them two instrument packages, their stakes, and the "embedding tool," which was a fancy name for a rubber mallet. The instrument packages were inside acrylic domes that looked like the sort you'd put cakes inside at a diner, but instead of cakes were several cameras and other scientific equipment.

Niamh and Aparna closed the cargo hold, gave me a thumbs-up, and then we all moved away from the copter. Satie was waiting for my thumbs-up; once he saw it he went straight up one hundred meters and held position.

"Watch out, it's slippery," Niamh said to me, through our headsets. I gave them a look. Then I turned to Aparna. "You come with me," I said.

"Safety first," Ardeleanu said, and undid the compartment on his bandolier that held the parasite pheromone. "Screamers and spray." I nodded, got out my own spray, and then sprayed down Aparna while he did the same to Niamh. Then I sprayed him and he sprayed me.

"We smell like fucking death," Niamh said.

"That's the point," Aparna reminded them.

I put the spray back and got my screamer out of my pocket, turned it on, and put it back. I watched as Aparna did the same, and gave a thumbs-up to Ardeleanu, who did the same once his and Niamh's screamers were switched on as well.

Ardeleanu looked at his watch. "That was a minute," he said. "We did this in practice in six minutes. Let's be back here in five forty-five." I saw Niamh roll their eyes at this; they were not on board with striving for a personal best. But they went off with Ardeleanu anyway.

I looked at Aparna. "Ready?"

"I'm not going to rush, if that's all right with you," she said.

"That's fine," I assured her. "Let's be quick but not stupid." We walked in the direction opposite of Niamh and Ardeleanu, toward our first chosen spot, roughly a hundred meters away. We walked carefully, because the algae and moss weren't getting any less squishy as we went along.

Our first destination was the farthest out because we wanted to work our way back in. As we walked, I kept an eye on the scenery, both at the landscape immediately around us, from which anything that might want to try to eat us would come from, and at the towering form of Bella. Walking around her was like walking around the Statue of Liberty, if the Statue of Liberty might, at any second, sprout wings and take to the sky.

Aparna followed my gaze. "She's amazing, isn't she?"

"*Amazing* is understating it."

Aparna nodded. "It still doesn't feel real, does it? All of this."

"Falling on my ass back there felt real," I assured her.

"Yes, all right, fine," she said. "But the *rest* of it. We're standing where a nuclear explosion went off two weeks ago. The ground is slippery with life." She pointed off to the side of us, where the natal jelly lay thick on the ground. I could see the eggs in it, spheroidal and the size of bowling balls. Vein-like growths came out of them and dissipated into the jelly. "There are things in that, that will grow up into *that*"—she pointed at Bella—"who still shouldn't physically exist, if you ask me, and yet, here we are. Unreal."

"You still think kaiju shouldn't exist physically?" I asked. I noticed around us things skittering about. The screamers and the parasite pheromones were doing their work, creating a bow wave of creatures determined to avoid us. Most of them at this point were insects and small lizardy creatures, none of which would have presented much of a threat to us. I suspected most of the real creature action was taking place in the natal jelly, where larger creatures were eating kaiju eggs and then being eaten by parasites in turn. Nature red in tooth and claw, as Tennyson once said; alternately, the circle of life, as Mufasa said.

"I read the precis," Aparna said. "The science checks out. It's just that it's so *convoluted*. The things that kaiju have to do to live is ridiculous."

"You mean like organic nuclear reactors," I prompted. I was having Aparna talk not just to have a conversation, but because I had an inkling that she was more on edge about this first away mission of hers than she was letting on. Having her talk would distract her from that.

"Yeah, but that's just one thing. And it's not the weirdest thing. The weirdest thing is they have fans."

I opened my mouth.

"As in to cool themselves, not Comic-Con nerds, Jamie, I *see* you."

I closed my mouth again, grinning.

"And the weirdest thing about *that* is that the fans aren't part of them. They're colonies of parasites—" And then Aparna was off and running about how the parasites drew air into the kaiju and cooled off its internals, including the reactor, and how this was just barely enough heat exchange, and how the constant intake of air meant there was always a breeze around a kaiju, and how this constant air exchange made the kaiju one of the most important pollinators on this planet, and so on and so forth, and Aparna didn't even have time to be nervous as we walked.

Until we got to where we planned to plant the first instrument pack and found a stack of tree crabs scavenging a carcass just where we planned to plant the thing.

"Oh, shit," Aparna said, pulling up.

"Keep walking," I said. "We have our screamers on. We're going to scare them off as we get closer."

And we did, most of them. They went skittering away as we drew up on them. But five tree crabs remained, policing the carcass, antennae waving threateningly at us.

I had been here before. But unlike before, I had now spent time under Riddu Tagaq's tutelage learning how to deal with the little fuckers.

Which was, you march right up to them, grab them mid-carapace where they have a blind spot, and then chuck them hard and far.

Which is what I did to the first one I came up to before it had time to react. I hurled it and it flew, chittering in alarm as it did. My crab fighting skills were impeccable.

Its fellows turned their antennae to follow its path into the air and back down again, and then turned their attention back to me.

"Who else wants some?" I asked.

In a movie, they would have all comically fled. In reality, I had to repeat the process of grabbing and chucking four more times. And then I had to pick up a rotted carcass and heave it some distance away, so that if the tree crabs came back, they would bother the corpse, not us. I came away from the whole experience smelling even worse than I had before, which was saying something.

I stood where we had planned to place the instrument package and made a *ta-da* motion. "Whenever you're ready, Dr. Chowdhury," I said. Aparna shook herself out of motionlessness and swiftly got to work, unzipping her bag, pulling out the stake and mallet, and getting to installing the package.

While she did that I scanned the area, canister launcher in hand. If there was anything larger than a tree crab, it was not making itself known. The one advantage of walking around in a nuclear explosion debris field, if one wanted to call it an advantage, was that there was very little verticality. Nothing would be coming at us from above. It was one less dimension to worry about.

"Done," Aparna said, standing up. The instrument package stuck up a few inches from the ground; its cameras were now at about the same height as a prone human.

"Is it sending?" I asked.

Aparna nodded and pointed to a green light on the package. "Sending to the nearest aerostat and receiving, too. They're probably already getting the signal back at Tanaka."

I waved to the package and then looked at my smartwatch. "That took four minutes. Come on, let's plant the other one and get to the chopper."

"It's going well so far," Aparna said.

"Come on, Aparna," I said. "Don't jinx it."

Ion Ardeleanu literally said, *That went better than I thought,* before he slipped and fell on the moss, and something the size of a panther came for him out of the natal jelly.

We didn't see it coming. Ardeleanu was walking up from a small sloping hill, and Niamh was ahead of him on the climb. It's fair to say my and Aparna's attention was on Niamh, not on Ardeleanu, on account that Niamh was our friend, and also because it was Ardelea-nu's role to be security, and thus, to be secure. Unlike the rest of us, this wasn't his first time on an away mission. We thought he knew what he was doing. We weren't prepared for his slip, his fall, and then the creature bursting out of the jelly to come for him.

Aparna and I were twenty meters away from Niamh when it happened; they were in turn ten meters ahead of Ardeleanu. We were close enough to Niamh that they saw our expressions change, and turned to see what happened. Niamh had their baton out, as had Aparna; once their instruments were planted, they were ready to assist in their own defense.

This came in handy for Ardeleanu because Niamh didn't waste any time. They sprinted to where he was, somehow not slipping and falling, and started whacking away at the creature that was now trying to yank Ardeleanu back down the slope, toward the kaiju natal jelly. Aparna and I ran to assist.

Niamh's baton whacking had managed to dislodge the creature from the fallen biologist, and now it, apparently pissed, started making threatening movements toward Niamh. Niamh was not impressed and swung at the thing again, and this time there was a notable pop as an arc of voltage went from the baton to what passed for the creature's face. Niamh had turned on the electric part of the baton. The creature backed off, rapidly, shaking its face, but didn't retreat entirely.

Aparna went to Ardeleanu and checked his wounds; I went to Niamh, who was looking pissed and ready to get into it with the creature.

"You okay?" I asked.

"What a stupid question to ask right now," Niamh said, which meant yes, they were okay.

The creature stood its ground several yards away, sizing us up.

I shouted back to Aparna, "How is it?"

"Left leg's torn up and bleeding," she said.

"I'm fine," Ardeleanu said, and tried to get up.

Aparna put a hand on his chest to keep him from moving. "He's really not fine at all."

I nodded at that and switched my headset over to Satie. "Chopper Two, come in."

"You don't have to tell me, I see it," Satie said. "Coming to you for an emergency extract."

"Thank you," I said.

The creature started making a noise.

"I think you should know there are more of those things on the way," Satie said. "I see them coming up through the jelly."

"Got it," I said. I raised my canister launcher, and per instruction, launched a canister past the creature and into the natal jelly beyond, where it went off with an impressive poof and cloud of metal dust and pheromones.

The creature looked back at the puff and then slowly and decidedly back to us.

"So, *that's* not great," I said. I handed my shotgun to Niamh. "If that thing moves, shoot it," I said.

"Fucking obviously," they said. I went back to Aparna and Ardeleanu, who was still trying to get up.

"I can move," he assured me.

"Jesus, shut up," I said, and took his shotgun and canister launcher from him. "Pick one," I said to Aparna. She took the canister launcher. I reloaded my own canister launcher from my bandolier and then picked up the shotgun. "Chopper is coming to us," I told her.

"I know," she said, and motioned up with her head. Satie was moving in position for descent. "I'm going to need help getting him into the helicopter."

"I can do it," Ardeleanu said.

"Shut up," we both said to him. "I'll send Niamh back when he gets here," I said to Aparna.

She nodded; I went back to Niamh.

"Fucker hasn't moved," Niamh said.

"No," I agreed. "It's waiting for backup." I pointed into the jelly, where several more of the creatures were making their way toward us. A few of them had gotten sidetracked by the delicious-smelling canister, but others were picking their way toward us.

"Thank God we set up those instrument packages," Niamh said. "Now base can watch us get eaten in high definition."

I nodded at this. "Go help Aparna with Ardeleanu," I said. The chopper was now close enough that it was about to drown out conversation. Niamh dropped back, and I was now the only one standing in front of the creature. Two of its friends were now about twenty meters away, moving up on us slowly.

I thought about my options, stowed the shotgun, and took out my canister launcher. The creature seemed to watch me do it but otherwise did nothing, waiting on its friends to close in.

I moved aggressively toward the creature, closing the meters between us and shouting, as if to threaten it. Then I started to wobble on the thick moss and algae.

This is what the creature was waiting for—for me to lose my balance, to distract myself and to be defenseless. It opened its mouth wide, its scream lost inside the noise of the helicopter rotors, and hunched itself up to leap.

Which was what *I* was waiting for. My footing was just fine. I just faked out the creepy fucker. And now its mouth was open.

I shot the canister directly into it.

Do you think you're going to be that good of a shot? I remembered Riddu Tagaq asking me when I asked about shooting a canister at a creature.

As it happens, I still wasn't that great of a shot.

But I was also shooting from a very, very close distance.

The canister burst in the creature's mouth, going off like the grenade it was, knocking the already off-center creature back and toward its oncoming companions. Who, once they got a whiff of their now stunned-or-dead pal, forgot all about me and decided their pal was an easier meal.

Tagaq was right; they'll eat us if we're convenient. So, make it more convenient for them to eat something else.

I suppose I could have used the shotgun to the same effect. But honestly using the canister launcher was so much more satisfying.

More of the creatures were picking their way out of the jelly toward their fallen comrade; I took that as my cue to take my leave. I walked back slowly to the helicopter, keeping situational awareness, until I was at the copilot's door. I opened it and got in. Satie took us up while I was still strapping myself in.

"What did I say about not needing emergency extraction?" he said to me after I was buckled in and switched over my headset.

"Sorry," I said. I looked back at the passenger compartment. Ardeleanu was on the floor, and Aparna was over him, cleaning out his wound with the antiseptic in the helicopter's first aid kit. "How is he?" I asked.

"It looks pretty bad," Niamh said.

"Tell base we're going to need medical," I said to Satie.

"I did that before I picked you up," he said.

I looked over to Ardeleanu, who didn't have a headset on. He was saying something drowned out by the cabin noise. It looked like, *I'm fine.* Aparna was ignoring him and treating him anyway. She was the sensible one here. I looked at Niamh, who still looked pissed. We weren't all good, but we were all alive. I was going to take that as a win. I turned back to the front, looked out of the helicopter, and let out a long, shuddering breath. Satie noticed it but didn't say anything.

Until several minutes later, when his curiosity got the better of him. "Hey, I didn't get a good look at it," he said, "but did you actually just shoot one of those things in the face with a goddamn *canister gun?*"

CHAPTER 16

When we arrived, we were greeted by a stretcher there to take Ardeleanu to medical. Tanaka Base had two doctors and two nurses, and one of the doctors, Irina Garin, was a surgeon. I suspected Ardeleanu might be visiting with her soon. He was efficiently removed from the helicopter and hustled off, decrying all the way that he was *fine,* actually, really.

"I'm glad he's safe now, but when he's better, I might punch him," Niamh said, watching him go.

"Seems fair," I said. "How are you?" I included Aparna in this. "How are both of you?"

"I need a drink," Aparna said.

"*A* drink?" Niamh exclaimed. "I need several."

Aparna smiled. "That's what I meant, but I didn't want to look like a drunk."

"To hell with that. After today's adventure, I'm going to get smashed and wear a fucking lampshade as a hat."

"Let me get the first round," I said. "After that, you'll be responsible for your own lampshade procurement." We said goodbye to Satie and promised to buy him a drink when he was done, then walked up the tunnel to the base, where it turned out almost everyone was waiting for us, cheering.

Kahurangi bounded out of the crowd and gave each of us a hug. "Thank you for not dying," he said.

"What the hell?" I asked, looking around.

"Mate, everyone saw the video of you three saving Ardeleanu."

"Everyone?"

"Well, it was a slow news day."

I looked around. "Apparently."

Kahurangi punched me affectionately on the shoulder. "Take the win, Jamie. Today, you three are heroes." He pushed me lightly into the waiting crowd; Aparna and Niamh followed. Hugs and back-slaps ensued.

As it turns out, Niamh was right. The cameras on the instrument packs were working and, thanks to their positions, caught the attack on Ardeleanu and our defense of him from several angles. So did the aerostat, which provided a top-down view. All of these points of view were beamed back from the aerostat to Tanaka Base in real time; additional video from Satie's helicopter would add to it when it was transferred over. By the time we got back to base, we had become must-see TV. Everyone saw Aparna go to aid her fallen comrade, Niamh zap the creature in the face, and me shoot it in the mouth.

"I had to go to another planet to go viral," Aparna noted as we watched the video of the attack, back at our own cottage. The three of us were told to take the afternoon off, and Kahurangi, presum-ably, was playing hooky.

"You're very famous to one hundred fifty people," Niamh said to her.

"That's about the level of fame I would ever want."

"What were you thinking when you started beating the shit out of that thing?" Kahurangi asked Niamh. We were at the point in the video where Niamh had gone ham on the creature, but not yet where they had zapped it.

"What does it look like I was thinking? I was pissed."

"You have very deep wells of rage, my friend," Kahurangi ob-served.

"You have no idea."

"What about you?" Kahurangi asked me.

"I was mostly thinking about how Satie was going to be annoyed with us," I said. "He told us not to have an emergency, and then we went and had one."

"You didn't have it. Ardeleanu did." Kahurangi scrubbed back to the biologist falling on his ass and the creature leaping apparently out of nowhere to get at him.

"Dude, *I* slipped and fell," I said. "It was the very first thing I did coming out of the helicopter. My knee still hurts. It was him that was attacked, but it could have been any of us."

"Not me," Niamh piped in.

"No, your deep wells of rage would have rendered you absolutely immune to attack if you had fallen," I said.

"Bang-on right they would."

All our phones made notification noises; Aparna got to hers first. "Update on Ardeleanu," she said. "Muscle tears but no ligaments torn or major blood vessels nicked. He's been given a full spectrum of antibiotics and a pair of crutches, and has been told no more field-work for the rest of this tour. He'll be fine."

"Just like he kept saying," I noted.

Niamh narrowed their eyes. "Don't you even."

"Sorry."

"Also," Aparna continued, "after dinner tonight there's going to be a special ceremony and party in our honor. The three of us, I mean. Sorry, Kahurangi."

Kahurangi grinned. "Considering what you had to do to get a party, I'm happy to miss out."

"What's the 'special ceremony' about?" Niamh asked.

Aparna looked back to the notice. "It says we're to be 'inducted into the orders.'"

Niamh's brow furrowed. "And what the actual hell do you think *that* means?"

"From time to time, now and again, here and there, we find in our ranks people who do extraordinary things at extraordinary times," Brynn MacDonald was saying in the dining hall. She was at the table where she had just finished her dinner before standing up and literally yelling at everyone to shut up and pay attention to her. If this was part of the "special ceremony," then it was deeply, deeply informal. "And when that happens, what do we do?"

"Induct them into the orders!" came the general response.

"Yes! That's it! And today is one of those days," MacDonald continued. "By now I'm sure you've seen the video of Ion Ardeleanu almost becoming a buffet, and then three of our newest Tanaka Base citizens coming to his rescue. To commemorate this event, it is time to make inductions. To begin, I yield the floor to my Blue Team counterpart, your friend and mine, Jeneba Danso."

There was applause as MacDonald sat and Danso rose from her own table.

"Our first induction of the evening goes to Ion Ardeleanu," Danso said. She pointed to where Ion Ardeleanu was sitting, and made him stand, which he did with the help of his new crutches. She held something in her hand which on slightly closer inspection revealed itself to be what looked like a cheap plastic medal on a ribbon. "Our chief biologist has had five tours of duty here at Base Tanaka and in his tenure has discovered, identified, and classified hundreds of the species of this planet. But as we learned today, in all that time, the one thing he has *not* discovered is that any of the creatures he's identified and named will be happy to eat him!"

Laughs all around, and why not. Ardeleanu wasn't dead; it's easy to make jokes when you live.

"To commemorate his escape from the literal jaws of death, and to remind him to be more careful the next time, I am proud to this evening induct Ion into the Ancient and Sacred Order of the Tasty Snack Cake." There was applause, and Danso walked over to Ardeleanu and placed the medal around his neck, and then gave him a peck on the cheek.

"That's an ancient and sacred order?" I said to Kahurangi, who was sitting next to me at our table, as I applauded.

"I'm guessing they make up the ancient and sacred orders as they go," he said.

"Thank you, Jeneba, and thank you, Tanaka Base," Ardeleanu said, after the applause died down. "I am proud to be known as a legitimate snack"—there were groans here, of the sort that emanate when your dad uses slang he shouldn't—"and I also hope this is the last time anything sees me as such."

More applause here.

"But wait! Because as it turns out I am next to award an order. When I fell and was the subject of attempted consumption, once the very rude creature was removed from my leg, I was treated to the compassionate attention of Dr. Aparna Chowdhury, who first protected me from additional nibbling, and then tended to me until we made it back to base. I remember telling her that I was fine, and I remember her response, which was, and I quote, 'Shut up.'"

There were more laughs.

"And it turns out she was right. I wasn't fine, and she knew it. I hate being the center of attention, even when it's because I was a tasty snack for a monster. But she kept me the center of *her* attention until I was safe at home. In recognition of her care of me—despite my attempts to pretend a shredded leg was no big deal—I am happy to award Dr. Chowdhury the Ancient and Sacred Order of the Very Persistent Nightingale. Aparna, you'll have to come to me, I'm still no good on my feet."

The applause came up and Aparna walked over quickly, got the cheap plastic medal and a hug, and then sat back down as quickly as she could. Being famous to 150 people was indeed her limit.

Ardeleanu negotiated himself back into his seat, and MacDonald stood up again. "Now it's my turn for an induction," she said. "Dr. Niamh Healy has been with us for—*Jesus*—just two weeks. And yet anyone who has spent time with Dr. Healy in those two weeks has learned, and I'm willing to bet, appreciated their absolute intolerance for bullshit. So when that parasite jumped on Ion, Dr. Healy did what Dr. Healy does, which is say, 'This is bullshit,' and then went to correct said bullshit. With an electric baton!"

Applause here.

"For their unwillingness to take crap either from humans or disgustingly large parasites, and their evident handiness with melee weapons, I am absolutely delighted to induct Dr. Healy into the Ancient and Sacred Order of Complete and Utter Bullshit."

More applause, and Niamh went over to get their medal and a

hug. Niamh turned to the assembled masses and held the medal up with their hand, ribbon looping around their neck.

"This is bullshit!" Niamh said. There was whooping and hollering as they sat back down.

This was Tom Stevens's cue to stand up.

"I believe I've told more than a few of you about how I recruited Jamie Gray," he said. "It involved food delivery and a last-minute need for someone to haul things around here on base." Laughs here. "So I got lucky, but I think Jamie also got lucky. Who else among us in their first two weeks was chased by a kaiju, narrowly escaped a nuclear explosion, and then, as a capper, shot a parasite right in the face with a canister launcher? I mean, this is my third rotation, and I haven't done a single one of those." He looked at me. "I admit it, Jamie, I'm totally jealous."

"You should be," I said. This got a laugh.

"Anyone who has ever had weapons training with Riddu Tagaq—which means all of us at this point—knows that her mantra with the weapons is 'Do you *really* think you're going to do that?' And yet, here is Jamie, who, when confronted with a parasite that would happily eat everyone on that away party, marched right up to it, yelled at it, and then shot a canister right in its mouth. Right in the damn mouth, people."

"I am going to talk to Jamie about that," said Riddu Tagaq, somewhere in the dining hall. This got a huge laugh.

"And so, for coolness under pressure, for giving the rest of the away team the time it needed to get Ion safely back to the helicopter, and for having the absolute nerve to ignore Riddu Tagaq, I am proud and happy to award Jamie Gray the Ancient and Sacred Order of Holy Shit Jamie Just Shot That Parasite Straight in the Mouth with a Canister Launcher."

"Definitely making it up as they're going along," Kahurangi said to me. I grinned and got my medal and hug and thanked everyone. Then MacDonald declared it was officially party time, and music went up and people went to get drinks. I thanked people as they came by to congratulate me, and when that slowed down, I took a closer look at my medal. It had the words *World's Okayest Dad* on it, which for many reasons was not terribly accurate, but I knew it was the thought that counted.

There was a firm tap on my shoulder. I turned and saw the impassive, unamused face of Riddu Tagaq.

"I can explain," I blurted out. This was a lie, I could not.

Tagaq held up a hand. "Explanations later. We have other business tonight."

"We do?"

"Yes, we do," Tagaq said. Then she broke into a huge toothy smile. "Karaoke!"

And then the next day, everything was back to normal. Aparna and Niamh went back to work, both of them going over the video and data from the instrument packages they'd planted. I think the thinking there was inasmuch as they were attacked by creatures planting the instruments, they deserved to take the lead in working what came out of them.

Likewise, I may have been inducted into the Ancient and Sacred Order of Whatever It Was That I Was Inducted Into, but also, people still needed to have things delivered or removed or lifted, and I didn't need Val to think I was basking in my glory. The day after the party, people still gave me congratulations, and told me the stories of their own inductions into the orders. The day after that, no one cared.

Which was fine. It was a heavy burden being the World's Okayest Dad, I didn't need to be thinking about it every moment of the day.

The day after that, I saw Tom coming up to me as I was coming out of the dining hall for lunch. He was holding his tablet as he came up to me. "First off, this is not my fault," he said.

"That's a hell of an introduction," I said.

"We have our first tourists coming in a couple of days."

"Yes, I know." I had gotten the lists of the incoming VIPs for the next three weeks, and they were what I was assured was a pretty standard mix of military brass, political sightseers, and scientists who might actually have something useful to add to our work.

"There's been a last-minute change to this week's lineup. It literally just came in from Honda Base, who literally just got it from back home."

"Okay, so?"

"They've swapped out Dr. Plait for one of our newer funders."

"All right, so I'm babysitting a billionaire. I'm familiar with the type."

"Well, that's the thing."

"Damn it, Tom, stop being vague."

He handed me his tablet. "Just remember, again, I had nothing to do with this."

I took the tablet and read the revised visitor list.

"You have got to be fucking kidding me," I said.

CHAPTER 17

The *Shobijin* slid into its dock, and immediately, the Tanaka Base airship crew started to work on it, securing it and preparing to unload the various supplies that it carried as our lifeline to Honda Base and, therefore, the real world. Once emptied, it would be filled up again, a little bit with scientific samples or things that we created at Tanaka that were requested by other bases, like canisters of specific kaiju pheromones—Tanaka was better equipped to make those than some other bases.

Mostly, however, the *Shobijin* would be filled with the trash we couldn't treat, recycle, or compost; it would go back to Honda and then make it back to our Earth for proper disposal. It might seem fairly extravagant to airlift refuse and then send it through a dimensional door to get rid of it, but that was KPS for you. We took seriously the idea that we were to leave as little a mark on this world as possible.

In a small change of pace, however, this trip the *Shobijin* would be bringing trash into Tanaka.

The gangway to Tanaka Base was extended and the door to the passenger compartment opened. Because this was mostly a cargo run, the passenger cabin of the *Shobijin* had been reconfigured, but there were still a few seats left for the tourists who had come to visit us. The first of these tourists finally appeared at the door and started down the gangway, followed by a second, and then a third and apparently final tourist.

Rob Shitmonkey Sanders. The former CEO of füdmüd.

"How the ever-loving Christ is *he* a tourist here?" I had demanded of Tom the day before, when he'd broken the news to me that Sanders was on his way.

"I don't know," Tom said. "The only thing I can guess is that he spent some of those billions you said he got from selling füdmüd and gave them to KPS, and they let him come over to see the place."

"So that's how it works? Shovel a couple of million to KPS and they let you pet the monsters?"

"Well, yes, actually," Tom admitted. I gave him a look, which he noticed. "This is how the game is played, Jamie. There's only so much governments can fund us before who we are and what we do becomes part of the public record. Getting money from the über-rich—"

"I see what you did there."

"—is part of how we do our job and still keep this mostly under wraps."

"It's a sketchy way to get funding."

"Wait until you figure out that at least some of that billionaire funding is actually government funding," Tom said. "They contract with the billionaire's company for a service on an expensive no-bid contract with the understanding that a cut of that revenue makes it here."

"Billionaires are *laundering government money* for us?"

"Basically."

"I reiterate my amazement this is all still somehow a secret," I said.

"Acknowledged," Tom said. "And remember what I said the first time we ever talked about it. It's secret, but not that secret." He pointed at his tablet. "Sometimes that means letting people we'd rather not in on the secret."

Watching Rob Sanders now walking down the gangway, I leaned toward Tom, who was standing next to me, along with Brynn Mac-Donald, as part of the welcoming party. "I can't promise I won't feed him to the tree crabs," I said.

"Resist the temptation," Tom suggested. "It would be bad to feed our funders to the fauna."

"Maybe just parts of him."

"Jamie."

"Fine," I said. "I will let him live. Today."

The three tourists made their way to where we were standing, and MacDonald greeted the first of them. "Major General Tipton," she said. "Welcome back to Tanaka Base." She nodded to Sanders and the other tourist. "I understand you're running with half of your expected team at the moment."

"We are," he said. "Dr. Gaines, who was with us from the Department of Energy, had a severe asthma attack after we crossed over to Honda Base. She's recuperating there in their medical facility, and the other two members of her team elected to stay with her."

"I hope she'll be all right."

"She'll be fine. They'll keep her people busy, I'm sure." Tipton motioned to Sanders and the other person on his team. "Allow me to introduce Colonel David Jones, my aide, and this is Robert Sanders, who is here representing Tensorial, one of our major contractors. He's taken on this role from his father."

I blinked at this and then remember Tom mentioning a couple of weeks back that Sanders came from a family that made its money from defense contracts. I suppose this meant he'd come back into the fold in the last few weeks.

"Pleasure," MacDonald said. "This is Tom Stevens, my aide, and Jamie Gray, who will be your liaison during your stay."

Sanders pointed to Tom. "You look familiar somehow," he said.

"We overlapped at Dartmouth," Tom said. "I was a couple of years behind you."

"Well, isn't it a small world," Sanders said. "Speaking of which"—he turned and faced me. "Look who this is!"

"It's me," I agreed.

"You know Rob?" Tipton asked.

"Jamie was one of my executives at füdmüd," Sanders told him.

"Oh! You must have been very pleased at your stock payout when Uber bought your company," Tipton said to me.

"Alas," I said, looking at Sanders. "I wasn't there when it happened and didn't own any stock when it did."

Tipton chortled. "Bet you regret that now."

"Well, I did get a fifteen percent discount at Duane Reade, so it wasn't all bad."

Tipton pointed at Sanders. "This one just became a billionaire from that. If I had his money, I'd be on the beach in Cancun with a big fruity drink in my hand. This one went back to work for his dad."

"To be fair, I was on the board of Tensorial when I was CEO of füdmüd," Sanders said. "I still kept a hand in. And now I'm here."

"Yes, sweating our asses off," Tipton said. "This place hasn't gotten any cooler since the last time I was here."

"No, I suppose not," MacDonald said. She pointed toward me. "Jamie here will be in charge of your stay here, so anything you need, you can just—"

"Actually—and I apologize for cutting you off here, Dr. Mac-Donald," Tipton said, and this is how I learned that Brynn MacDonald had a doctorate in something, "I've been tasked with getting a comprehensive overview of the KakKasuak Event—"

"The what?"

"It's what we're calling your exploding kaiju on the other side," Tipton said. "I've been tasked with getting a comprehensive overview of the event as quickly as possible and returning as quickly as possible." He nodded to Jones, who reached into the bag he was carrying and presented MacDonald with a clipboard with paper on it. "Here are the things we'll need to be briefed on. We'll need to have those briefings today."

MacDonald took the clipboard and passed it to Tom without looking at it. "We have a full suite of briefings scheduled for tomorrow—"

Tipton shook his head. "Apologies again, Dr. MacDonald, but we have to be back on our way tomorrow morning." He held a hand up, anticipating the objection she was about to make. "This isn't me pushing you around and disrupting your schedules, I promise you. This is coming from my bosses, and also from their boss, and his boss. All the way up."

"I don't understand," MacDonald said. "It's not like we haven't had kaiju go up before."

"You have," Sanders said. "But they're not visible from Canadian airspace."

I remember Niamh pointing out the flash that the Canadian drone was able to spot from the air, corresponding to where Bella was sitting on our side of the fence.

"It's not a threat," MacDonald said.

Tipton smiled. "You're probably right about that. But it's only a matter of time before it gets spotted by a commercial flight, or tourists—"

"There are tourists in Newfoundland? In October? In a pandemic?" I blurted out.

"—or by residents nearby," Tipton said, looking at me, displeased. He was less thrilled about being interrupted than he was with interrupting. "And with no disrespect to your people here, Dr. MacDonald, not everyone back home is convinced that a pregnant kaiju squatting on the barrier between our two worlds is not a threat. I'm sure you are right, but I need information to convince others. And I need to have it today, because I'm expected at the White House early Monday morning."

"The White House," MacDonald said, skeptically.

"I'm reporting to the chief of staff. He'll fill in his boss as necessary."

MacDonald nodded. "Tom here will set up the meetings for today, then."

"Thank you," Tipton said. "And when can we see the site?"

MacDonald looked at me. "Martin's ready," I said. "We were going to take up one group as soon as possible. As soon as possible might as well be now."

"Colonel Jones will stay behind to police our luggage and to coordinate with Mr. Stevens here," Tipton said.

"All right." MacDonald looked over to me again. "They're all yours, Jamie. See you all in about ninety minutes." She and Tom and Colonel Jones headed off, with Jones already pointing to things on the agenda.

I turned back to my charges. "You've been in helicopters before?"

"Of course," Sanders said.

"And you?" I asked Tipton.

Tipton gave me a look. "I'm a major general in the United States Air Force. What do you think?"

Not too far off from the site, and while Satie and Tipton, who was in the copilot seat, were talking incessantly about helicopters, Sanders tapped me on the shoulder, took off his headset, and motioned at me to lean in. I took off my headset, was immediately reminded how much a pair of good aviation headphones blocked out helicopter engine noise, and leaned in as well.

Sanders said something.

"What?" I said.

Sanders got closer and pretty much yelled in my ear. "I said, I hope there are no hard feelings about me firing you in March."

Really, you're doing this now? was what I thought but I did not say. "It's not what I had hoped out of that performance review," is what I did say, into his ear, once he had turned for me to yell into it. This is how we would have our conversation; clearly Sanders didn't want the others to be privy to it.

"I can understand that," he said. "But you landed pretty well."

"I wouldn't have minded having the stock payout."

"The stock buyout was only for the class A stock. You and most employees had class B. They were just swapped over for Uber stock."

"So I wouldn't have been a millionaire."

"Not unless you were one already. Does that make you feel better?"

"Not really."

"This is better anyway," Sanders said. "And actually I'm jealous of you. You get to be here every day. This is only my first trip here."

"But you knew about it before?"

Sanders nodded. "Tensorial and its predecessor companies are invested in nuclear energy technologies. Ever hear of a radioisotope thermoelectric generator?"

"Radio what?"

"It's a type of nuclear power generator. We make 'em. KPS uses them."

"We do?"

"Not at your base. Other places. Point is, we've been working with KPS for decades. My dad told me about it when I was a kid."

"And you believed him?"

Sanders shook his head. "Not at first. Too wild, right? But then I realized it was real. I told him I wanted to see it."

"What did he say to that?"

"He said, 'When you make your first billion.' So I went and made füdmüd."

"You did füdmüd so you could come *here*?"

"Dad made me a deal."

"füdmüd could have been a failure."

Sanders smiled at this. "It was never designed to *succeed*. It was designed to *sell*."

"I don't know what that means."

"When you start up a company, you can do it to dominate a sector, or you can do it to cause someone else so much pain that they buy you out. I made füdmüd to cause Grubhub and Uber Eats pain. And one of them bought me out. For billions."

I considered what this meant, and how cynically Sanders had designed his company. Then I remembered the suggestions that I had given him in the meeting where I had been fired. He used them, which was bad enough, but he also used them just to annoy someone else to pay him to go away. My sole attempt at business genius worked only to antagonize another company into buying a competitor that had no real interest in competing.

"Well, aren't you a massive prick," I said, quietly, under the roar of the helicopter.

"What?" Sanders asked.

"I said, 'That's a nifty trick.'"

"It's the art of the deal, my friend."

I did not say the next thing in my brain and instead changed the subject. "So, why *did* you fire me?" I asked. "Now that we're here and it doesn't matter."

"It wasn't personal," Sanders said. "You remember Qanisha Williams?" I nodded. "She and I were talking about the pandemic and how it was going to mess with the economy. She said she hoped it wouldn't be too bad. I said it was so bad that even people who had good jobs that week would be signing up to be deliverators next week. She didn't think it would happen. So I made her a Duke bet."

"A what?"

"I bet her a dollar. You know, like the Duke brothers in *Trading Places*."

I racked my brain on this one. "The old Eddie Murphy film."

"Yes. I made her the bet, and then I told her to pull up the employee directory, and I picked ten names at random. Then I called them into my office and fired them."

"Including me."

"Sorry. Qanisha put up a fight for you, you should know."

"We were friends," I said. And we had been.

"That's what she said. I told her she could take you off the list if she replaced you. She didn't."

"I wouldn't have wanted her to," I said. I knew Qanisha was supporting more than herself on her salary.

"So, then I swore her to secrecy, and I told her that if half of the people I fired were deliverators a week later, I'd win the bet."

"And?"

Sanders looked smug. "Six out of ten."

"You must be proud," I said.

"I just understand people."

"Do you?"

Before Sanders could answer, Tipton waved at us to put on our headsets. We were close to the site.

"Do you think the pilot will let us land and walk around?" Sanders asked me, before we put on our headsets.

"I wouldn't bet on it," I said.

"Want to make a Duke bet on it?"

"Not really."

"I'm going to try anyway. Watch this." He put on his headset, and then quickly took it off and leaned in again. "What's the pilot's name again?"

"Martin," I said.

"Got it." The headphones went back on and he patched back through into the intercom just as Bella became visible, looming in her nest.

"Well, that's a hell of a thing," Tipton said, looking at Bella. "And she's been there for two weeks now, just sitting."

"Not just sitting," Satie said. "Making eggs. The first run of eggs are going to hatch in the next week. Lots of little kaiju going to be born, eat their brothers and sisters, and then run off into the woods. Then she'll make more eggs. She'll do that a few times before she's done."

"And not move a muscle while she does."

"She doesn't have to move. She has all her creatures to move for her."

"How close are we going to get to her?" Tipton asked.

"Depends on your nerves, General," Satie replied.

Tipton chuckled at that.

"How about you let us out to look around?" Sanders said.

"I don't recommend that," Satie said.

"Why not?"

"Jamie knows."

"I landed here with some scientists about a week ago, and one of them almost got eaten," I said.

"I don't mind the risk," Sanders said.

"That's easy to say when you're not being chewed on," Satie said.

"I'll pay you ten thousand dollars to land for five minutes."

"Do you have the ten thousand dollars on you? In cash?"

"No."

"Then no," Satie said. "And anyway, what would ten thousand dollars do me here? Kaiju Earth is a socialist paradise, Mr. Sanders."

"A hundred thousand dollars, Martin," Sanders said. "Wired to your accounts at home, the minute we get back."

Satie turned and looked at Sanders, who looked back, a small smile on his face. He was sure he had just found Satie's price. Satie turned back to his instruments. Sanders turned to me as if to say, *See?*

The helicopter dropped violently. If we hadn't been strapped in, we'd have been on the ceiling. Satie took us all the way down and nearly put us on the ground, hard, before he stopped, hovering inches above fallen trees and new green.

Satie turned back to Sanders. "All right, out," he said.

Sanders looked around. We were still a distance from Bella. "What, here?"

"Here is as good a place as any."

"Well, if I'm paying a hundred grand, I want to be close to *her*." Sanders pointed toward Bella.

"I'm not taking your money," Satie said. "I'm just letting you out."

"I don't understand."

"I know you don't. Get out."

Sanders glanced over to the copilot's seat. "General Tipton—"

"You're not talking to him," Satie interrupted. "You're talking to me. He's not going to say a goddamn word. He's not in charge of this mission, or this aircraft. I am. And I'm telling you to get out."

Sanders was visibly confused. "I don't see what the problem is here."

"You insulted me, Mr. Sanders."

"Offering you money is an insult?"

"You didn't insult me by offering me money. You insulted me by thinking I could be bought."

Sanders blinked silently at this. He clearly didn't understand the distinction.

I looked out the window. In the medium distance, away from the wash of the rotors, creatures were looking in the direction of the helicopter, curious about it, wondering if it might be food.

"When you made your first offer, I was willing to let you pass it off as a joke," Satie said. "You're not the first billionaire I've ferried around. I know how you all like to wave around your money dick to see who might be willing to suck on it. If you had let it go when I gave you the opportunity, I was willing to ignore it. But you had to push it. You wanted to see how much it would cost for me to compromise the safety of everyone on this aircraft, me included, to assert your dominance. So, now here is my answer, Mr. Sanders. I will let you out for free. And there is no amount of money, on this planet or the other, that you or anyone else could pay me to let you back in."

Sanders gaped at Satie, then looked at Tipton, then at me, and then out the window, where, I believe, he saw the curious creatures for the first time.

"Now. Out you go." Satie pointed to the door.

Sanders looked back at Satie. "I've changed my mind."

"You still don't get it," Satie said. "It's not *your* mind you have to change here."

"Martin—"

"Dr. Satie, if you please," Satie said, and this is how I learned how he had a doctorate. I very briefly wondered if in fact I was the only one on this whole planet who did not possess a terminal degree of some sort.

Sanders gathered himself. "Dr. Satie, I have clearly offended you, and for that I am profoundly sorry," he said. "Please accept my full and unreserved apology for what I said to you."

"I accept it on the condition that for the entire rest of this trip, I do not hear a single goddamn peep out of you," Satie said. "Not to me, not to General Tipton, not to Jamie. You just *sit* there, Mr. Sanders. Do you accept? You can nod if you do."

Sanders nodded.

"Well, then, we have a deal," Satie said, and turned away from

Sanders. "Now let's go look at a big damn creature, what do you say?" He lofted us back into the air and back toward Bella.

I looked at Sanders, who was pale and sweating.

Damn, I thought. *I could have won a dollar.*

CHAPTER 18

The tour of the site over, it was time for things to be explained.

"Here's a thing I'm confused about," Rob Sanders said, at the first of the briefings we had set up for him, General Tipton, and Colonel Jones with our scientists and staff. If Sanders was showing any residual psychological damage from being humiliated by a helicopter pilot a couple of hours earlier, he wasn't showing it now. The resiliency of the billionaire ego was truly something to behold. "We know that the kaiju, the big ones, have organic nuclear reactors. But when we were flying over Bella today, looking at the field of eggs, it occurred to me that I've never heard of baby kaiju having the reactors in them, too. Do they?"

"Yes and no," Aparna said. Because she was the one gathering the data from the nesting site, and this meeting was ostensibly about that, she was the one from the biology lab leading the briefing. Aside from her and the tourists, the briefing included Brynn MacDonald and Tom Stevens and me. We were holding it in the very small conference room in the administration building. It was a very cozy meeting. In addition to my role as visitor liaison, I was also, once again, supervising snacks.

"That's vague," Sanders said, smiling.

This got a head shake from Aparna. "Not vague at all. Yes, because even at a very early age—even as an embryo in the egg—there are certain precursor structures in the kaiju body that will develop into the reactor in later stages of life. No, because those precursor structures are not yet a reactor. There are other things that have to happen first."

"Like what?" Tipton asked.

"Certain hormonal changes, to start."

"The kaiju has to hit puberty," Sanders said.

"If you like," Aparna said, in a tone that suggested that she didn't, in fact, like. "It would be incorrect to imagine kaiju development being an exact analogue to mammalian or even earthly vertebrate development, however. It's much more complex than that."

Sanders nodded. "Tell us how, please."

"All right. As just one example, the nuclear reactor development is not only contingent on the *age* of the creature—that's where the puberty metaphor goes wrong—but also contingent on parasite load. If a kaiju doesn't have enough parasites, or enough of a certain sort of parasite, then the nuclear chamber development doesn't happen."

Tipton frowned. "So, these things don't go nuclear if they don't have the right sort of fleas?"

"Again, if you like," Aparna said. "But it's really more complicated than that." She motioned to MacDonald. "When I first got here, Dr. MacDonald here told us not to think of the kaiju as animals and instead to think of them as ecological systems in their own right. This is accurate in a way that's difficult to convey. The creatures we call 'kaiju parasites' aren't all strictly parasites. Some of them are, but more of them are in a commensal relationship with the kaiju, while others are in a mutually beneficial relationship. And not just with the kaiju, with each other as well. In fact, there are some who have a commensal relationship with the kaiju but a mutual relationship with other parasites. They live *on* the kaiju, but they survive *with* these other creatures."

"That's great, but what does that *mean*?" Sanders said. It was clear Aparna was going over his head more than a little bit.

"Basically, if they don't pick up the right parasites from their environment, certain developmental stages can't happen," Aparna said. "In the case of the nuclear chamber, a developing kaiju has to—among many other things—acquire the sort of parasite that acts as an internal cooling system from the kaiju, bringing in air from the outside and routing it through the kaiju to take away heat. Gaining those parasites creates the conditions that allow the kaiju to grow larger. Growing larger introduces stress on the developing kaiju because its ability to continue living through metabolic functions alone quickly decreases. That type of stress causes the kaiju body to release specific hormones and initiate other processes that, among other things, create and activate the nuclear chamber."

"And if they don't find the right parasites?"

"Then they don't become kaiju. Either they die from growing too large—they fall victim to the square-cube law"—Sanders frowned here, which I assume meant he'd never heard of that particular law—"or they simply stay at an earlier stage of development. It's not quite right to think of the massive kaiju as the only viable stage of the creature. They can live quite happily at earlier developmental stages for their entire lives, where they are 'only' as large as, say, an elephant or a tyrannosaurus rex. Only a small percentage of all kaiju actually get to what we would consider true monster size."

"So, if you want a kaiju, you need some parasites," Tipton said.

Aparna nodded. "And not only *some* parasites, *specific* parasites, for specific species of kaiju. One of the really interesting things about Bella, and Edward, the kaiju who impregnated her, is that they are in the wrong place. Their species is endemically from what we'd think of as Mexico and Central America. There are some parasites critical to their development that don't exist this far north. Which means they had to have come here from the south as fully developed kaiju, because they wouldn't have been able to develop here."

"What does that mean for their children?" Sanders asked. "Will they develop into full-size kaiju?"

"It depends," Aparna said. "If Bella stays in the area as they develop, or if they can get close to Edward without him or some of his parasites eating them, then they might get those critical creatures from them and grow into large kaiju. If Edward and Bella leave, they'll stay at an earlier development level. Mind you, most of them won't even get that far."

"They'll get eaten, you mean."

"Yes, or they'll starve. The kaiju at every stage of life are predators, and the larger they get, the closer they get to their ecological

apex niche. An ecological system can support only so many predators. And when you have a full kaiju in the area, things get even
worse."

"Why?" Tipton said. "They're nuclear powered. They're beyond
eating."

Aparna shook her head. "They derive energy from their nuclear
processes, but they still need things like nutrients for their biological systems. They still *hunt*. They hunt other kaiju. They hunt less-
developed kaiju. But more significantly from an ecological point of
view, they also have their legions of parasites, many of whom hunt,
and all of *them* have metabolisms. A kaiju is a walking mountain of
mouths. They and their parasites can and will eat their local countryside bare. Or would, if the countryside didn't fight back."

"It fights back?" Sanders said.

"Oh, yes," Aparna said. "Everything here is ridiculously lethal,
because all of it that's not a kaiju parasite has evolved to defend itself
from kaiju parasites. Some things even prey on the parasites directly.
It's constant war. Sometimes the countryside even wins, and routs
the parasites."

"And then what happens?"

"Well, remember: The kaiju aren't animals, they're ecological systems," Aparna said. "What happens when you kill off a critical part
of an ecological system? Chances are good the rest of it dies, too."

"It's this intense competition that makes this version of Earth so
interesting, from a chemistry point of view," Kahurangi said, in the
next scheduled meeting, where he was briefing Sanders and Tipton
in the latest from the chem lab. "Everything is signaling to everything else, and most of it is some variation of 'Leave me alone or I'll
cut you.'"

"And this differs from our Earth how?" Tipton asked.

Kahurangi grinned. "Volume, mostly. Everything is shouting
here."

"So, how do we shout back?" Sanders asked.

"We don't shout back, we shout what they're already saying. I
don't know if you've ever done any work on the jungle floor—"

"Not yet," Sanders said, dryly. Yep, he'd definitely recovered from his earlier moment.

"—but one of the things we do is use scents and pheromones that mimic kaiju parasites, so everything will give us a wide berth."

"We were told by your associate Dr. Chowdhury that there are things here that kill the parasites, not run from them," Tipton said.

"She wasn't lying to you," Kahurangi said. "But just like home, there are qualifications for that. Some creatures are prey to those parasites. They'll run away. Some want to prey on the parasite, and they'll come for a look. But like all predators, they'll size up the situation. If it's too much trouble, they'll leave us alone. We try to make it too much trouble. But it's not perfect." He motioned to me. "Jamie here just had a mission where a predator took its chance."

"We heard something along that line." Tipton turned to me. "How did that go?"

"Jamie shot it in the face," Kahurangi said, proudly, before I could answer.

Tipton looked me over, reassessing. "You don't look like the face-shooting type."

"We all have hidden depths," I said.

"So, if we have the right chemicals, we can control these things," Sanders said, bringing things back around to the subject at hand.

"Control? No," Kahurangi replied. "We don't talk in terms of control."

"Why not?"

"Because these aren't people, and we're not talking to them. When these things smell the pheromones or scents, it's not like they're getting orders. They're getting *suggestions*. If we have a pheromone that's designed to invoke a fight-or-flight response, we want them to flee, and ninety percent of the time, they will. But then there's that other ten percent of the time where they want to fight."

"And you can't perfect this any."

"Not really," Kahurangi said. "And even if we could there's still no way we could guarantee they'd do what we wanted every single time. They're biological creatures, not machines. I mean, we can speak to other humans perfectly well, right? We don't have to spray them with chemicals or anything. We can just *talk* to them, and they can understand exactly what we want. Do *they* do what we want them to do every single time?"

"Not always," Sanders admitted.

"There you go."

"Let me take this in another direction. Could we *drug* a kaiju?"

Kahurangi grinned. "Do you want to get a kaiju stoned, Mr. Sanders?"

"I don't want to do anything with one. I just want to know if it's theoretically possible."

"I'm sure it is, although as far as I know we've never done it."

"Never?"

"Well, I'm new, so I would have to check," Kahurangi admitted. "But in a larger sense, again, these are biological creatures, even if they are mostly nuclear powered. I'm sure you can create compounds that have specific effects on them."

"And for other creatures from here, too."

"Sure, although everything will react differently. Heck, there are some drugs that work on adult humans that don't work well on children and vice versa. Also, it would take a brave person to dose a kaiju or even a kaiju parasite to see what their invented pharmaceutical compound would do."

"You already do that when you spray them with pheromones," Tipton pointed out.

Kahurangi grinned again. "Yeah, but then we usually run the hell away."

"Is there anything in your current arsenals of smells and pheromones that can keep a kaiju in one place?" Sanders asked. "Bella is sitting right on top of a fluctuating barrier between our worlds. If she gets up, she might get up on the wrong side of the barrier."

Kahurangi shook his head. "No," he said. "But as I understand it, Bella isn't likely to cross over, and she's acting to keep the other kaiju away."

"How so?"

"Well, speaking of pheromones, ever since she nested, she's been emitting a huge amount of them, and they all say the same thing to the other kaiju in the area."

"What's that?" Tipton asked.

"'Stay the hell away.'"

"And what happens if she *does* get up?" Tipton asked Niamh, in the third briefing of the day, this one updating the two of them about current physics work at the site.

"You mean, is she coming through to our Earth?"

"That is the concern, yes."

"Well, even if she could, and I'll get to that in a moment, the question is: Why would she?"

"Because she's a stupid animal that might lean in the wrong direction getting up?" Sanders said.

"She's not a stupid animal, first off," Niamh said. "None of these creatures are."

"They're not *intelligent*."

"Of course they are," Niamh said, in a tone that expressed disappointment that something so obvious had to be said. "You don't think of Bella as intelligent because she's not playing the stock market or some other utterly irrelevant standard. But in fact, she's a perfectly intelligent creature, within the context of being driven by her own needs. Right now, her *need* is to stay in one place and squirt out eggs. She has no need to get up, and the only way she *will* get up is if something bothers her. And anyway, if she *does* get up, it'll be to respond to something on this side of the barrier, like another kaiju crashing into her territory. The moment that happens, your barrier problem is on its way to being solved."

"That," Tipton said suddenly, and pointed at Niamh. "*That's* what I need to know. Explain this to me."

"The barrier got torn when the other kaiju blew up," Niamh said. "It's just part of the release of that much nuclear energy. The thing is, no matter how large a hole you punch in a dimensional barrier, it immediately starts to heal up."

"Why does it do that?" Sanders asked.

"Because the release of nuclear energy that thinned it out stops, and the surrounding nuclear activity starts to decay away. The barrier heals up in a predictable manner tied to the ambient nuclear activity in the area. Unless more energy is added, it will eventually close up entirely."

"But this one's not closing," Tipton said.

"Right, because you have a big damn living, breathing nuclear reactor sitting right on it," Niamh said. "Bella's nuclear powered, and that energy is keeping the barrier thin. Or at least, thinner than it would be. But the moment she moves—"

"Then her energy moves away with her."

Niamh nodded at Tipton. "And even now, the amount of energy she's adding into the mix isn't enough at this point to let her punch through. Maybe it was in the first few days, when the ambient radiation levels at the site were still high enough. But it's been weeks, and those levels are way down. She's keeping the barrier thin, but not enough for her or any other kaiju to get through on their own."

"But what about that flash?" Sanders asked.

"See, that's *really* interesting," Niamh said, animatedly. "I thought the flash was a brief tear between our worlds where something might get through. But then we got some instruments in there. Turns out that what's happening is that as she sits there, feeding energy *into* the barrier, something akin to a static charge is building up. And at some point, something happens to agitate it, and all that static energy just goes *pop,* and it discharges on both sides of the barrier."

Sanders paused at this. "It's *static electricity?*"

"No, it's something *much weirder,*" Niamh said. "We've never seen it before because we've never had a kaiju sit still near a nuclear site long enough to have it happen. And since I am the first to describe its nature, I am calling it *the Healy effect,* and one day when I can actually publish about it, I will get a Nobel Prize, and all the other physics postdocs at Trinity will just have to suck it."

"That was quite a journey you just took us on," Sanders said, smirking.

"Let me have my moment, please," Niamh replied.

"I want to make sure I understand you," Tipton said. "The barrier between our worlds right now *is* thin, and this kaiju *is* feeding energy into it, but it's not thin *enough* for this or any other kaiju to get through, and if any other kaiju comes along, she will move to fight it and in doing so remove the energy that's keeping the barrier thin."

"That's right."

"But *could* it open up again?" Sanders asked. "Enough to let her through?"

"Not unless she goes nuclear herself," Niamh said. "And there's no evidence she's at risk for that."

"So it would take a nuclear blast, is what you're saying."

Niamh thought about it a minute. "No? But effectively yes on this side of the barrier, since we don't have any concentrated fissionable material over here. But if Bella goes up over here, that will solve your problem entirely. She's dead and the other kaiju only cross over if the nuclear explosion is on the other side."

"That's just weird," Tipton said, almost muttering to himself.

"What is?" Niamh asked.

"How something over *here* can sense something back home. How there's an alternate Earth and the way we discovered it was through nuclear bombs."

Niamh smiled. "Mate, if you want your noodle *really* baked, then think about this: Any time we play with nuclear energy, we're thinning the dimensional barrier not just between our world and this one, but with *every* potential alternate Earth and our own."

Tipton frowned. "What?"

"Every single one of them," Niamh said. "Millions. Billions. Trillions."

"How do you know that?"

Niamh shrugged "It's just math."

"Then why do we only see this one?"

Niamh grinned even more wildly. "You're going to love this. Because as far as I can tell, it's because our two Earths are the only ones with nuclear creatures. The kaiju got there naturally. We used our brains."

"Then why did it take a kaiju coming over for us to realize this world existed?" Sanders asked.

"Because we think we're smart," Niamh said.

"Come again?"

"We think we're smart," Niamh repeated. "And because we think we're smart, we only looked at what we wanted to look at and didn't think to look past it. We were looking at creating nuclear bombs and didn't think about how nuclear energy might mess with a multiverse. We didn't consider there *was* a multiverse. It's not built into our model."

"And the kaiju *did* consider this," Sanders said, skeptically.

"Of course not," Niamh said, the "I can't believe I have to say this" tone returning. "They didn't consider anything like that. It never occurred to them to create a model of a universe where alternate worlds would or wouldn't exist. They just acted intelligently, within the context of their needs. They sensed a food source and they moved toward it. They didn't consider that it was across a dimensional barrier. They came through to our world because it never occurred to them that they *couldn't*."

CHAPTER 19

"I have a couple of questions for you, if you don't mind," Brynn MacDonald said to General Tipton, after Niamh had finished their presentation and headed out, and we were coming to the close of our meeting schedule.

"Of course, Dr. MacDonald," Tipton said.

"I was curious what your takeaway is and what you'll be reporting back, for a start."

Tipton glanced over at Sanders. "I think it's clear your people know their stuff," he said. "This wasn't really in doubt; KPS always finds good people. But this is an unusual event, and you can understand why back in the real world we would have some concerns. It's been decades since a kaiju came through, and the world has changed in the interim. To have one just sitting on a barrier? It's a security issue, or so it would seem, at first."

"And you think it's less of one now," Tom Stevens said.

"I do." Tipton pointed. "Let me be clear that these presentations need to be backed up with data that I can share with my scientists back home. If they come to different conclusions from the data, I *will* let you know, and, bluntly, I'm not going to be happy about it. But you've never fudged the data before. I'm not sure why you would start now."

"Thank you for the compliment, General."

"You're welcome. Of course, Dr. MacDonald, you would do us all a favor if you could find some way of getting Bella to move, so that breach can seal up entirely. Spray her with some pheromones or something. You do that sort of thing all the time."

"We thought about it," Tom said. "But since she's not in danger of crossing over we decided it's not an issue. Also, brooding kaiju are touchy."

"Touchy?" Sanders asked.

"Bella would rip apart any other kaiju she felt was threatening her eggs. If one of our helicopters goes in and tries to get her to move, she's going to see that as a threat and try to destroy it. And she'd likely chase it until she *did* destroy it, which would risk leading it back to Tanaka Base."

"We'd like not to get stomped by Bella," MacDonald said, dryly.

"So, we think it's better to let her stay where she is for now," Tom continued. "We have those cameras and equipment monitoring her, and we do live observations with the helicopters as well. If something happens that we need to worry about, you'll know."

"How much longer is she there for?" Sanders asked.

"Until she stops producing eggs. She's due to lay more soon, and she'll probably have another session after that."

"So, weeks? Months?"

"Probably another month at least."

"I understand you're curious about these creatures, Mr. Sanders," MacDonald said.

"Of course," Sanders said.

"Enough so that you tried to bribe my pilot to land near Bella," MacDonald continued. "You do understand that Dr. Satie filed an incident report not long after you landed. As he's obliged to whenever something unusual happens on a flight."

Sanders looked uncomfortable but not unduly so. He was back on land and in a conference room environment, which was his usual playing field. "Dr. MacDonald, I realize now that I let my enthusiasm get away from me—"

"Yes, you did," MacDonald said. "Please tell me why."

"It's my first time here," Sanders said. "Seeing this. Seeing all of this. I got carried away. It was wrong of me. I'm sorry."

MacDonald looked at Sanders levelly. "You understand your family has a less-than-shining reputation with regard to Tanaka Base."

Sanders appeared confused about this. "I . . . didn't, actually."

"In the sixties, as the KPS was getting underway, your grandfather pushed your company's radioisotope thermoelectric generators as a way to power our bases, including the first version of Tanaka. There was a report noting the kaiju here seemed especially attracted to that version of RTGs and would go looking for them, but his counterpart at the time"—MacDonald motioned to Tipton—"approved it anyway, in no small part because your grandfather bribed him. Would you like to guess what happened next, Mr. Sanders?"

"I'm guessing a lot of kaiju visitations."

"Yes, including the one with a defective reactor that destroyed the base," MacDonald said. "The old Tanaka Base was by the water, and kaiju with defective reactors often try to get to water, maybe as a way to cool themselves down before they go critical. This one went to the water and then went to the base. Even in the middle of a critical event, it couldn't help looking for what it thought was food. Dozens of people died, Mr. Sanders. Ironically, those RTGs are still there, under the rubble. Not active, of course."

"I don't know how to respond to that," Sanders said, after a minute. "Except to say I'm not bribing General Tipton."

"I can vouch for that, I still have a mortgage and school tuition for three kids," Tipton said.

"You've never struck me as the bribable type," MacDonald said to Tipton.

"Thank you," Tipton replied, sardonically.

MacDonald turned her attention back to Sanders. "But we know *you* are the type to bribe. Just like your grandfather. So, one more time, Mr. Sanders, tell me why you tried to bribe my pilot to let you land."

"Dr. MacDonald, I swear to you that it was just personal curiosity," Sanders said. He sighed, exasperated. "Look, I know I can come across as an asshole sometimes. Just ask Jamie." He pointed at me. All eyes swiveled in my direction.

"Yes, he can," I affirmed. "If I remember correctly, I told him so the day he fired me."

"Yes! *Thank* you," Sanders said to me, then looked back to Mac-Donald. "I was in smug asshole mode earlier this morning. I got called out for it. Fair enough. And also, I've learned my lesson. Being a smug asshole here doesn't fly. Literally, in the case of your helicopter pilot. I'm sorry. I can promise it won't ever happen again."

MacDonald stared at Sanders and then looked over at Tipton. "General?"

"Well, having spent the last two days with him, I can vouch for him being an asshole," Tipton said. "I can also say I was as taken by surprise by his request as your pilot was. I have no reason to believe it was anything other than a spur-of-the-moment thing."

"Jamie?" MacDonald turned to me.

"Huh?" I said, because I am just that smooth.

"Martin says he saw you and Mr. Sanders conversing privately in the helicopter just before he attempted bribery. What was the conversation about?"

A thought occurred to me, and I filed it away for the moment. "It was about *Trading Places*."

MacDonald looked confused. "About the two of you trading places?"

"No," I said. "There was a movie called *Trading Places*. It's from the eighties."

"The Eddie Murphy flick," Tom volunteered.

"That's the one," I said.

"And you were talking about his movie why?" MacDonald asked.

"It was just part of the conversation. Rob's a big Eddie Murphy fan."

MacDonald looked over at Sanders for confirmation. "It's true," he said. "Early Eddie, not later Eddie. Although *Dolemite Is My Name* was pretty good."

"And you talked about nothing else," MacDonald said to me.

"Before that, we talked about füdmüd, which was the company he founded and that I worked for before he unceremoniously fired my ass," I said. "He was trying to tell me that firing me wasn't personal."

"What did you think about that?" Tom asked.

"Well, I suddenly had no job and no money and spent the next six months delivering food in the middle of a pandemic. It sure felt personal."

"Did you tell him that?"

I looked at Sanders. "I mean, he already knows I think he's an asshole."

MacDonald nodded. "All right," she said. She turned back to Sanders. "Congratulations, you've had your one strike, Mr. Sanders. You get no others. Step out of line again, annoy or interfere with any KPS staff again, and I don't care how much money your family has or what your connections are, I'll make your life miserable. And you will certainly never come back to this side ever again. Are we clear?"

"Yes," Sanders said. "Thank you. Sorry."

"Good." MacDonald looked at her smartwatch. "We have a couple of hours until dinner, so unless there's something else you need, General, I'm going to suggest we break. I would be delighted to have you and Mr. Sanders here accompany me for the meal, if you're willing."

"That would be wonderful, thank you," Tipton said.

MacDonald nodded. "Six thirty, then," she said. "I'll have Jamie come collect you at your quarters." Everyone got up and exited the room, except for me, who still had to clear the refreshments. I cleaned everything up, put them on my dining cart, and headed out the door toward the dining hall.

Along the way, I saw Tipton and Sanders standing there, talking. I navigated my way toward them; I could see Tipton being animated and poking Sanders in the chest in a pointed way. Tipton saw me coming up, stopped his conversation with Sanders, nodded to me, and wandered off.

"Everything okay?" I asked Sanders.

"I'm being chewed out by everyone today," he said.

I nodded. "What did the general say?"

"He was telling me that what I did today was the stupidest thing he's seen a civilian ever do on this side of the fence, and also that the KPS doesn't care whose son I am or how much money I have, you guys can always find other billionaires to fund you because you have fucking Godzillas, and nerds with cash will line up at the door for that shit. 'Fucking Godzillas' is an actual quote, by the way."

"I'm sure it is," I said. "Probably also 'nerds with cash.'"

"You would be correct!" Sanders smiled ruefully. "So, yes, not my best day."

"It's not the worst thing in the world to be served up some humility," I suggested.

"I don't know about *that*," Sanders said, and then remembered something. "You lied in there today for me. About what we talked about before I offered the pilot money."

"I didn't lie," I said. "I was merely selective about our conversational topics."

"Why did you do that?"

"Why shouldn't I?"

"Well, for one, you think I'm an asshole."

"You *are* an asshole," I confirmed. "But after a certain point, I think the beatings made their point. Beyond that, it's just piling on. I think you get it."

"I've certainly learned things today," Sanders said. "This place isn't like I expected. Anyway, thank you."

I nodded again. "What's your plan now?"

"Got me," Sanders said. "It's not like you have a lot of activities here. I might go back and stare at a wall until dinner. Why?"

"Well," I said. "It's fair to say you've had a disappointing day, yes?"

"Yes. So?"

"Let me make it up to you."

"How?"

"Let me deal with this," I said, motioning to my cart. "Then let's go for a walk."

"Are we going to get in trouble for this?" Sanders asked, as we tromped down the stairs to the jungle floor. We could have taken the elevator, but several weeks constantly schlepping things around the base plus six months of delivering food to East Village walk-ups meant stairs were not an issue for me. Sanders was beginning to look a little winded, however, and this was us walking down.

"Not at all," I said. "If you had stuck to your original schedule, I would have taken you down here tomorrow anyway. Since you chucked that schedule, this was no longer on it. I'm just putting it back on."

"Maybe we should have told Tipton," Sanders said.

"Nah. He's been here how many times before? I think he's probably seen this bit." We got to the landing, and I stood before the bolted door. "For you, this is all new. Ready?"

"Ready," Sanders said, panting. I unbolted and opened the door, turned on the screamer I had in my pocket, and we went out onto the jungle floor.

"This is amazing," Sanders said, looking around.

"It is," I agreed.

"Is it safe?"

"*Safe* is a word we don't much use here," I said. "But this is as safe as it gets. Just, you know. Don't wander off too far from me, please."

Sanders grinned. "You're my bodyguard, then."

"Something like that," I agreed again.

We wandered out some distance from the door, toward the trees. As we got closer, I reached into my pocket and turned off the screamer. About ten seconds later, the first crab popped around a tree and pointed its antennae at us.

"Whoa," Sanders said, and then the jackass actually reached out to the thing. I turned the screamer back on, and the thing scuttled away. "Did you see that?"

"I did see that," I said.

"What are those?"

"*Tree crabs* is what we call them. Not very imaginative, I know."

"Are they dangerous?"

"They're venomous," I said. In the time since my first encounter with them, I learned that tree crab venom is mostly harmless to humans; it's painful, and enough of it will make you miserable for a day, but it probably won't kill you. It's one reason why Riddu Tagaq used them to scare the shit out of new people. I wasn't telling Sanders that at the moment, however.

"So, I probably shouldn't have tried to touch one," he said.

I turned the screamer off. "You do you," I said, and motioned toward the tree, where the crab had scuttled back around again. This time, Sanders backed away from it, and slightly away from me as well.

I quietly took a step in the other direction, away from Sanders and the tree. "Careful," I said.

"Why?"

"They travel in packs." I pointed to the tree, on which three more tree crabs had scuttled into view.

"Okay, I think I've seen enough," Sanders declared. He wasn't taking his eyes off the tree crabs, who, to be fair, weren't taking their antennae off of him.

I took another quiet step away from Sanders and the tree. "Rob?"

"Yeah?"

"Why did you want to land out there at the site?" I asked. "*Really,* I mean."

"I already said why," he said. More tree crabs had appeared at this point, and they had begun chittering among each other.

"No," I said. "You lied about why, and when they asked me, I deflected enough that they believed your lie. But *I* know you're lying."

"Yeah? How do you know that?" Sanders looked at me when he said that, and one of the tree crabs took that opportunity to scuttle down the tree to the jungle ground. It tapped the ground gingerly with one leg, as if testing it for solidity. Sanders caught the movement out of the corner of his eye and brought all his attention back to the tree full of crabs.

"Because you wanted to make one of your damn 'Duke bets' about it," I said. "You went in confident that you could get Martin to do what you wanted. Which means to me you probably planned it. Which means you had a plan."

"That's a lot of supposition," Sanders said.

"Okay, have it your way," I said, and then turned to walk away. Behind me, I heard a soft plop; one of the crabs had dropped off the tree and was now fully on the ground.

"Wait!"

I turned; Sanders spared me the briefest of panicked looks. By this time, three of the crabs were on the ground, and one of them had begun walking, at a very casual and measured pace, toward him.

"This is just between us," he said.

Despite myself I had to admire his need to try to bargain while he was, or so he thought, on the verge of being eaten. "Go on," I said.

"I wanted to get a sample," he said.

I frowned at this, and noticed the crab nearest to Sanders was now within jumping distance of him. I flicked the screamer on and off; the crab stopped and reared, confused.

"What do you mean, you wanted to get a sample?" I asked.

"I brought a syringe with me," Sanders said. "I told them it was for my insulin."

"You're diabetic?" I asked, pulsing the screamer again.

"No, I just told them that."

"Where's the syringe now?"

"It's in my pocket."

I pulsed the screamer. "Show me."

Sanders fished into his jumpsuit pocket and produced a sealed package that included a syringe and needle. It was very small. I laughed.

"What?" Sanders said.

"You weren't gonna get that into Bella, my dude."

Sanders looked annoyed, or as close as one could be to annoyed while panicking. "It wasn't for Bella."

The tumblers fell into place in my brain. "Ahh, I get it," I said, and pulsed the screamer again. I might have been imagining it, but it seemed to me the crabs were getting exasperated by that point. "You wanted to get a sample from one of her eggs."

"Yes," Sanders said.

"But we already have kaiju genetic material on file."

Sanders shook his head. "Not on the other side. We have the *data* about the genetics. But not the genetics."

"And you thought you would just get your sample *past* everyone on the way back."

"I have the insulin bottle," Sanders said.

The forward crab had finally had enough waiting and leapt at Sanders. He screamed and pivoted, and the crab sailed past him. I turned on the screamer full blast while the crab was midair; it landed and ran off and the rest of the crabs did likewise.

I walked up to Sanders. "So you thought you would just land, at an active kaiju site, stroll over to the natal jelly, which is crawling with creatures like these"—I waved in the direction of where the tree crabs went—"but much, *much* worse, take a sample without any of the rest of us noticing, and bring it back to the other side."

"Yes, basically, that's it," Sanders said.

I turned off the screamer. The crabs poked out from around the tree again.

"It must be *amazing* to have that much confidence," I said.

"In retrospect, I see this plan had flaws," Sanders said, eyeing the crabs.

"A few," I agreed. I turned the screamer back on. The crabs ran away. A slow dawning look on Sanders's face indicated he finally figured out the tree crabs' actions seemed all too well synchronized. I smiled and pulled the screamer out of my pocket. "Keeps them away," I said. "Unless I turn it off."

"You brought me down here on purpose," he said, eyes narrowing.

"I sure did," I agreed.

"Why?"

"Because I know you better than the rest of them, and I was curious. And also, you were an asshole to me. I wanted to return the favor."

"Well, nicely done," Sanders said. "You've definitely done that."

"Not done yet," I said, waggling the screamer, and then putting it back in my pocket before Sanders thought to try to take it from me. He couldn't—I was better in shape than he was; I lift things—but why let him think about it.

"What else do you want?" Sanders asked.

"There's the matter of your punishment," I said.

Sanders's eyes widened. "You *wouldn't*."

I gave him a look. "What, leave you out here to be eaten by the tree crabs? Not very subtle. I mean, I *could*, and I could make them believe me. You were stupid enough to want to land at the kaiju site. No one would doubt me if I said you just ran off in the trees and left a skeletonized corpse behind." This wasn't true, of course; the tree crabs wouldn't kill him, even if they would happily strip his corpse to the bone. I was not telling him that. "But then you would be dead, and you couldn't *learn*."

Sanders rolled his eyes. "For Christ's sake, stop with the movie villain thing and just *tell* me."

"You've lost your Kaiju Earth privileges," I said. "This is your one and only trip."

"You can't do that," Sanders said. "MacDonald makes the rules here."

"This would be between you and me," I said. "That is, unless you want me to tell MacDonald."

"It would be your word against mine."

"Well, see, MacDonald already has your number, so I would win that one. But just in case—" I reached into the jumpsuit front waist pocket that didn't have the screamer and showed Sanders my phone, which had its audio recorder on. "This is already uploaded to my account on the local cloud, so don't try wrestling me for it."

"So, you want me to just never come back here."

"Yup, that's pretty much it," I said. "Or I could just give MacDonald the audio file and she could tell you never to come back, and also, you'd probably get strung up for smuggling or whatever it is that they would charge you for—I don't know, but it would be interesting—and I imagine they use secret courts or something for this because, well." I motioned to encompass the world. "Your choice."

"You really are an asshole," Sanders said.

"What can I say, you were a role model," I replied. "Now, come on, we have to get you back for dinner."

"Wait," Sanders said, and I could feel him centering himself. "You won this round. Fine. Well done. But—if you *don't* do this, I could make it worth your while."

"Tempting," I said. "But nope! Also, I'm walking now, and I'm turning off the screamer. You can keep up with me. Or not." I started walking. After a second, Sanders followed me. I kept the screamer on the whole time. Even if they won't kill you, tree crabs are the worst.

As we got to the door, Sanders looked up at the stairs. "Isn't there an elevator?" he asked.

"No," I said. "No, there is not."

CHAPTER 20

After the drama of our first set of tourists, the next two sets of tourists were delightfully sedate. They were scientists and politicians, with only one billionaire, who, thankfully, behaved himself just fine and did not require a mock feeding to tree crabs. As requested, I acted as cruise director, and kept them all engaged and entertained. I answered their basic questions, made sure they were where they needed to be when they needed to be there, and on one occasion volunteered to do a karaoke duet of "Under Pressure" with a shy winner of the Nobel Prize in Chemistry. It was not rocket science to babysit rocket scientists.

When I wasn't playing cruise director, I was trying to make up the workload as a Lifter of Things, on account of Val having to take the majority of our shared work when I was ferrying about our spectators. Val never complained about me doing the other work and leaving her to pick up the lifting slack. That didn't mean I didn't feel bad about it anyway.

My commitment to guilt, and lifting things, did not go unnoticed. "You're going to wear yourself out," Tom warned me. "You're barely just a month through your tour. You keep this up, there's not going to be anything left of you but a nub five months from now."

I considered this. "It's really only been a month?"

"A month and a week, but yeah."

"Wow."

Tom grinned at this. "Feels longer?"

"Not longer," I said. "Just, like I've always been here."

Tom nodded. "Time works differently over here. We're cut off from the rest of humanity and pretty much nothing they do reaches here. Remember news? Like, when was the last time you thought about COVID? Or the election?"

"Well, I *voted*," I said. KPS had delivered absentee ballots for Tanaka's Americans on the same trip Sanders had been on, and we sent them back when they left.

"Sure, but are you *thinking* about the election anymore?"

"Not really," I admitted. "I'm actually vaguely surprised it hasn't *happened* yet."

Another nod from Tom. "That's what I mean. Time means almost nothing over here. You're going to get home to New York in March, and your first two weeks back are basically catching up with news and saying, 'They did *what*?!?'"

"I'm not sure I'm looking forward to that."

"It's been especially bad the last few years, for sure. That being said, time *does* still happen over on this side, and you should pace yourself. Almost nothing we do over here is so critically important you have to exhaust yourself to do it."

I looked at Tom, shocked. "Where is your Protestant work ethic, young man? You went to business school!"

"I know, I know. I'm an embarrassment to capitalism. But I'm about to slightly reduce your work schedule by adding slightly to my own, so we can both feel better about me."

"You're going to lift something for me?" I asked.

"Oh, hell no," Tom said. "I'm going to take you off the mission to replant the instrument packages at the kaiju site and put myself on it."

"Really?" After three weeks, most of the instrument packages at the kaiju site were low on power, or had experienced glitches, or their images were useless because some creature or another had knocked them over or slimed them up. The science folks were preparing updated instrument packages; we'd send them out once the last of the tourists were gone and Honda Base shut down its dimensional gateway device for maintenance. "Why are you doing that?"

"I would like to say it's because I'm a good guy and I'm concerned about you, but actually it's because Riddu Tagaq has told me it's time for me to recertify for ground and weapons training. If you actually go on a mission right after you recertify, the recertification lasts longer."

"No one told me that," I said.

"You got certified *to* go on a mission, so it was implied."

"It was not, not in the least."

"Well, congratulations, Jamie, you won't need to be recertified for ground and weapons until two tours from now. And once I go on the mission I'm taking you off of, I will be the same. Unless you were really wanting to go."

"No, you take it. I want you to have it. And while you're doing that, I'll be here lifting things."

"You're intentionally ignoring my advice, I see," Tom said.

"No, no, I listened and considered it fully and with gravity," I said. "And then I rejected it."

"This is what I get for trying to be helpful."

"You want to be helpful, I have some things you can deliver for me. Heavy things."

"I'd rather not."

"Coward."

"Damn it, the feed's down again," Niamh said. They were staring angrily into a monitor in the physics lab. The monitor that was arousing their ire was blank.

"What feed?" I asked. I was in the physics lab to pick up equipment to take to storage. The labs at Tanaka Base were small, and anything not directly in use was schlepped away to make room for what was in use.

"The one from the kaiju site." Niamh pointed at the screen.

"Well, it would be down, wouldn't it," I said. "They're swapping the instruments out over there right now." It was the Tuesday after we had sent away our last set of tourists, which was the day after they had been sent back to Earth, and the day Honda Base shut down the dimensional gateway for maintenance. Kaiju Earth was on its own for two weeks.

Niamh quickly disabused me of my misapprehension. "No, it wouldn't," they said. "Or shouldn't be, anyway. The individual instrument packages are shut off when we switch them out, but the feed is routed through the aerostat, which has its own camera and instruments as well. *The aerostat* is not being swapped out, and it's what out."

"Does that happen a lot?"

"It's been happening more. The aerostats are like any other machine, they're finicky and they should probably be brought in for maintenance more than they are." I grinned at this. "What?" Niamh asked at the grin.

"I'm listening to you complain about the aerostats like you knew they even existed six weeks ago."

"Look, mate, time is weird over here."

"Tom was telling me that just the other day."

"Also, I'm not wrong," Niamh continued. "We've been using the same aerostat over Bella since she squatted her ass down there. That's a long time. If we lose the feed from the aerostat, we can't get the data from the instrument packs."

"You'll lose the data?"

"No, they all record locally if they can't connect. But eventually their memory will max out, and *then* we'll lose the data." Niamh was grumpy about that. Having installed the previous instruments, they were proprietary of the data feed.

I nodded. "How long has the feed been out?"

"Just now," Niamh said. "I was watching the overhead feed, waiting to check the connections on the new instruments. The helicopter had just dropped everyone off, and they were swapping shit out. Then you came in and distracted me, and when I looked back, it was out."

"Sorry."

"You'd better be." They mused at the screen. "It usually drops for a few seconds at most before it comes on again. This is way longer than usual. It's annoying. I want more data. Data from an instrument pack that's not been smeared with parasite mucus."

"I'm going past the administration building," I said. "Do you want me to tell them the aerostat feed is out? They have a radio connection with Chopper One. They can probably check to see if there's something obviously wrong."

"I'm sure it will be fine," Niamh said. "By which I mean *obviously* go and complain to Administration, so you'll be the one they'll be annoyed with and not me."

"On it," I said.

I got to Administration and found Aparna and Kahurangi there. "The aerostat feed's out," Aparna said to me.

"I know. I was told by Niamh to complain about it."

Kahurangi pointed at Brynn MacDonald's office. "There's another problem," he said. "They can't raise Chopper One, either."

I frowned at this. "For how long?"

"Since we've been here to complain about the aerostat feed being down."

"So not that long."

"No, but it's weird to have both the aerostat feed down and a helicopter out of contact at the same time," Kahurangi said.

"Especially near a kaiju," Aparna added.

I nodded. I hadn't quite made that connection myself. Something or someone might have bothered Bella enough that she roused herself out of her brooding torpor. If that happened, that could be very bad news for the aerostat, the helicopter, and everyone on the mission, which included Kahurangi's Blue Team counterparts. Niamh's, too.

And Tom Stevens, I just remembered.

MacDonald came out of her office, looking displeased. She was about to say something to Aparna and Kahurangi, saw me, and stopped.

"I know about the feed and the chopper," I said to her.

"Then I want you to go to the airfield and talk to Martin Satie," she said. "Quietly and discreetly. The airfield has its own radio equipment, maybe he can raise Chopper One from there."

"And if he can't?" I asked.

"One thing at a time," MacDonald said. She turned to Aparna and Kahurangi. "I need you not to talk to anyone else about this yet."

"Niamh Healy knows something's up, too," I said. "I just came from talking to them."

"We can talk to Niamh," Kahurangi said.

"It's not something we can keep quiet for long, though," Aparna warned. "We're not the only ones with access to the aerostat feed. Ion will be back in the lab soon, and looking for that data."

"It's not the aerostat I'm worried about," MacDonald said. "They go down every now and then. It's Chopper One out of communication that bothers me." She looked at me. "Why are you still here? *Go.*"

I headed out the door and went to the airfield in enough of a rush that I almost forgot to grab a hat and gloves.

Martin Satie did not seem surprised to see me. "You come from Administration?" he asked.

"Yes," I said.

"They can't raise Chopper One either."

"No. The aerostat feed is down, too."

"How long?"

"As long as Chopper One's been out of contact."

"Anything on the feed before it went out?"

"I didn't see it. I was talking to Dr. Healy, who was looking at it before it went out. They didn't see anything either."

Satie nodded. "Okay. Well, let's go, then."

"What?"

"We have a chopper out of contact and an aerostat down near a kaiju," Satie said. "We need eyes. You have eyes."

"You have eyes, too," I said. "I need to report back."

"Right." Satie pulled out his phone, opened the screen, and texted something. "Okay."

"What was that?" I asked.

"I just texted Dr. MacDonald and told her I was borrowing you for a moment."

"And she knows what that means?"

Satie looked at me. "Dr. MacDonald sent you here instead of texting. She wants this quiet. She also wants answers. If I tell her I'm borrowing you, it says to her that I am going to give her answers, and anyone looking over her shoulder when she gets that text isn't going to know there's a problem. I'm always borrowing someone."

"Got it," I said.

"Thought you might."

"What do you think happened?"

"I have no idea what happened, that's why we're going out there. But if we see that kaiju on the wing, I know exactly what we're going to do."

"What's that?"

"Hope she doesn't see us before we get the hell out of there. If she's up and moving around, something's really pissed her off. If she sees us, she'll drive us right into the ground."

"Tell me what you see," Satie said as we circled the site.

Here's what I saw.

Chopper One, a wreck on the ground, still smoking and burning, near the shore of the lake.

The ground near the kaiju site and the crash, crawling with jungle creatures. If anyone had made it out of the helicopter crash, those creatures had already taken them.

Our friends were dead.

I told this to Satie.

He nodded. "Now," he said. "Tell me what you don't see."

"I don't see the aerostat," I said.

"What else?"

"I don't see the eggs Bella laid."

"What else?"

"I don't see Bella."

She was gone. Her eggs were gone. All her parasites and companion creatures were gone.

Everything was gone.

"This isn't right," I said.

"It's not," Satie agreed. "Now tell me why."

This was why: Because when I looked down at where Bella used to be, it didn't look like Bella had been there and had left.

When I looked down at where Bella used to be, it looked like Bella had never been there at all.

CHAPTER 21

"So, where did she go?" Brynn MacDonald asked. We were in the administration office conference room: Brynn, Jeneba Danso and Aparna, Niamh and Kahurangi, along with Martin Satie and I. Satie and I were there because we'd taken the trip to the site and reported back. My friends were there because they had been the leads on the site data, and because, in the case now of Niamh and Kahurangi, after the apparent deaths of their colleagues in the Chopper One crash, they were nominally in charge of their labs.

It was fair to say we were all still in shock, as were all of our colleagues across the base. MacDonald and Danso informed the Tanaka Base personnel as soon as Satie and I returned about the apparent accident; by that time the rumors were already flying, even with my friends keeping their mouths shut. There was no point in allowing them to continue.

Everyone was grieving. In a base as small as ours, everyone knew everyone, and we had just lost five of us. Those of us in that conference room at least had something to do to keep us busy.

"We don't know," Aparna said to MacDonald's question. She had her laptop casting an image onto the conference room's larger wall monitor; it was a map of the "local" kaiju, spread out across hundreds of kilometers of the nearby Labrador Peninsula. "Bella was marked and tagged, and even without the aerostat that appears to have gone down at the site, we're still getting readings from the rest that we know about. We have a small blind spot where the coverage from the downed aerostat isn't overlapped by the others. So it's possible she's in there. But if she is, Martin and Jamie should have been able to see her."

"We saw nothing," Satie said, and I nodded. After we had surveyed the site from the air, recording as we did so, we made a wide circle of the area to see if we could locate Bella. "She isn't there. And there's nothing to indicate where she might have gone."

"She does fly," Danso noted. "She wouldn't leave a trail or take a path like some other kaiju do."

Aparna nodded at this. "She wouldn't have left a trail, but she would have shown up on our map, whatever direction she'd gone. Even to the southwest, where we have the fewest aerostats, she would have been pinged for least a few minutes."

"Her tracker could have fallen off," Kahurangi said. "That happened to the kaiju we saw when we were coming to base the first time."

"Kevin," I said.

"That's the one," Kahurangi agreed. He didn't smile when he said it. For the first time, the commonplace names of the kaiju just weren't that funny.

"So you think she flew the coop and her tracker fell off," Satie said to Kahurangi.

"I don't know, but it seems possible." He nodded to Aparna. "She said we have a tracking blind spot right now. If it fell off there, that would explain a lot."

MacDonald looked at Satie. "How long until we can bring another aerostat into the area?"

"We can assign the one immediately southwest at any time," he said. As head of Tanaka Base's aviators and aircraft, he was also responsible for the aerostats under the base's control. "But they move slowly. It will take most of a day for the nearest one to move."

"We need answers faster than that."

"I can't make them go faster than they go," Satie said. "But in the meantime, if you like, we can assign the *Shobijin* to act as a temporary aerostat. It's not doing anything else at the moment. Put aerostat guts in it and float it there until we can move a real one into place."

MacDonald looked at Danso, who nodded. "Let's do that, then," she said.

Aparna raised her hand. "There's another issue."

"What's that, Dr. Chowdhury?"

"It's possible Bella is either hiding in our blind spot, or maybe her tracker fell off in it," Aparna acknowledged, "but that doesn't answer the question of where her eggs went. They're gone. All of them."

"Other creatures ate them after she left," Danso suggested.

"I'm sure they would," Aparna said. "But not that *fast*." She turned to me. "You said that you saw no eggs, no natal jelly at all."

"No," I confirmed. Satie also nodded. "We were up pretty high, so maybe we didn't see everything. But where we knew Bella had been, there's nothing. No Bella. No eggs."

"Bella wouldn't have left her eggs except in case of an emergency or imminent threat," Aparna said to MacDonald and Danso. "We know that's basic roosting behavior for her species. But if she did move out of her roosting posture, she wouldn't—and she couldn't—take the eggs with her." She pointed at the screen. "Bella is missing, and that's strange. But her eggs are completely gone, and that's impossible."

Danso looked over to Niamh. "Unless," she prompted.

"Unless Bella went through the dimensional barrier," Niamh said, finishing Danso's thought.

"Is that possible?"

"It *shouldn't* be," Niamh said, slowly. "Her nesting behavior kept the dimensional barrier thin, but not thin enough to get her over. And her physical state hasn't changed since she started brooding. No data we have indicates any change at all. And even if there had been a change"—Niamh pointed at Aparna—"she's right, the eggs would still be there. The eggs wouldn't have gone with her."

"Why not?" Kahurangi asked.

"Because they don't have little nuclear reactors of their own yet, basically," Niamh said.

"But Bella's parasites would have gone with her," MacDonald said. "And they don't have biological nuclear reactors."

"If they were physically on her at the time, sure," Niamh said. "They're literally along for the ride. But the eggs Bella laid aren't attached to her anymore. They wouldn't have gone with her to the other side any more than they would have gone with her if she flew away on this side."

"So the question is not 'Where is Bella?' but 'Where are her eggs?'" MacDonald said.

"That's right."

"So, where *are* her eggs?"

"I have no idea," Niamh said, then paused to reconsider. "No, that's not true. I have an idea, but it's not one I like."

"Tell us."

"You're not going to like it either."

"What is it?"

"Bella and her eggs did go through the dimensional barrier."

"You just said she couldn't get through," Danso said.

"*She* can't," Niamh confirmed. "And her eggs definitely can't. Not on their own, anyway."

"Spit it out, Dr. Healy," MacDonald said.

"I'm not trying to draw this out, I promise," Niamh said. "I'm just still trying to figure out the logistics of this in my brain. But no matter what, it stands to reason that if no conditions on this side of the dimensional barrier have changed enough to get Bella and her eggs through, then something on the other side *did*. I just have no idea what it would have been."

"A nuclear explosion could do it," Kahurangi said.

"Mate, if we have nuclear bombs going off in rural Canada right now, we are all mightily fucked."

"If not a nuclear bomb, then what?" I asked.

"I don't *know*," Niamh repeated. "Getting through the dimensional barrier requires a huge amount of nuclear power, either applied all at once, or built up over a sustained length of time." They pointed to the map that was still up on the wall monitor. "Where Bella is, or *was*, there is nothing on the other side. It's forest. There are no cities or roads. No people. And definitely nothing with the nuclear oomph to suck Bella and her eggs over to the other side."

"So it doesn't make any sense that she's over in our world," MacDonald said.

"It does not," Niamh agreed. "But it's also the only thing that makes sense for what we're seeing."

"Unless we're missing something," Kahurangi said. He pointed to Aparna's computer. "May I?"

Aparna nodded. Kahurangi took it and accessed the restricted folder for the meeting we were in, into which Satie had placed our flight video. Kahurangi scrubbed through the video, to a part where the helicopter camera had an unobstructed view of the ground, and the creatures swarming around on it.

"What are we supposed to be seeing here, Dr. Lautagata?" Danso asked.

"I was looking at this video earlier and something about it was bothering me, and I couldn't quite place it," Kahurangi said. "It just now came to me. All of these creatures are swarming around, and none of them are attacking each other."

"Okay, so?"

"Correct me if I'm wrong, but at least some of these creatures are prey for some of these other creatures." He looked at Aparna. "Right?"

Aparna squinted at the screen, trying to make out the various species. "That looks right."

Kahurangi nodded and pointed at the screen again. "This would be our equivalent of alligators ignoring helpless baby gazelles at the edge of the water. This doesn't happen unless the alligators think there's something much better around." He looked over to me. "You've shot a canister gun. You know how creatures react to a canister once it bursts open. They ignore everything else to go after it."

"More or less," I said. "Although don't discount 'less' here."

"It's not an exact science," Kahurangi agreed. "But the principle stands."

"Are you saying there's something pheromonal going on here?" MacDonald said. "And if there is, what does that have to do with what Dr. Healy was saying?"

"Not pheromonal," Kahurangi said. "Pheromones are part of

what we put into the canisters. The other part is actinides. The local fauna go wild for them. And of course uranium is the one they like the most." He paused the screen. "That's what they do when there's a lot of the stuff around, or at least they think there is."

"Is there a significant amount of uranium at this spot on the other side?" Niamh asked.

"I don't know, I would have to check a map," Kahurangi said.

"And you call yourself a geologist."

Kahurangi smiled at this, and it was, I think, the first genuine smile in the whole meeting. "This was the site of a nuclear explosion just a few weeks ago," he said. "So it's still going to be highly attractive to the local creatures. That's one reason why we think Bella brooded here, so that her parasites would find enough food for them and her. But this activity suggests something else happened that either directly brought more actinides into the area, or gave an at least temporary impression that there were."

"What would that be?" MacDonald asked.

"I'm not sure," Kahurangi said. "But whatever it was, I'm willing to bet it wasn't natural. It's something we did. Humans. Maybe not a nuclear exchange." He nodded over to Niamh. "But still involving humans for sure."

"Curious timing," Satie said.

I caught what he meant, and turned to MacDonald and Danso. "How long are we out of communication with the other side?" I asked.

"When Honda Base shuts down the gateway, it's usually for a couple of weeks," Danso said.

"Can that be made any shorter?"

"It's not like flipping a switch," she said. "They pull things apart for maintenance. They've already started doing that. Even if it was an emergency it would still take several days for them to put it all back together and into working order."

"This kind of *is* an emergency," Niamh said.

"We need more than what we have now to get them to speed things up," Danso said.

Niamh was incredulous. "A fucking kaiju on the other side *isn't enough*?"

Danso pointed to Aparna. "Dr. Chowdhury has told us we have blind spots. We need to be able to see into those blind spots first. This is a situation where we do not want to cry wolf."

"Wait a minute," I said. "Camp Century isn't the only place where people come through to this side. There are other gateways on other continents."

"Yes," MacDonald said.

"We can't get a message through by sending it to them?"

MacDonald shook her head. "Our aerostat networks aren't that extensive. They cover a local area—local in this case meaning this chunk of North America. If we need to get a message to Europe or Asia or Australia, we usually send it through Camp Century, which relays it through the other side."

"There has to be something else we could do."

"We could use the *Shobijin*," MacDonald said. "Send it to the KPS base in Europe. But it won't be any faster in the long run, and we want to use the *Shobijin* here. No matter what, there is going to be a gap of at least a week before we could say or send anything to the other side."

"By which time, if Bella *is* over there, they will have already figured that out," Aparna said. She had a point. Eventually a kaiju was going to be hard to miss.

"We still need answers," Danso said. "For ourselves, if not for anything else. We have to know what happened to our people. And we have to know, as best we can, what happened and why."

"The instrument packages," I said. "Are they operating?"

"Maybe," Niamh said. "It depends. The old ones are running low on power and they've been dinged up by the local wildlife, but they still work. Unless they were powered down when the mission team switched them for the new ones. The new ones should work just fine, but they need to be powered on. Also the old ones might be lost if they were on Chopper One when—" Niamh stopped, because there was no easy way to say what would come next. They took a moment before continuing. "But either way, we can't get at the data until the *Shobijin* gets there to receive their data and transmit it back to us. *If* they're transmitting."

I looked over to Satie. "How long until the *Shobijin* will be ready?"

"Several hours to prep at least," he said.

I nodded and stood up. "Well, let's go, then," I said to him.

He grinned, again, the first for him that I had seen for the day. "That's my line," he said, standing up.

"What's going on?" MacDonald asked.

"We need answers," I replied, nodding to Danso. "And there are still a few hours of daylight left. So I'm going to go looking."

"At the site," MacDonald said.

"Yes."

"Which you know is crawling with creatures who will be happy to eat you," Kahurangi said.

"Yes," I said. "Want to come?"

"Want? No. But I *will*," he said. "Because you'll need someone to watch your back. Just let me stop at the lab first. I've been working on some new pheromone formulas. I've got some things you might want to try out."

"Are you going to try them out with me?"

"No, I should be the control subject."

I blinked. "Really, dude?"

Kahurangi grinned again and shook his head, chuckling. "Sorry," he said to me. "It's been a bad day. I really needed that look on your face right now."

CHAPTER 22

"This is the new stuff," Kahurangi said to me as we approached the site. He leaned forward from the back of the passenger compartment of Chopper Two and handed me an applicator bottle of something that could have been suntan lotion.

I took it. "What is it?" I asked.

"You don't want to be surprised?"

"I'd really rather not be, no."

Kahurangi nodded at that. "These pheromones should make everything think you're an actual kaiju."

I frowned. "Why would I want that? Those things have parasites. Big ones. Some of them almost as big as I am."

"They do," Kahurangi said. "But all of Bella's are with her right now. Most of them anyway. And the rest of the creatures here will think of you like a mountainside. You'll just be part of the scenery. They'll ignore you."

"And you're sure about that," I said.

"I tried a batch on the tree crabs back at base. They acted like I wasn't even there."

"Yeah, but the tree crabs won't kill you."

"They would if they could," Kahurangi pointed out.

"And if there are any parasites in the area?" I asked. "You know, like, left behind when Bella went wherever she went?"

"I'm guessing that you'll confuse them. They might approach you, but since you're not a kaiju, they'll ignore you and look for the actual kaiju that has to be around somewhere."

"You're *guessing*."

"I was planning to field-test it soon," Kahurangi said. "I got rushed a little, here."

"You're not filling me with confidence," I said.

"Well, that's why I also have this"—he held up another bottle—"which is the stuff you already know about and use. And also, I have this." He lifted a canister launcher.

"Are you two ready?" Satie asked me.

I looked at Kahurangi. He nodded.

"We're ready," I said.

"Don't waste time," Satie said. "Look fast. Whatever you find, get it back to the chopper and then we head back. The *Shobijin* will be here this evening and can take over collecting data. Whatever happened here, I don't want to give it a chance to happen again."

"We'll be quick," I promised. Satie nodded, and we headed down. Satie hovered as Kahurangi and I got out, grabbed our spray bottles and weapons, and retrieved exactly one instrument package from storage. No matter what happened to the other instrument packs, there would be something on the ground here reporting back. I gave Satie a thumbs-up, and he headed upward, just enough to keep us from being whipped around from rotor wash. He was absolutely going to make sure we had a quick getaway if we needed one.

"Okay, hold still," Kahurangi said, and sprayed me down with his kaiju camouflage.

I choked on the smell. "Jesus, that's awful," I said.

"Wouldn't work if it smelled like flowers," he said, and continued spraying me head to toe, front to back. When he was done, he handed me the spray. "Now me." I likewise hosed him down with the pheromone. He gagged as I did so.

"If this doesn't work, at least we won't taste good when they eat us," I said, handing back the spray.

He packed it away. "Where to?" he asked.

"I remember where Aparna planted her instrument packs," I said. "Let's start there." I headed in the direction of where I knew the first of those packs would be.

We found it just a couple of minutes later, along with its replacement. "Tell me I'm not imagining what I'm seeing," Kahurangi said to me.

I shook my head. "You're not imagining it." Both instrument packs were smashed and their contents broken. "Their storage drives are missing," I said, after I looked more closely.

"They could just be dispersed," Kahurangi said. "Things have gotten moved around by now."

"Does this look like the local creatures did this to you?" I asked him.

"I don't know," he admitted. "I know the instrument packs have been designed to handle what this planet throws at them, and they've been tweaking the design for years. But it's possible they just got stomped on."

The next placement and the exact same thing had happened with both the instrument packs there: destroyed and data storage missing.

"Yeah, all right, that's *definitely* not a coincidence," Kahurangi said.

"Let's leave the new pack here," I suggested. Kahurangi nodded and got to work setting the pack while I kept watch. Usually by this time we would have attracted the attention of the local critters, who would either be running away from us due to the predator pheromones, or sizing us up regardless. This time, aside from the small, bitey insects that were never not in one's face (and other areas), nothing was either dodging or trailing us. They just . . . left us alone.

"I'll be damned," I said, when I realized it. "Your cocktail works, my dude."

"Well, so far anyway," Kahurangi said as he wrestled with the pack. "This is actually the second version. The first version was a mess."

"What do you mean?"

"Instead of everything ignoring you, it just made everything really pissed off. I think I was signaling the kaiju was under attack or something. I barely made it back to the stairs on that one. It was like a tree crab zombie horde."

"Thank you for not mixing up the canisters," I said.

"You're welcome," Kahurangi said. "Just never give me a reason to spray you with it."

I smiled at this and then looked in the direction of where Bella used to be, just in time to catch a big flash of . . . something.

"Whoa," I said.

Kahurangi looked up. "What is it?"

"I don't know." I connected through my headset to Satie. "Did you just see anything?"

"Other than the two of you moving slow enough to become snacks? No."

"Keep an eye on the area Bella was in," I said.

"What am I looking for?"

"You'll know it when you see it."

"Are you two almost done?"

"We have two other sites to look at," I said.

"Don't waste time talking to me," Satie said, and clicked off.

"Done," Kahurangi said, then looked in the former direction of Bella. "What are we looking at?"

"I thought I saw a flash."

"It's daylight."

"I know," I said. "That's why I only think I saw it. I might have imagined it."

"Let's keep an eye out while we walk," Kahurangi said.

"You keep an eye out for it," I said. "I'm going to keep an eye out for things trying to eat us. Just in case your new batch of pheromones stops working."

The next pack location had only one pack at it, the older one. It was, not surprisingly, smashed and broken.

"Where's the other one?" Kahurangi asked.

I scanned the area and saw something several meters away. "Come with me," I said. We walked toward the thing. It was the newer instrument pack. Like the others, it was smashed and broken.

Unlike the others, there was a bullet lodged into the shattered instrument package.

"Hello," I said, and showed it to Kahurangi, who took one look at it and summed up what we were both feeling into a single word.

"Fuck," he said.

"You think Riddu Tagaq let anyone out here with something that fired bullets?" I asked.

"No. Shotgun? Yes. Rifle? No. She doesn't have that much faith in our ability to aim."

"This means you were right," I said. "Someone came through. Someone came through and shot this thing."

Kahurangi nodded. "And probably took down the aerostat. And Chopper One. *Fuck*." He looked away, disgusted.

I turned and dropped the shattered instrument pack. As I did, something glimmered in my peripheral vision.

"Shit, I think I just saw that flash you're talking about," Kahurangi said.

I turned to look at him. He was looking in the direction opposite of where I saw the glimmer. I went to where I thought I saw it.

"Where are you going?" Kahurangi asked.

"All right, I *did* see something that time," Satie said, through my headset. "What the hell was that?"

I ignored both of them and crouched down by a fallen tree. There was an object there, partially obscured by moss and algae. I picked it up.

It was a phone.

A phone that appeared to have been intentionally placed, with its camera in the direction of where Bella had been.

"Hello," I said again, more quietly this time.

"Jamie?" Kahurangi said, coming up on me.

I turned and showed him the phone.

"What is that doing here?" he said.

"I think it was left here on purpose," I said. I pressed the power button. Nothing. It was dead. I opened a channel to the helicopter. "Martin," I said.

"I saw that flash thing," Satie repeated.

"Okay," I acknowledged. "Unrelated question. Do you have a phone charger on Chopper Two?"

"What?"

"A phone charger."

"You planning to make a call or something?"

I looked at the bottom of the phone. "Preferably a charger that has USB-C."

"Chopper Two has two USB outlets, and I have one of those cords with multiple ends, including USB-C. Why?"

"We're going to be done in about two minutes. Be ready for us." I clicked off and looked at Kahurangi. "I already know what we're going to find at the last installation area, but we have to be sure," I said.

He nodded. "All right."

We jogged to the final installation site, where we found two smashed instrument packages. We didn't even stop, we just confirmed they were smashed and destroyed and immediately went back to the pickup site, where Satie was waiting for us. We jumped in the chopper, and Satie took off, straight up.

He motioned to the console between his seat and the copilot's one I had strapped in and put on the cockpit headset. "Cord and charger in there," he said, and glanced over as I produced the phone and plugged it in. "Why do you need to charge your phone so urgently?"

"It's not my phone," I said.

"Whose is it?"

I shook my head. "I don't know. But I'm betting that whoever its owner was, they were smart enough to have it record whatever was going on at the site. And I hope they were smart enough to do something else."

"What?"

"Turn off the lock screen."

* * *

"This isn't easy to watch or listen to," I warned everyone in the conference room.

There were nods all around. The earlier group had reassembled and was aware that I had found something, but only Kahurangi and Satie had any idea what I had. I opened my laptop and cast to the wall monitor, and then pulled up the first video file. In the first still image, Tom Stevens was looking into the camera, which he'd already placed into position. An instrument pack sat on the ground by him.

I started the video.

"I don't think I have much time," Tom said, into the video. "We landed and started planting instrument packs when we heard a bang and saw the aerostat get hit by something. Almost as quickly, the helicopter got hit. Then we saw what looked like soldiers coming through with equipment, heading toward Bella. They saw us and some of them started firing at us. We all ran. They're hunting us now. I think they're going to kill us. I don't know who they are or where they came from. I have this phone pointing at Bella. I'm going to let it run. Hopefully they don't find it. Hopefully someone at Tanaka will. I don't know what else to say. I'm walking away now."

With that he picked up the instrument pack, stood, and walked purposefully away from the phone and out of frame.

A few seconds later someone else crossed into frame, wearing camo and carrying some variation of a military rifle, yelling at Tom to stop. The soldier crossed out of frame, still yelling. I paused the video.

"At this point the sound is a little difficult to follow so I'm going to have to turn up the volume," I said. Everyone nodded. I cranked up the volume and then resumed the video.

The ambient noise was much louder, but the voices that came next were barely audible.

First there was Tom. "I'm unarmed."

There was some not-quite-comprehensible growling on the part of the soldier, followed by Tom. "I came from Tanaka Base. Who are you, and why are you here? Where did you come from?"

More incomprehensible.

"We're here to do science. What are you here for?" Tom said.

"He's doing it on purpose," Niamh said.

"What?" asked MacDonald.

"Talking clearly. Enunciating. He's trying to make sure what he's saying gets recorded."

MacDonald looked ready to respond, but then Tom said something else, which was, "How did you come through? How did you know to come here?"

More growling in response.

"I'm just trying to understand what's happening here," Tom said.

There was more muttering from the soldier, like he was having a conversation with himself, and then a more aggressive set of mumbles.

"I can't take apart the instrument pack," Tom said. "We seal them up at the base and make them hard to destroy, so we can get data no matter what happens. Why do you want me to take it apart?"

Yelling, and this time, *fuck* was definitely part of the conversation.

"I'm not trying to argue with you," Tom said. "I'm just telling you what I can and can't do."

More muttering.

"All right, I'm going to put the pack down over here, and then I'm going to step away from it," Tom said.

Silence, and then the flat bang of the rifle being shot.

"I told you they were tough," Tom said a couple of seconds later.

Another bang.

"I would like to go back to my teammates now," Tom said, after a moment. "I know they are scared. I'm scared. You've destroyed our data, and you've made sure we can't talk to our base. We can't stop you from doing whatever you plan to do here. We're not going to be a problem."

Muttering, and a few seconds later, the soldier showed back up in the frame, walking backward to keep his weapon trained on Tom, talking urgently into a headset.

"Look, what the fuck do you want me to do with this guy?" he was saying, intelligibly now that he was closer. "We were told there weren't going to be people here. We were told they wouldn't be here until we were long gone. Now I've got this fucker, and others in my squad are babysitting his pals."

He stood, listening into his earpiece.

"Well, but that's my point," the soldier replied to whoever he was talking with. "We already took down the helicopter. We don't *have* to do anything to these assholes. Just strip them down and send them out into the jungle. They'll be dead before any of their pals show up. Why waste the bullets?"

Another pause, and then a sigh.

"Jesus. Fine," the soldier said. "We're being paid extra for this. And I want even more for taking down the chopper."

Every eye in the room turned to Satie, who sat there, grimly. He had already heard this part before.

"Yeah. Yeah. Fine. All right," the soldier said, and then walked out of frame again.

A few seconds later, Tom said, "You don't have to do this."

Then there was another flat report from the rifle. And another.

The room was silent except for a few quiet sobs. Everyone knew what had just happened off-screen.

Unexpectedly the soldier returned into frame, looking about.

"Fucker is looking to see if he got caught," Niamh said.

Before he could spot the phone, he had another problem on his hands; the jungle creatures, attracted by the noise and the sudden release of blood, were converging. The soldier raised his rifle, threatening, and went out the opposite side of the camera frame in a hurry. In a few seconds, there was the image of creature limbs hustling by, chasing him.

"I'd like to think they caught him and ate him," Danso said.

"You didn't see anything of Tom when you got there," MacDonald said to me and Kahurangi.

We both shook our heads.

"We didn't see any remains, either of us, or any of the invaders, whoever they are," I said, pausing the video. "The soldier was right. The creatures would take anything they could get with them into the trees."

MacDonald nodded, unhappy.

"What the hell are they doing?" Danso asked. "Why are they even there?"

"I have the answer," I said. I closed the video file we were watching and pulled up another. "There's a few videos in between the one we just watched and what I'm showing you," I said. "The phone automatically chops up the videos into about five-minute chunks. It's a memory-saving thing. This is good because it means that when the battery died we didn't lose all the video." I pulled up the particular video I was looking for.

"What are we looking at?" MacDonald asked as I let the video play.

I pointed to several barrel-size objects in the field of view, arrayed several meters from each other. "These things," I said.

"What are they?"

"I don't know. But I think they're being used to create a perimeter around Bella and her eggs."

"Okay, but why?" Danso asked.

"Because of this," I said, pointing at the video.

In the video, the barrel-looking things suddenly started glowing. Then there was a flash that overwhelmed the camera sensor, and a crack like lightning had just struck.

When the sensor was clear again, Bella, her eggs, the barrels, and all the interlopers were gone.

"All right," Niamh said, after the video had stopped. "How the fuck did they just *do* that?"

23

My day had been long, and exhausting, and inexpressibly soul crushing. After barely tasting my dinner, I decided I needed to go to bed early and try to get some sleep. This resulted in a few hours of not sleeping, running the day's events in my head, and staring at the potted plant gifted to me by Sylvia Braithwhite.

"This is not working," I said to the plant. The plant, while sympathetic, I'm sure, said nothing.

The door to my room opened, and Niamh appeared in it. "Hey."

"It's called knocking," I said.

"I know what it's called, I just didn't do it."

"I could have been sleeping."

"No one's sleeping tonight."

"Or rubbing one out."

"Definitely no one's doing that tonight."

"You have a point."

"We need you in the living room."

"What's up?"

"We need your help on something."

"What is it?"

"If you get out of bed and come to the living room, you'll find out, won't you?" Niamh disappeared from the doorframe but left the door open, so the light from the living room was still flooding in. After one more minute of lying there just to show Niamh they were not the boss of me, I got up and went into the living room, which my cottage-mates had strewn with documents and laptops.

"Let me guess, you need me to pick up after you," I said.

"Well, you *do* lift things," Kahurangi said. "But that's not it."

"We need your advice," Aparna said.

"Not so much advice as we need you to listen to us and tell us we're not completely off our crackers," Niamh added.

"All right," I said, and sat at our table. "What is it?"

Aparna sat as well. "Bella has to get back over to this side of the fence. Somehow. Tonight, if possible."

"Why?"

"Because if we don't, I think she's going to explode."

"You mean, explode like an atomic bomb."

"Yes."

"In *Canada*."

"Yes."

"There are . . . *challenges* to getting her back over here," I said, after a moment.

"No shit," Niamh said, sitting down as well. "But we might have something. Sort of."

I held up a hand. "Hold that for just a second," I said to Niamh. I brought my attention back to Aparna. "Explain the whole 'Bella's going to explode' thing to me, please. I thought she was fine."

"She *was* fine," Aparna stressed. "Over here. But she's not over here. She's over *there*. And over there, on our Earth, things are very different, environmentally. The atmosphere is not as thick or as oxygen rich. And it's much, much colder. It's late October in Labrador. It's literally freezing there."

"And that affects the kaiju."

Kahurangi cocked his head. "It does. But it affects the parasites more."

"It's already killing them." Aparna grabbed her laptop and opened up a file to show it to me, as if I were going to read the whole thing. "Specifically, the parasites that act as her cooling and airflow system. These parasites are common across a bunch of kaiju species, so we know a lot about them. What we know about them is that they're hugely susceptible to cold. When the temperature drops below ten degrees Celsius, they start dying off."

I looked at Aparna blankly.

"That's like fifty degrees Fahrenheit," she said, barely repressing her exasperation.

"Got it," I said.

"It's not just the temperatures," Kahurangi said. "A kaiju and all of the parasites are used to a thicker atmosphere and more oxygen. Going to our Earth for them is the equivalent of us going up to six thousand meters and then trying to run a marathon."

"So lack of oxygen is killing them, too."

"Not killing them directly but it makes them do their thing much less efficiently," Niamh said. "And that affects the kaiju. Affects Bella."

"Bella is a flying species of kaiju," Aparna said. "Flying kaiju have especially complex airflow systems. They're part of how they fly. And those airflow systems are intimately connected to cooling their internal reactors. Impair and kill off the parasites that control the airflow systems—"

"Bella goes boom," I finished.

Aparna nodded. "Right."

"Tonight."

"Within the next day for sure."

"And we know this how?"

"This is where I come in," Niamh said. "Although you helped."

"I did?" I said, surprised.

"Only a little, don't get a big head about it."

"Okay. That's better."

Niamh smiled. "When you and Kahurangi were on-site, you both noticed that flash. Martin Satie, too. It's the same sort of flash that we saw earlier, except now it's *much* stronger—you saw it in daylight—and it's happening more frequently. We're getting data from that one instrument pack you put back on the ground, thank you for that—"

"You're welcome."

"—and from the *Shobijin*, too. That flash is discharge being generated by the processes of Bella's reactor, compounded with the energy of whatever the fuck it was they used to pull her over to the human side of the barrier."

"The flash is getting stronger and happening more often," Kahurangi said. "Niamh thinks it has something to do with Bella's reactor getting hotter and more stressed."

"Yeah, that," Niamh said. "There's another thing, too. Right before the flash happens, the dimensional barrier between worlds is at its thinnest. These flashes are so strong that the math suggests that right before they happen, the barrier is hardly there at all."

"Hardly," I said.

"It *is* still there," Niamh stressed. "But I'm betting that it's easily disruptable. A little more energy in there and someone could walk through."

"Or be sent through," I said, thinking about Bella.

"See?" Niamh said to Kahurangi. "I told you Jamie wasn't completely addled."

I looked to Kahurangi. "You called me *addled*?"

"I did not," Kahurangi protested.

"The problem is," Niamh continued, plowing through Kahurangi's clearly weak-ass defense of his calumny toward my person, "as these things get stronger and more frequent, they're pointing to Bella's reactor overheating and then, well."

"Are the flashes showing up or getting stronger randomly?"

"What a good question," Niamh said. "Once again, you are outstripping Kahurangi's estimation of you."

I looked over to Kahurangi. "All lies," he whispered.

"They are *not* random," Niamh said. "The strength is increasing as the time between the flashes decreases. I've been charting them, and something is definitely going to happen about sixteen hours from now."

"What?"

"You heard Aparna."

I nodded. "How does the perimeter thingy play into all of that?"

Niamh looked disgusted. "Oh, that fuckin' thing."

"This is my bit," Kahurangi said. "I have a theory about it."

"He has a *hypothesis*," Niamh spat out. "It's not the same thing."

"You're just irritated that I extended on your metaphor."

"I'm irritated because it's a shit idea and that as a physicist, you're a very fine geologist."

"Children," I said.

"Actually only a passable geologist," Niamh finished.

I looked over to Kahurangi. "Well?"

"Niamh described the flash as being a bit like a static electricity discharge." And here, Kahurangi stared at Niamh, daring them to contradict him, which they did not. "It's not *exactly* like static electricity, but as a metaphor goes it's a decent way to think about it. I watched the video of the perimeter going active and taking Bella and her eggs, and I thought about electromagnets generating an electric current. I'm guessing something like that is happening here, but instead of creating a current, it's collapsing the wall between our world and this one, without having to use a nuclear reaction to do it."

"Trash hypothesis," Niamh said.

"Except that it fits the available data," Kahurangi countered.

"The available data being ten seconds of video."

"And the fact that creatures are swarming the site like it's been dusted with uranium."

"And the fact that the evidence points to the barrier being thinned out more than it could be just from Bella's reactor alone," Aparna added.

"I see how it is," Niamh said. "Take his side, why don't you."

"His side has the data on it."

Niamh gasped.

"You're . . . not really angry at Kahurangi, are you?" I asked.

"Obviously not, I'm just pissed he came up with a reasonable hypothesis before I did." Niamh narrowed their eyes at Kahurangi. "Lousy mingy *chemist*."

Kahurangi grinned at this.

"So what's the plan here?" I said. I nodded to Aparna. "You're telling us Bella is going to die if we don't get her back over here, and take a chunk of Canada with her when she goes." I looked over to Niamh. "You're giving us a timeline of less than a day before it happens." I pointed to Kahurangi. "And you're telling us that the only way we get her back is to use the same perimeter that took her over to the other side to begin with."

Kahurangi blinked at this. "I didn't say that."

"You sure *implied* it," I said. "I'm guessing the thing isn't on now, but that Bella's reactor is keeping the barrier thin. But even as thin as it is now, it's not enough. If she's going to get back, it needs to be turned on again."

"Sure," Niamh said. "So, that's one problem. Then there are all the rest of them."

"Like the fact we can't get over there to start with," Aparna said.

"And that if we do get over, there's going to be a welcoming committee," Kahurangi added.

"You mean the people who stole Bella in the first place and killed some of us to get her," I said.

"Yes, those."

"Even if we could get over, MacDonald and Danso aren't going to say yes," Aparna noted.

I nodded at this. After our last meeting, the two of them agreed to send an urgent message to Honda Base informing them of the events at Tanaka and asking to make reassembling the gateway a priority. Even if Honda agreed to it, it would be days before anything would happen through that. In the meantime, MacDonald and Danso had placed Bella's site off limits, excepting the personnel on the *Shobijin*, who would leave the site when the new aerostat had been repositioned.

"We've lost more people today than we have since the sixties," MacDonald had said. "These people were trained to kill and had no compunctions about doing so. We can't risk a chance they come through again with our people there."

MacDonald and Danso were right, of course. Even if anyone on our side could go over, these killers would be waiting for them when they did. It would be foolish and possibly suicidal to attempt it.

Except that if some of us *didn't*, Bella would die, and take a fair chunk of Labrador with her when she did. A mostly unpopulated chunk, to be sure.

Unless she *moved*.

"Can Bella fly over there?" I asked Aparna.

"Not *well*," Aparna said after a minute.

"So, that's a *yes*."

"She doesn't want to fly right now," Kahurangi said. "She's got eggs."

"She doesn't *want* to fly, but she *will* if she's threatened or if she feels like she's in danger, right?" I asked. "Like, for example, feeling like she's slowly suffocating and burning up because the parasites that keep air moving through her are dying off from the cold and lack of oxygen."

"There's not much on the other side she could get to, is there?" Aparna asked.

"Tanaka Base is more or less in the same place as Happy Valley–Goose Bay in Labrador. That's about ten thousand people," I said. "Plus there's a Canadian military base there. And they're both right by a river and an ocean inlet."

Aparna nodded. "And Bella will be looking for water."

"Looking?" Niamh said. "She's right up against some now."

"Not necessarily on the other side," I said. "And if she's hurting in her current location, she'll be looking for somewhere else to be. Like the only patch of light within a hundred kilometers, right next to a huge body of water."

"It's not going to look great for a Canadian military base to be attacked by a kaiju," Kahurangi admitted.

"Which then *explodes*," Niamh said. "Taking ten thousand Canadians with it."

"Is it likely she moves?" I asked Aparna.

"I don't know," she said. "We've literally never had any of this happen before. But Kahurangi is right. She's not going to move. Not unless she absolutely feels like she has to. So, if she moves, there's probably not a lot of time before she goes up."

"And what happens if we get her back? Does she still go up?"

"If she's back, then her parasites stop dying, and they're able to move more air through her no matter what," Aparna said. "If we get her over in time, she'll live. She won't be happy for a while. But she'll live. I think."

"Do we care about that?" Niamh asked. "Whether she lives?"

"Well," I said. "We *are* the Kaiju Preservation Society."

They all stared at me for a moment.

"Just like you to name-drop that shit on us, Jamie," Niamh said, eventually.

"Sorry," I said, although I was not. "So, we're agreed we're going to do this, right? Bring Bella back?"

"There is still the minor problem of not being able to get across," Kahurangi said.

"And not being able to get to the site in the first place," Aparna continued.

"Plus the soldiers who will be happy to murder us *if* we get over," Niamh finished.

"This is why you all had me come in here," I said. "You all know what has to be done. It's all there in your data. You just needed me to come in here and say it out loud. So, this is me telling you. You're right. You're not off your crackers. Bella needs to come back to this side. It *has* to be done tonight. And since she can't do it herself, we have to help her. And it has to be *us,* since I don't think any of *you* want to risk anyone else. Or ask permission, which we won't get. Right?"

They all looked at each other, then back at me.

"I mean, I don't know that I was actually *planning* to possibly die tonight in order to protect a kaiju," Kahurangi said. "But I might be willing to possibly die to save a kaiju and ten thousand Canadians."

"Now we know what motivates you," I said. "Ten thousand Canadians."

"I'm in," Aparna said, simply.

I nodded.

"Look, I'm not saying I'm not in," Niamh said. "I'm in. Why

not. But this happy team-building moment doesn't change the fact *we* still don't know how to get across or how to even get to the goddamn site."

"You three work on the first one," I said. "I have an idea for the second."

Martin Satie came to the door of the cottage he shared with other members of his aviation crew. It was clear by his face and how quickly he answered the door that he hadn't been sleeping at all.

"I was expecting you," he said.

"You were?" I asked.

He nodded. "I'm in."

"You . . . have no idea what I'm going to ask."

"Yes, I do," Satie said. "I don't know the exact words you are going to say. But I know you. I know your friends. I knew you wouldn't leave it. And you didn't. You need a ride. So you need me. I'm in."

"I don't know what to say."

"You could say 'sorry.'"

"Why would I say 'sorry'?" I asked.

"I figured you'd be here earlier than this," Satie said. "I stayed up waiting for you. I could have taken a nap."

"Would you look at that," Aparna said, through our headsets, as we approached the site.

The entire site was aglow, faint and golden. It increased in intensity until there was the flash that we had come to expect. Then it disappeared, to slowly build again until the next flash. The underside of the *Shobijin,* which was hovering above the site, reflected the glow dully back onto itself.

"Guess we didn't need torches after all," Kahurangi said. We had flashlights with us, in the packs we were carrying, along with pullovers, canisters of various pheromones, first aid and emergency supplies, protein bars and water, screamers, electrified batons, canister launchers, and shotguns. The projectile weapons were apportioned between us according to who was better at what. I was given the canister launcher, because I had a reputation for those now.

"We'll need them," Niamh said. "If nothing else, we can club things with them."

"You seem tense," Kahurangi said to them.

"Of *course* I'm tense," Niamh snapped back. "We have a stupid plan."

"You're just saying this because it's my plan."

"I'm not *just* saying it because it's your plan, and also, yes."

I left the two of them to bicker and turned my attention to Satie. "You clear on your end of things?" I said, more to reassure myself than to remind him.

In the glow of the instruments I saw him nod. "Wait until you step through, if you can step through. If all of you step through, go back to Tanaka. If only some of you get through, pick up the rest and go back to Tanaka. If none of you can get through, wait for you to contact me, then pick you up and go back to Tanaka. If you all go through, then I tell MacDonald and Danso what you're up to. If only some of you get through, whoever's left will do it."

"They're not going to be happy with you," I said.

"They're already not happy with me," Satie said. "My radio to base has been off this entire time. They've probably been calling me since we left. The *Shobijin* crew are almost certainly on the lookout for us."

"Remember to tell them to clear out. We don't want them to be there if we get Bella back. They might spook her."

"I'll tell them. Whether they listen to me is another story."

"I'm sorry you'll be in trouble."

"You'll be in more trouble. I'm just giving you a ride."

"Thank you anyway."

"This is what we do," Satie said. "Or what we're supposed to do. I lost friends just like you did. Getting Bella back from those who took her and our friends is what they would want us to do."

"I'm sure of it."

"If you want to shoot a couple of them as well, I wouldn't mind."

I grinned at that. "You'll have to talk to Kahurangi about that. He has the shotgun."

"If it comes to that, I'm not going to use the shotgun," Kahurangi said. He had been listening in because the headsets were on an open channel in the passenger area of Chopper Two. "I have something else ready for us."

"Good enough," Satie said. We were now almost over the site. "Let's get you on the ground."

He maneuvered us down, taking care to avoid the *Shobijin* as we went in. As we descended, I looked over at the airship and thought I could see its crew, waving frantically at us. I waved back.

Once down and the chopper away, Kahurangi and I first sprayed Aparna and Niamh and then each other with the "I'm a kaiju" pheromone, applying it liberally to ourselves and our packs.

"Mate, that shit is *rank*," Niamh said to Kahurangi.

"Don't blame me," he said. "I don't make kaiju biology, I just exploit it."

"Do some genetic engineering. Make the kaiju smell nice. This whole version of Earth smells like a wet dog."

"You know what actually smells nice? The pheromone that puts kaiju and their parasites in murder mode. If you smell something that reminds you of oranges, you should run."

"I'm going to remember that."

"Do." Kahurangi put the spray back in his pack, hiked it up on his back, and took a look around. "This is amazing," he said.

He was right. On the ground, the "glow" wasn't a single blanket of light, but thousands and possibly millions of tiny light particles floating in the air, glowing slowly brighter in sync.

"They look like fireflies," Aparna said.

"Not fireflies," Niamh said. "Look closer."

We did. The points weren't points at all, but irregular rings whose size and shape changed as we looked. I moved, and the rings moved with me.

I mentioned this to Niamh, who nodded. "They're not moving with you," they said.

"They're three-dimensional," I said.

"They're more than that, but that's all you can see."

"Pedant."

"Physicist," Niamh corrected, and pointed. "And they get larger closer to where Bella is. Was. Should be."

I followed their finger. They were right. Incrementally the glowy holes took up more space, glowing commensurately more diffusely the larger they got.

"These are all where the barrier thins out," Kahurangi said, of the holes.

Niamh nodded, and passed their hand through one, to no effect. "Not enough, though."

"Not yet," Kahurangi agreed.

They all flashed, and went out.

"*Now* we need a flashlight," Aparna said.

The glow started up again, very low now.

"All right," Niamh said, bleakly, to Kahurangi. "Where do you want to do this stupid attempt of your stupid hypothesis?"

Kahurangi motioned toward where Bella should have been. "The effect seems stronger near where Bella used to be. Let's try it there."

We set off in a group. Around us, creatures acted like we weren't there, except for the insects that were always and forever trying to drain us of every drop of blood that we had.

"This looks good," Kahurangi said, at one point. We were at a spot where the spectral holes were now almost as long as a forearm, and barely visible. "They don't look like they're getting any bigger from here. Any objections for trying here?"

Aparna and I had none. "I have *several*," Niamh said.

"Go ahead and get them out of your system," Kahurangi said, taking his pack off his back and unzipping it to rummage through it.

"First, or more accurately, *again*, this isn't even a hypothesis, it's a *guess*," Niamh said. "Based on nothing but a hunch, which is itself based on nothing but you pulling an idea out of your ass."

"Yes," Kahurangi agreed. He pulled a small canvas bag out of his pack.

"Second, this is bad science. What we're about to do isn't experimentation, it's like a séance. It's like homeopathic physics, and I resent that I have to be here for it, and that I agreed to go along with it just because we all felt like we should do something."

"Okay," Kahurangi said. He unzipped the bag, and reached into it.

"Third, and for all the reasons previously noted, if this does work, I will absolutely hate you forever."

"Noted," Kahurangi said. "Hold out your hand."

Niamh groaned and did as they were told. Kahurangi dropped four small cylindrical objects into Niamh's hand.

Uranium fuel pellets.

"This is so stupid," Niamh groused.

"We know the barrier thins and disappears through nuclear reactions," Kahurangi said. He fished out another four cylinders. "We also suppose that whoever took Bella found a way to power her over without actually using a true nuclear reaction *but* using nuclear material." He motioned to me; I held out my hand. "We know the barrier at the moment is thinner than it would be just on Bella's power alone, which means there's some residual effect going on." He dropped the cylinders into my hand, cool and flat gray. "So it's not unreasonable to hypothesize that some refined nuclear fuel might have a pronounced effect on the barrier. Maybe even enough for us to push through."

Niamh grimaced. "I hate this."

"Also, you didn't come up with a better idea."

"Yes, shame on me for feeling bounded by *actual science*."

"If it doesn't work, at least we tried," Kahurangi said. He'd fished out another four cylinders and offered them to Aparna.

"Reassure me my hand isn't going to fall off if I take those," Aparna said.

Kahurangi smiled. "These are unused fuel pellets. If they had been used, they could kill you. As it is, they're safe to hold for as long as we're going to use them for."

Aparna looked over to Niamh. "Kahurangi is a comprehensive load of pants, but this much he has actually got correct," they assured Aparna.

Aparna nodded, held out her hand, and took the offered fuel pellets. Then Kahurangi fished out the final four pellets, set them down briefly on the ground as he returned the bag to his pack, zipped it, and placed it on his back. He retrieved his four pellets and stood up.

"Ready?" he asked.

"For what?" Niamh said. "To stand around with fuel pellets waiting to see if our hands slip over to our home planet?"

"Basically, yeah."

"Uuuunnnnngh, this is the *worst*."

"I know," Kahurangi said.

"The *actual* worst. I feel like they're going to rescind my doctorate for doing this."

"I can't believe I'm the one saying this to you," Aparna said to Niamh. "But, wow, you're sure whining a lot right now."

"This is what *bad science* does to me! Now you know!"

"Okay, all right, enough," I said. "It's a wild and possibly terrible idea, it probably won't work, and if it doesn't, then we go back to the base and face our very angry bosses. Until then, let's hope. Just hope. Fair enough?"

"Works for me," Kahurangi said.

Aparna nodded again. Niamh rolled their eyes but nodded, too.

"Great," I said, and closed the fuel pellets in my hand. "Fist bump, everyone."

Kahurangi grinned and leaned in.

"Love you, kaiju nerds," Aparna said, both paraphrasing the movie *Pitch Perfect* and putting out her fist. I was pleased to have caught the reference.

Niamh sighed and leaned in. For the briefest of seconds, all our fists touched.

The world lit up like a fireworks display.

"Oh *come* the fuck *on*," Niamh yelled, and then there was an immense crack, the sound of a sequoia being snapped in half by a lightning strike.

Aparna pointed up, and moved her mouth in a way that said, *Look*. We all looked.

A vast and bright pillar of light was blasting straight up seemingly out from nowhere. At what appeared to be its base, very faintly, we could see the outline of what would have been Bella's mouth. All around the dimensional holes were brightening and growing, and in their centers we could see another world.

The barrier was breached. There was a way through.

Wind started whipping up as the hot warm air of Kaiju Earth was sucked into the colder, thinner atmosphere of the human Earth. As it hit, it immediately condensed, forming a cloud of vapor.

I looked around near us and a few meters away saw a vaporous hole, big enough to run through. I started running.

"Come on!" I yelled, although I could only barely hear myself. I hoped the other three were following, but I had no time to check.

I was almost to the hole when the lights suddenly went out. The vaporous hole in front of me immediately began to close.

I leapt into it, closing my eyes as I did so.

And then I was through and tumbling on the ground, which was soft and gave way, cushioning me.

And then I was kicked in the head by Niamh as they barged through, followed by Aparna and Kahurangi, neither of whom, I'm happy to say, followed up on the kick.

"Sorry," Niamh said.

"It's all right," I assured them. I looked up to where we had come through.

The hole was gone.

"Everyone okay?" I asked.

"Okay?" Kahurangi said. "I'm awesome. We're through. It worked!" He unclenched his fist to show his fuel pellets.

"It did *not* work," Niamh said. "We got through because of Bella's atomic belch making the barrier fall."

Kahurangi nodded. "And the fuel pellets."

"The place we went through was meters away from your godforsaken fuel pellets, you impossible man."

"Still counts."

Niamh held up a hand. "I'm not talking to you about this anymore."

"Hey," Aparna said. "Look where we are."

We looked. Right next to us was Bella, all hundred-plus meters of her, going straight up. All across her body, things shifted and moved; her parasites and personal ecosystem. There was a pronounced breeze as Bella's body sucked air into itself. Around us was a thick layer of something rubbery. Natal jelly.

"We landed in *goo*," Niamh said, looking down.

I stood up. The jelly did not stick to me, thankfully. I reached into my pocket and pulled out my cell phone and, for the first time since we had gone over to Kaiju Earth in September, switched over to cellular mode to see if I could find a signal.

There was none.

This was not terribly surprising; we were in the forests of Labrador, and the nearest human population of any size was a hundred kilometers away. The trees did not need cell service. It was too bad. If ever there was a time for the Royal Canadian Mounted Police, this was it.

I looked at the time: 2:20 a.m.

"It's cold," Aparna said. She fished in her pack for her pullover. We all did the same, as well as retrieving, checking, and loading our various weapons.

"We came through at two twenty," I said to Aparna.

She nodded, knowing why I was telling her the time. We were now waiting to see what the interval was between Bella's ventings.

"Anyone else feeling a little woozy?" Kahurangi asked.

"You got used to the atmosphere on the other side," Aparna said. "Just breathe."

"Right, got it."

I looked around. Bella was illuminated by the moon, which was nearly full and to the west. We were too close to her to see anything else, but I could hear faint noises in the distance.

"I think we landed on the far side of Bella," I said. "Away from whoever took her, I mean."

"That's a bit of luck," Niamh said. "It would have been inconvenient to pop into existence in front of the people we were trying to surprise."

"So, how are we going to do this?" Aparna said. "Get to the perimeter thing and turn it on to get Bella back?"

We all looked at Kahurangi.

"Why are you looking at me?" he asked.

"You're the one who got us here," I said.

"He is *not*," Niamh retorted.

Kahurangi held up his hands. "I was kind of focused on getting us here," he said, and then pointed at me. "I thought Jamie was the one with the plan after that."

I was going to respond to that, but at the moment, someone came around Bella and stepped in front of us, carrying some sort of equipment. He took several steps toward us before he looked up and realized there were four people in front of him.

We all stared at each other for a good ten seconds.

"All right," he finally said. "Who the *fuck* are you people?"

CHAPTER 25

"Let me show you some ID," Niamh said, closed the distance on the interloper in an instant, and zapped him with a stun baton.

He stiffened, gurgled in surprise, and fell to the forest floor, unconscious.

The rest of us stared, shocked.

Niamh noticed. "*What?*"

"You have rage issues," Kahurangi said, after a second.

"If I had rage issues, he'd be dead."

"Are you sure he's *not* dead?" Aparna asked.

"I can hear him whimper when he breathes," Niamh said.

We all stared some more.

Niamh sighed, looked to the heavens with a *help me Jesus* expression, and looked back at the rest of us. "What do you want me to say? This asshole could have given us away. We didn't cross a friggin' *dimensional barrier* to get popped by the first joker who saw us. I zapped him. It needed to be done. And frankly I'm pissed that you all are giving me shit about it."

"It's not that," I said. "It's just now we have an unconscious dude to worry about."

"What do you mean?"

"I mean if we leave him here, Bella's parasites are going to make him into cold cuts."

Niamh shrugged. "Fuck 'em."

"Niamh!" Aparna said.

"It's not like he wouldn't leave *us*."

"This is what I mean by rage issues," Kahurangi said.

"I may be working through some residual annoyance that your

plan worked," Niamh admitted to him. "Sort of worked, anyway. But I'm not *wrong* about this shithead."

"Maybe you're not," I allowed. "But maybe *we* should try to be better people than the faceless henchman of an evil organization."

Niamh sighed again. "You're not *wrong*," they said. "But look. We can't do this every single time we meet up with one of these assholes. We'll be here all night stuffing bodies away. Bella will go up by the time we're done."

"Let's deal with this guy right now and we'll figure out the rest of this as we go along," I said.

"Figuring things out as we go along is our *problem*," Niamh said.

"We really should have had a better plan for once we came through," Aparna agreed.

"I'm feeling suddenly blamed," I said.

"A little, yeah," Kahurangi said.

I motioned. "Well. For now, let's drag this dude out toward the tree line. Put him out there, spray him with the 'I'm a kaiju' pheromone. So they leave him alone."

"Good idea," Niamh said. "And that way when he wakes up, he'll smell like shit."

"I'm open to a better plan," I said.

"I have none, so let's do this."

"You two do that," Kahurangi said. "I need Aparna's help with something."

"What thing?" Niamh asked.

"Preparing a backup plan. So we don't have to drag everyone's body into the tree line."

"Fine." Niamh turned to me. "You want the arms or legs?"

"Your choice," I said. Niamh took the legs. I hoisted the dude's arms. I lift things.

"What are you doing?" Niamh asked, after we'd tossed him into the trees and sprayed him down. "Are you *looting* this poor bastard?"

"I'm not *looting* him," I said, fishing through his pockets.

"Whatever, just remember I get half."

I produced the dude's phone. "There we are," I said. I turned it on; it needed a fingerprint. I took his hand and acquired one. He murmured as I did so. I patted his cheek. He smiled sleepily and went back to wherever his brain was at the moment.

"I thought there was no cell phone signal out here," Niamh said.

"There isn't," I said, and showed them the phone screen. "There is, however, a Wi-Fi connection. This weird little place brought its own intranet."

"You going to send an email?"

"No," I said. I looked through the apps to find one for shared files. I found it, and opened it up. "I'm looking for secret plans. And I think I just found some."

Niamh peered over. "This will be useful until the moment you close this phone and walk away from his fingerprint."

I gave them the phone. "Hold this." I fished out my phone from my pocket. "I'm not going to send an email. However, I *am* going to use near-field communication to transfer these files."

"Look at you being a computer nerd," Niamh said, not quite admiringly.

"I *did* work at a tech start-up, once," I said. "I learned at least a couple of things."

"Then make it go faster," they said. "Or I'll have to zap this poor bastard again."

When the files were transferred over, I turned off the guy's phone and chucked it far into the woods. "Come on," I said to Niamh. "We need to get moving. Whoever this guy is, he's probably going to be missed soon. We don't want to be there when anyone comes looking for him."

We started walking and found Kahurangi and Aparna coming toward us. "We heard voices," Aparna said. "I think they're looking for their friend."

I looked up toward Bella and saw flashlights waving about. "Right," I said. We headed out, away from the unconscious henchman and the flashlights of his pals.

We hunkered down a couple of hundred meters away, and everyone else looked out while I went through the files I downloaded. "Here," I said. "It's a dos-and-don'ts document about that perimeter. They call it a *trans-dimensional portal*."

"Mate, they did *not* just rip off *Doom Eternal* for that," Kahurangi said.

"I'm afraid they did."

"Copyright violation for sure."

"I don't think they're going to try to sell this," I said, continuing to read. "It looks like it requires a ridiculous amount of energy to work, so it needs to be primed before it can be activated. Those barrel-looking things are capacitors. Once there's enough energy in the system it can be discharged into these components at the top of the barrel, which thins out the barrier between worlds to nothing."

"Exactly how?" Niamh asked.

"It doesn't say. It's not a schematic or anything. It's just describing how it works enough so that some jerk doesn't get himself killed working around it." I flipped the screen over so they could see it. "Like, 'Don't go near the capacitors, they're not actually safe and might accidentally discharge a hundred thousand volts into you.'"

"That's . . . good to know," Aparna said.

"Seriously, it looks like a really bad design," I said.

"If the capacitors are charged, then something is charging them," Kahurangi said. "There's a generator here somewhere. And if there is, that's probably where the switch to discharge them is."

"Find it, discharge the capacitors on the perimeter, send Bella home," Aparna said.

I nodded and flipped through the document until I found a rough design illustration. "There's where a generator would be," I said. "I'm guessing, since we didn't see it immediately, that we'll find it on the other side of Bella, along with all the rest of whatever camp they have set up."

"So, let's go and flip the switch," Niamh said.

"It's probably guarded."

"Why would it be guarded? Do you really think these assholes are expecting visitors?"

"Maybe they weren't, but then one of them went missing because someone who shall remain nameless zapped the shit out of them," I pointed out.

"I acknowledge your point even as I defend its necessity," Niamh said. "But what that just means is that whatever we do, we need to do it quickly."

"That, I agree with."

"What if we just told them?" Aparna said.

"What?"

"I know we're going with the assumption that these are bad people—"

"They actually *are* bad people," Kahurangi reminded her. "They killed our friends."

"I know that," Aparna acknowledged. "I'm not forgetting that at all. But I also don't think they intended for Bella to go nuclear when she came over. I don't think they understand the danger here, to themselves even if they don't care about other people. I think it's possible that if we just told them, they might send her back."

"Do you *really* think that?" Niamh asked.

"I'm not sure if I do," Aparna admitted. "But I think at least one of us should say this out loud before we do anything else. We should be at least willing to entertain the notion these people, even if they are evil, are rational actors."

"I admire your optimism," I said.

"Yeah, I admire it, and I also think they will murder the shit out of us the first chance they get," Niamh said. "So, no, let's just go for the generator."

Kahurangi nodded. "I'm with Niamh, here."

"All right," Aparna said. "It was worth saying."

We made our way around in the woods, moving counterclockwise against Bella's bulk. As we did so, the human encampment made itself known in a stand of lights, and a collection of shipping containers that had been repurposed for whatever activities the crew down there was doing. At least a dozen people were out in the open, collecting material from the natal jelly and from Bella herself. More milled among the containers. One container wasn't a container at all, but a small trailer. I suspected whoever was running the operation would be in there.

Kahurangi pointed. "I think the generator's in there."

I followed his hand to a storage container set a bit away from the rest. The doors of the container were closed, and a thick cable snaked out of it, leading several meters to a large box out in the open, which itself connected to the first of the barrels of the perimeter.

No other cables came out of the container; whatever was powering the rest of the encampment was somewhere else. It all pointed to this being, indeed, the generator we were looking for.

"Anyone see guards or others near there?" I asked. I didn't see any, but it didn't hurt to have confirmation from others. No one saw anything; the nearest person moving about was tens of meters from it and moving away.

Still moving in the tree line, we picked our way around until we were directly behind the generator container, with Bella towering up in front of us.

"We ready?" I asked.

"Should we all go?" Aparna said.

Niamh looked at her. "Do you want to stay behind?"

"Not really."

"We all go," I said. "One."

Bella shifted, monstrously, lifted her head, and screamed.

"Two," I whispered, entirely lost.

A beam shot from her again, nearly straight up, followed by a reverberating *crack*. The beam abruptly cut short some tens of meters above her head as it punched through to Kaiju Earth, tearing a hole in the sky.

Around us, the world started to glow. The portal effect, so pronounced on the other side, was hardly noticeable here, except for when Bella released so much nuclear energy at once. Bella herself was drenched in fog as the moist, warm air of Kaiju Earth whipped through the far larger dimensional holes near her and collided with the freezing, dense air of this one.

She looked in the moment like every kaiju you'd ever seen in a movie. Large. Angry. Terrifying.

Primal.

Bella stopped screaming and the beam of light stopped. The world stopped glowing and all the holes went away. I had the presence of mind to glance at my smartwatch, to record the interval between Bella's eruptions.

"Three," I said, looking at the time.

Everyone else ran.

That's not what I meant, I thought, and then ran to catch up.

The door to the generator container was slightly ajar, and lights glowed from within. We entered, and I closed the door as quietly as possible once we were all inside.

Inside was strip lighting along the top of the container walls. A long, modern-looking object was inside, with an instrument panel reading out data and a laptop attached to it via a USB-C cable.

"This is the generator?" Aparna asked.

"I think so," I said, looking at the instrument panel, which was showing the amount of electrical output and other indicators.

"It doesn't look like a generator. It looks like an overgrown iPhone."

"It doesn't smell like a generator either," Niamh said.

"You're right," Kahurangi agreed. "I've been around diesels when I've done fieldwork. This isn't one of those. You can hear around it, for one."

"It's outputting power," I said. "At least that's what the panel says."

"Does the panel say anything about discharging the capacitors?" Niamh asked.

"No." I looked up at the laptop. "But this might." The laptop had up a window that featured an image of the capacitors, chained together. There were several dozen of them; moving the computer cursor over each of the icons noted how close to capacity their charge was. They were all at 95 percent or above.

In the bottom right of the window was a large red button with the words *Discharge Capacitors* on it.

"Well, that's convenient," I said, showing the button to the rest of them.

"What are you waiting for?" Niamh asked. "Do it."

"Give me a second to make sure I'm not missing something," I said.

"Seems straightforward."

"Look, do *you* want to press the button?"

"If you don't do it this decade, maybe."

I pressed the Discharge Capacitors button.

A dialogue window popped up: *Confirm discharge.*

"Oh, for fuck's sake," I said, and confirmed.

Nothing happened.

"Well?" Kahurangi asked.

I shrugged. "It didn't go."

"You pressed the button?"

"I pressed the button," I said. "And I confirmed with the dialogue window."

"Well, shit."

There was a knock on the door of the container.

We all jumped, and then stared at the door.

There was another knock.

"In retrospect, maybe one of us should have been a lookout," Aparna said.

There was another knock, and then someone said, "Last knock before tear gas."

"Coming," I answered.

They all looked at me.

"What?" I said. "You want tear gas?"

"We could go out the other side of the container," Kahurangi said.

"We have the other side of the container covered," the voice said.

"Stop saying things *out loud*," Niamh hissed at Kahurangi.

"Seriously, come out now, before we have to shoot you all," the voice said.

"We're really bad at this," Aparna said. None of us could disagree.

We came out of the container, hands up. Five men with military rifles were waiting for us. They rapidly divested us of weapons and backpacks and put us on our knees, hands behind our backs.

"Which one of you tased Dave?" The one directly in front of us asked.

"That was me," Niamh said.

"That was mean. He's new. Barely above an intern."

"Sorry, you all look like people who murdered my friends to me."

The man smiled at this. "I'd be murdering you, too, but we were told not to, for now."

"By whom?" I asked.

"By me," a voice said, coming up from behind us.

I turned to look.

It was Rob Sanders, because of course it was.

"Just so you know, the plan here is to tie you up and feed you to the kaiju parasites," Sanders said to us. Our packs and weapons were arrayed in front of him; one of his flunkies had found him a folding chair, and he was sitting in it. Then that flunky and the others returned to training their weapons on us. "We obviously can't let you *live* now. But if you answer my questions, we might kill you painlessly instead of letting the parasites eat you while you're still conscious."

"Did you practice that?" Niamh said. "It sounds like you practiced that. A lot. In a mirror."

"Dr. Healy," Sanders said, regarding Niamh. "I remember you being rude the last time we met. It doesn't surprise me you've kept in character. And no, that was all spontaneous. Also, true. So, first question: How did you manage to come across?"

"Fuel pellets," I said.

"Excuse me?"

"Uranium fuel pellets," I said. "You'll find mine in my pack."

Sanders frowned at that and started digging through my pack, eventually finding a couple. "You're shitting me," he said, looking at the tiny gray cylinders.

"Ask Dr. Lautagata," I said.

"I figured there was some sort of field that would be excited by purified actinides," Kahurangi said. "We brought some, and we were able to come across."

"And how did that work, exactly?"

"We held them up in a witchy circle," Niamh said.

Sanders looked over to me for verification. I shrugged. "We all stood closely together, held up our hands with the fuel pellets in them, and we were able to step through." I didn't feel the need to tell him that the hole that we stepped through was several meters away from us and activated by Bella blasting nuclear energy out of her throat; that seemed extraneous information.

Sanders looked to Aparna. "You're the only one here that I don't remember being a smart-ass," he said. "Is this accurate?"

Aparna nodded. "It happened like Jamie said."

"And your bosses agreed to this?"

"We didn't ask permission," I said.

"I can see why," Sanders said. "Seems *super* sketchy."

"We were desperate to get across," Aparna said.

Sanders regarded Aparna. "And why was that?"

"Because we need you to send Bella back. She's a danger to you and to herself."

Sanders smiled. "Oh, you mean because of the nuclear burps."

Aparna frowned at this characterization. "Yes."

"We know all about them. We're not worried about them."

"You're not *worried* about a kaiju going nuclear on you?" Kahurangi asked, incredulous.

"We're counting on it," Sanders said. "Dude, we just brought a kaiju over to this side of things. Do you know how *illegal* that is? She goes nuclear, she wipes out every bit of evidence of what we were doing here, including herself. There's nothing left but a crater."

"And flash fires, and nuclear fallout," Kahurangi pointed out.

Sanders waved this away. "Into a national park no one goes to anyway."

"Bella might move," Aparna said. "If she's in too much pain or is confused, she might leave here. If she leaves here and heads to Goose Bay, then thousands of people might die."

Sanders grinned widely. "Which is even *better*," he said. "There's a Canadian military base there. A nuclear attack on Canada's military? In Labrador? Shit, that's confusing for everyone. They'll spend months trying to figure out who did that and why. I figure they'll eventually settle on China, because why wouldn't they. A nuclear attack on North America, during a pandemic, right before the United States election—right before *this* United States election. That's going to be *amazing*. Martial law for the U.S., for one. Stocks will crater, for two. I have short sellers standing by."

"Martial law and the economy cratering is a nice opportunity for you," I said, sarcastically.

"Don't be angry that I have a *plan*, Jamie," Sanders said. "It's more than you had, clearly. You really thought you could just send Bella back by fiddling around with my laptop?"

"Maybe," I said, realizing how ridiculous it sounded now.

Sanders reached into his shirt and pulled out something tiny on a chain. "USB security key, my friend. The capacitors don't discharge without this physically plugged into the laptop. I mean, come on, that's just basic CEO-level security right there."

"Why do you even have your perimeter still on, then?" Niamh asked.

"Perimeter?" Sanders looked confused.

"Excuse me, your *trans-dimensional portal*," Niamh spat, disgusted.

"It's a good name," Sanders said. "I thought it up myself."

"Dude, it's from fucking *Doom*," Kahurangi said.

"You do have a history of stealing terms from science fiction classics," I pointed out.

"I have no idea what either of you two are talking about," Sanders said. "As for your question, Dr. Healy, it's still active because it's a fail-safe. If Bella became unruly before we had an indication she would go nuclear, we could send her back. We don't need it now. In fact, when I'm done here I'll go turn it off. Strand Bella over here for good."

"How does it work, anyway?" Niamh pressed. This session was meant to extract answers from us, but Sanders was an egotistical shit and liked to talk. Clearly the plan we'd all decided on without discussing it in advance was to keep him monologuing.

"You like it?" Sanders asked Niamh.

"I want to *understand* it."

Sanders casually looked at his watch. "For all the good it will do you, given how much time you have left."

"I want to know how you thought of it, prototyped it, and had it ready for this"—Niamh motioned with their head to encompass everything—"in a couple of weeks. And by *you,* I mean whatever scientists you employ, because you clearly have no capability for it."

"Ouch," Sanders said. "I have an engineering degree."

"You have a bachelor's from a college where you're a legacy," I said. "Your family probably endowed the building and they let you skate through."

Sanders narrowed his eyes. "I could feed you all to parasites right now, if you want."

"Then you wouldn't get answers to your questions," Aparna said.

"I'm not getting any answers now!" Sanders said. "You have me monologuing, I'm guessing, to stay alive longer. Yes, I *know* about monologuing. I've watched *The Incredibles.*"

"The trans-dimensional portal," Niamh promoted. "Monologue on that, please."

"Clearly we had it before now."

"Since when?"

"Since the 1960s, if you must know." Sanders turned to me. "Remember that bit of drama back at Tanaka Base? Where your administrator tried to lecture me about my family's involvement in the old version of Tanaka being obliterated? She was more right than she knew. That kaiju didn't just happen to be near the base. We lured it in."

"So you've killed KPS people before," I said.

"We didn't know the kaiju had a malformed reactor," Sanders said. "We can't be blamed for *that.*"

"No, just for putting the kaiju in a place where it could kill dozens of people."

"If you like," Sanders said, conceding the point because he didn't seem to care about it very much. "We were trying to get it into an earlier version of the portal, which was powered like this one is, with our company's RTGs." Sanders jerked a thumb back at the generator container. "That one's a prototype polonium-210 RTG. Outputs a ridiculous amount of energy really quickly. Perfect for this use case. Fuel doesn't last very long, though."

"You've tried this before?" Aparna said.

"It didn't work," Sanders said. "We could make a tear in the dimensional wall, but it wasn't significant enough to bring anything through. We needed more residual thinning, and we could never get it. Until now. That first kaiju going nuclear and thinning the barrier, and then Bella sitting at the edge of the crater and having her reactor keep it thin?" Sanders made a chef's kiss action with his hands. "Perfect. My family's been waiting for actual generations for this moment." He motioned around. "We've had this prepped to go for years. We update the components from time to time, obviously. But we've been ready."

"Yeah, all right, but *why*?" Kahurangi asked. "What good does bringing a kaiju over do you? You can't control them. You can't harness their energy. They can't survive here more than a few days. What's the point?"

Sanders smiled at this. "Dr. Lautagata, I would think of all people you would understand."

"I don't."

"Then let me help. Which is your pack?" Kahurangi pointed out his pack. Sanders rummaged through it and fished out a spray bottle. "What is this?"

"Kaiju pheromones."

"Which you use to keep the parasites off you."

"Mostly."

Sanders waved at all four of us. "Which is why the four of you currently smell like fermented gym shorts."

"Yes."

"So you are less interested in the kaiju than what you can get *out* of the kaiju," Sanders said. He sniffed the spray bottle nozzle, made a grimacing face at it, set it down on the ground, and continued to rummage through Kahurangi's pack. "For you, the kaiju isn't the kaiju. It's a bunch of compounds and smells and pheromones that you can fiddle with to give you what you want." He pulled what looked like a remote control out of the pack, puzzled at it, set it down. "I'm the same way. Just not about smells and pheromones."

"You want the reactor," Aparna said, suddenly.

Sanders smiled at her. "Dr. Chowdhury, clearly the smartest of the four of you. Yes. My family's been in nuclear and nuclear-derived power generation since just after the end of World War II. Imagine the competitive advantage we could have if instead of *building* viable nuclear reactors, we could just *grow* them. Safe. Effective. Organic. Wind and solar are only going to get us so far, you know. I don't care about the kaiju one way or another. I just want to know how their bodies make their reactors."

He looked over to me. "Although *you* should have figured that out by now. You caught me trying to smuggle out kaiju genetic information."

"I didn't know this was plan B," I said.

"I'm glad you didn't figure it out," Sanders said. "But that does bring up the question of how you figured out how we were here at all. When my people went in, the first thing they did was take out the aerostat."

"And the helicopter," I added.

"We weren't expecting the helicopter," Sanders admitted. "Or your staff. We thought getting the aerostat and then the instrument packs would be enough. Even with the downed helicopter, you still should have thought it was Bella attacking, not us. What happened?"

"You were sloppy," Niamh said.

"Evidently, but how, is what I'm asking."

"You remember Tom Stevens," I said.

"The guy who said we went to Dartmouth together."

"That's the one. Your people murdered him."

"That will be an awkward note in the alumni magazine, but continue."

"Before that happened, he hid a camera," I said. "We caught your people. We saw your perimeter."

"Trans-dimensional portal," Sanders corrected.

I ignored this. "And we knew it wasn't an accident or the result of a kaiju attack. *We* know. Our people know. And as soon as the gateway at Honda Base comes back online, people on this side will know, too."

Sanders looked up to one of the men who had weapons on us, the one who asked which one of us zapped Dave. "You said the site was clean."

"I thought it was," the man replied. Now that I knew, the voice matched what I remembered from Tom's video.

"Well, obviously it wasn't," Sanders snapped. "This complicates things."

"There's nothing that ties this to you or your company," the man said. "We don't have any identifying clothes. The portal doesn't have brand marks. They can't know."

"Except that you've done this before," I said. "Your company, I mean. Eventually KPS will figure that out."

"No, they won't," Sanders said, almost distractedly. "They were never told what we were doing. It was between us and the Department of Energy."

"Then *they* will know," I said.

Sanders smirked at me. "You know who's in charge of the United States right now, right? Do you think they'll *care*? Especially if I give them an excuse to declare martial law and scrub the election? Dude, I'll get the Presidential Medal of Freedom for this shit."

I ground my teeth. "I hate that you're right about that," I said.

"I know you do," Sanders said, placatingly. "But I don't think it will get that far. Evidence or not, we can make sure it doesn't come back to us." He turned back to Aparna. "We've spent the last several hours extracting genetic material from Bella's eggs," he said. "And we've taken some of the eggs themselves, to raise in a controlled environment. We'll be able to look at the young kaiju as they develop."

"But that's not going to help you," Aparna said.

"I know that," Sanders said. "I know that because you told me how the parasites are needed to spur the development, and I know that because of our company's own research. All the more reason to bring Bella over. We've been harvesting her parasites, too, both for their genetics and for individuals."

"And they haven't eaten any of you?" Niamh asked.

"A few have tried, but the cold and the thinner air makes them less active," Sanders said. "They've mostly just been clinging to Bella for warmth."

"Which makes your threat of feeding us to them less terrifying."

"Well, we'll deliver you to them directly, that'll help." Sanders checked his watch again. "And soon, because it's only going to be a couple of hours before Bella goes up, by our estimation."

"The Canadians have to know you're here by now," Kahurangi said.

"Of course they do; they gave us permits," Sanders said. "They think we're doing radio interferometry out here. We told them a week ago that tonight they might see some intense light coming from here as part of our work, so they're expecting that."

"And the massive fucking kaiju?" Niamh asked.

"We have permission to build structures as long as we don't permanently alter the site. Bella is a structure, so far as they know."

"No one's going to buy that," Aparna said.

"They might not if we were doing this in the middle of Montreal. But we're sixty miles from the nearest town of any size, in Labrador, in the middle of a pandemic. We're not even on any flight paths. I don't think you understand how incredibly perfect this location is for this."

"You are planning to permanently alter the site, though," I said. "A nuclear explosion will do that."

"Well, that's true," Sanders conceded. "But they'll think we went up with it. But in fact, a cargo-size copter is coming to take away our lab container and me and my crew. It'll be here presently. You folks came just as we were wrapping things up." Sanders slapped his thighs and stood. "So, let's go ahead and put a pin in things, shall we?"

"You don't want to ask us any more questions?" I asked.

"Not really, no," Sanders said. "I thought I did? But I know how you came through, I know no one knows you're here, and I know no one knows I or my family's company is behind this. You're all going to die and be vaporized. What else do I need to know?"

"*We* have more questions," Aparna said.

"I'm sure you do, but that's not actually how this works. But I hope that you enjoyed the monologuing."

"We did," Kahurangi said. "And so will KPS headquarters."

Sanders paused. "Come again?"

Kahurangi nodded to the remote control–looking thing on the ground. "That's been recording the whole time, and sending everything you've said to a device I hid on Bella. It's being stored there for right now. It's on a dead man's switch. If I don't press *that* button," he pointed to a red button on the remote, "at least once an hour, it sends everything."

"That's a cute threat in an area where there's no cell phone coverage," Sanders said.

"You have a Wi-Fi network up," I pointed out.

"It's local," he said. "And how do you know that?"

"Because I used Dave's phone to download your shared files, and uploaded them to the same device."

"Which has no connection," Sanders reminded us. "You're bluffing."

"Oh, for Christ's sake," Niamh said. "They're called *satellites*, you asshole. Your pal Elon just put a few thousand of them up."

"We're *not* friends," Sanders said, sounding defensive.

"Actually this one works with the Iridium satellites," Kahurangi said. "They're old and slow, but they're reliable. And they'll receive everything in"—he checked his watch—"five minutes."

Sanders reached down and picked up the remote. "This button?" he asked, pointing to the red disk on the remote. He pressed it. "Bad monologuing," he said to Kahurangi. "You only reveal your secret *after* it's too late."

Kahurangi smiled. "You don't think that works without my fingerprint, do you?"

Sanders frowned and looked at the remote. "What?"

"I mean, that's just basic security right there," Kahurangi said.

Sanders presented Kahurangi with the remote. "Press it," he said.

"Or what?" Niamh said. "You're going to kill him? Mate, you've already played *that* card."

Sanders turned to Niamh. "How about I have you shot in the gut, so he can hear you scream in agony until he presses the button?"

"Wow, *that's* dark," Niamh said. "Also, fuck you."

"Have it your way." Sanders looked up at his lead minion. "Would you, please?"

"Hey, hey," Kahurangi said. "No gut-shooting anyone. Give me the remote." He held out his hand. Sanders put the remote into it.

Kahurangi looked at all of us. "So, I guess this is it," he said.

"I guess it is," I replied.

"I just want to say that no matter what happens, I'm glad I met each of you," Kahurangi said. He looked up at Sanders. "Not *you*," he clarified. "*You* can die in a fire. But you, Jamie. You, Aparna. You, Niamh. I'm glad for our friendship."

"I'm glad for yours," Aparna said.

"Me, too," I concurred.

"I didn't plan to go out with this much mush," Niamh said. "But yeah. You're all the best." They looked up at Sanders. "Again, not you. You are the worst."

"Just the worst," Aparna agreed.

"History's worst monster," I said.

"I can still have you shot in the gut," Sanders said. "Like, *all* of you."

"Oh, right," Kahurangi said. He pressed the button, and then tossed the remote back to Sanders. "By the way, I lied."

"You what?"

"He lied," I said. "So did I."

"We *all* lied," Aparna said.

"Not about liking each other," Niamh said to Sanders. "We do. And not about you being an asshole. You are."

"I lied about what that remote control does," Kahurangi said. "One, it doesn't record anything. It's just a remote control."

"Two, it doesn't control a box that sends data to a satellite," Aparna said.

"No, I lied about that, too," Kahurangi agreed.

"Three, it's not a dead man's switch," I said. "When you pressed the button, you activated it."

"Activated what?" Sanders asked.

From the direction of Bella came yells and screams.

"You said that the parasites are sluggish here and are clinging to Bella," Kahurangi said. "I planted a pheromone bomb that should wake them right up."

Around us, the lightest scent of oranges and citrus cut through the smells of pine and dirt.

"What do you mean you woke them up?" Sanders asked.

"I told you once that pheromones aren't a perfect language," Kahurangi said. "And that's true. This pheromone, though, is as close as it gets to saying one thing very loudly. And what it says is, 'We're being attacked. Kill everything that moves.' You just set it off. And *we* just gave them time to get here."

"Shit," Sanders's man said.

I turned my head to see a flood of parasites had come off of Bella and at least some of them were galloping toward us.

I looked up at Sanders, who watched them come, mouth gaping.

I jumped up, grabbed Sanders, and yanked the USB key off of his neck.

I turned to my friends.

"Run," I said.

CHAPTER 27

We scattered as the parasites hit around us.

The men who had trained their weapons on us had forgotten we existed. We weren't the scary alien creatures running at them full bore; we were just people, unarmed at that, and we weren't going to do anything to them. The men swiveled and started firing their rifles at the parasites.

It turns out that Riddu Tagaq was right. It's hard to hit a fast-moving parasite with a tiny bullet.

Two of the men went down almost immediately, yelling and fighting. The others did what we did and ran.

Looking back, I saw Rob Sanders flinch, then look around.

What is he looking for? I wondered.

He saw me. He took off after me, pausing only to grab the shotgun Kahurangi had brought with him.

Oh, right, I have his key, I thought.

Then I was running again, toward Bella, running into what everyone else around me was running away from.

As I ran, parasites galloped around and past me; the "I'm a kaiju" pheromone was still on me, and, I hoped, on my friends as well.

Around me, I saw Sanders's people running, dodging and screaming as the flood of parasites tracked them down. In my peripheral vision, I saw a parasite barrel into a human, forcing him down to the ground; immediately several other parasites were on him as well. I stopped paying attention to what happened to him after that.

I looked up at Bella, who chose that moment to do something I didn't expect.

She *moved*.

Her body, which hadn't budged at all except to eject nuclear screams, shuddered and shook. What parasites that hadn't already come down from her were flying off her in waves, their homes disturbed by Bella's motion.

Kahurangi had explained this to us earlier. *Aparna and I planted the pheromone bombs where Bella takes in her air,* he had said as we'd walked toward the generator. *The pheromones are going to get sucked right into her and go to every part of her body. Her parasites are going to react to it first, but eventually she'll feel it, too.*

What then? I'd asked.

Stay the hell out of her way, he'd said.

I ran harder toward Bella.

I felt the buckshot hit me before I heard the crack of shotgun, peppering my back and head.

Sanders was too far away for the shot to do me any real damage, but it stung like hell and knocked me out of my rhythm. I stumbled and fell to the ground, giving Sanders time to close the gap between us.

"Give me back my ke—" was as far as he got before he started spitting out the clod of dirt I flung directly into his face. There was a small rock nearby; I grabbed it and pitched it at him. He cursed as it hit him in the chin, causing him to bring his hand up to his very minor injury.

"Really?" I heard him say, in disbelief, but anything after that I missed because I was running again.

As I ran, I realized I had done something to my left ankle when I'd fallen. It felt hot and sore, and every step was making it worse.

I looked up and I realized that Bella was now looming directly in front of me, with nothing more between me and her. I realized something else, too.

She was looking right at me.

Those big, glowing, unearthly eyes had rotated across her head and were now intently peering down to where I was.

I froze, because I suppose that's what you do sometimes when you're prey.

"I have one more shot, Jamie," Sanders said, coming behind me. "Don't make me use it."

I looked back to him. "I got news for you, Rob. You're the least of my problems right now." I pointed up. He followed my hand to see Bella staring down at the both of us.

"Oh, *shit*," he said.

I held out my arm in warning. "Don't run."

"Why the fuck *not*?"

"It won't do you any good anyway," I said.

We both stared up, transfixed, at Bella.

Who decided that she wanted to get a closer look at the both of us.

I'm not sure how to describe the geometry that was involved in how a more-than-one-hundred-meter-tall creature maneuvered her head down close to our level. But it happened. Bella's head was the size of a largish suburban home, and her eyes just slid around until they found us. In and around the head, things moved; parasites that still had not been dislodged or had been moved to attack.

"Oh, fuck," Sanders said.

"Stop *talking*," I said.

Bella's eyes split, considering the both of us severally.

As Bella gazed on us, I felt the heat of her internals blasting into me, forced out of her body through the network her parasites had created for her. It was almost unbearable, like standing in front of a furnace that was well on its way to overheating.

There was something else, too. Something in the way Bella held herself while she was considering us. She seemed . . .

Exhausted. Tired. Out of her element.

Sad.

Maybe I was reading more into it because I knew she had been taken to a place she didn't belong. It's possible my brain was ramping up a pathetic fallacy just to hope against hope that this monstrous creature with the head the size of a house wouldn't eat me or step on me. Alternately, perhaps I was just having a psychotic break, pure and simple. Some or all of those things could have been true in the moment.

It didn't change the fact that, at that very second, what I most wanted to do in the world was put my hand on Bella and tell her it would be all right.

"You poor girl," I whispered to her.

"Are you fucking kidding me?" Sanders said behind me. He had clearly heard me.

I turned to him. "Shut it, Rob," I said. "You brought this thing over here. You brought it to a place where the only thing it can do is die. You *want* it to die. And for what? So you can have a bio-industrial process you and your family business can monopolize."

"The world needs limitless bio-nuclear power—"

"Dude, don't even pretend you're doing it for *the world*," I said. "You don't give a shit about the world. This one or hers." I pointed toward Bella. "Tom Stevens told me once that part of the job of the KPS was keeping the kaiju safe from humans. We joked about which of us were the real monsters. But it turns out it's not a joke after all, is it?"

Sanders looked over nervously at Bella, who was still considering us, then back at me. "Give me the key, Jamie, and I'll send her back," he said. "I have everything I want or need from her. Give me the key and I'll power up the portal. She can go back. You can go back. You can *all* go back."

"What about the part where you were going to feed us to the parasites?" I asked.

"I can change that part of the deal."

"Or the part where you just fired a shotgun at me."

"Mistakes were made."

"And you would just let us go on living, knowing what we know, knowing that we would be *asked* about what we know."

"I think I can sufficiently motivate the four of you to tell a mutually beneficial story."

"This is where you offer us money," I said.

"Not just money," Sanders said. "But money *is* a part of it."

I smiled. "It's tempting," I said. "Until I remember that right now, you're just making a Duke bet with yourself about whether I'm stupid enough to accept your offer."

Sanders smiled back. "You remembered that."

"I did."

"Did you remember I still have a shotgun?"

A blast of superhot air came from Bella, knocking the both of us down. Bella's head disappeared, going up, up, up into the sky.

Sanders stood himself and leveled the shotgun at me. "Jamie Gray," he said. "Let's do this."

Bella screamed, a beam shot from her, and the world went golden.

I looked up, and a dimensional hole had opened up behind Sanders. Fog formed around him, obscuring his view.

I rolled away as he pulled the trigger, the buckshot too tightly packed to find me.

As I rolled and turned, I saw something race toward my face.

A parasite.

My pheromone's run out, I thought.

It leapt over me, catching Sanders in the chest.

He shouted in surprise and terror as the parasite knocked him into the hole. I lost sight of him in the fog.

Somewhere on the other side of the fog, Sanders stopped yelling and started screaming.

I got up, testing the soundness of my ankle, and looked up just as Bella stopped her beam. The hole around the beam started to close up, and something came through it, disrupting the fog.

A helicopter. Chopper Two.

"Fucking *Martin Satie,*" I said, and started waving for him, hopping as I did so.

Bella spotted Chopper Two and took a swipe at it. Satie avoided it and put distance between himself and Bella.

Bella stood up, slowly, reaching her full height.

She unfurled.

And then she started to *go.* In my direction.

I decided I could worry about my ankle hurting later. I ran ninety degrees from the direction Bella seemed to be going.

Her first steps took her out of the perimeter of the capacitors.

Her second steps crushed most of the containers that Sanders's people had been using as labs.

With the third steps, a noise like jet engines started coming from Bella.

Bella flapped, huge wings hoping to find purchase in our planet's thin air.

Eventually they found it.

Bella was airborne.

I looked back down to the ground and saw three forms running toward me: Aparna, Niamh, and Kahurangi.

"Mate, you okay?" Kahurangi asked, reaching me first.

"My ankle's shot, but I'm fine," I said. Aparna and Niamh had reached us. I showed them Sanders's USB key. "We can fire up the perimeter now," I said.

"That's great, but there's a small problem," Niamh said. "Our bird has flown the coop."

"The longer she's out, the harder it is to send her back," Aparna said.

"I have an idea," I said. I turned to Aparna. "How long was Bella's interval this time?"

"A little over twenty minutes," she said.

"How will her flying affect the interval?"

"She's putting in a lot of effort to fly, expending a lot of energy. It'll be a lot shorter."

"How much shorter?"

"I don't know."

"Guess."

"Ten minutes at most."

Niamh looked up. "Is that fucking Chopper Two?" Satie was coming down where we were.

I gave the USB key to Kahurangi. "You and Niamh get down to the generator and be ready."

He took the key. "Ready for what?" he yelled, as Chopper Two got louder around us.

"To send Bella back," I yelled. "We're going to go get her for you."

Kahurangi grinned. "You're mad and I love you."

He grabbed Niamh, showed them the key, and motioned toward the generator. They set off.

Satie hovered low enough for Aparna and me to get in, Aparna in the passenger area and me in the copilot seat. "I thought we agreed you were going to go back," I said to Satie, once I was strapped in and my headset connected.

"I decided I could wait to get into trouble," Satie said. "And then I noticed that when our Bella burped, she made a big hole. I wanted to see how big it was. I found out."

"You know what we're doing now, right?"

"I thought you'd never ask," Satie said.

"I haven't asked, yet."

"Sure you have, you just phrased it badly. Now, let's go chase down our lady. Dr. Chowdhury, we have about ten minutes, am I right?"

"Less than that now," Aparna said.

Satie swung us violently into the early morning, chasing Bella.

"She's not very fast," Satie observed as we came up on her, laboring in a northwesterly direction. She was heading in the direction we thought she would, toward Goose Bay.

"The air here isn't giving her a lot of support," Aparna said. "She's compensating with her airflow systems, but they're probably faltering, too. It's amazing she can fly at all."

"You're saying she could drop out of the air at any second," I said to Aparna.

"It wouldn't surprise me."

"That's no good," Satie said. "She's not going to be able to walk back to where we need her."

"What are you going to do?"

"Let me try being polite first," Satie said. He flew ahead of Bella and, once he had enough distance, turned and hovered in her path.

"Playing chicken is polite?" Aparna said, alarmed.

"As polite as we have time for," Satie said.

Bella flew directly at Chopper Two, tacking at the very last moment to avoid it. We were buffeted by the turbulence of her wings and airflow systems. Satie evened us out and went to follow Bella, who had resumed her northwesterly direction.

"So much for being nice," he said.

"You're not going to do what I think you're going to do," I said.

"I don't know what you think I'm going to do, but yes, probably," Satie said.

I looked back at Aparna. "You're strapped in, right?"

"I thought I was, but now I'm not sure," Aparna said.

I nodded. "That's the right attitude." I looked over to Satie. "All right, do it."

In the glow of the instruments, I could see Satie grin. He made Chopper Two climb in altitude, and then started a rapid descent toward Bella's head.

"Oh, I do not like this. I do not like this at all," Aparna declared.

"Yuuuup," I agreed. I was trying very hard not to wet myself.

Chopper Two came in hard on Bella's head, scraping the landing skids across it. At one point, it felt like one of the skids caught and that we would pitch forward and die, but then whatever the skid was caught on let go. Bella screamed at that.

"That got her attention," I said.

"Not enough," Satie said, and dropped Chopper Two directly in front of Bella's face, so the tail rotor was inches away from making contact.

From the screaming, I could tell this was enraging Bella. I looked up at the monitor to see the rear view.

"*Teeth*," I said, urgently.

"On it," Satie said, and we dived suddenly and in a very unsafe manner.

Bella followed, determined to make us pay for annoying her.

"She's not flying slow anymore," I said as I watched her gain on us, with what I hoped was not complete panic in my voice.

"How much more time, Dr. Chowdhury?" Satie asked.

"She's ready," Aparna said. "I'd be guessing any minute now."

The faint lights of the wrecked site were visible now.

"Your friends had better be ready," Satie said to me.

"They'll be ready," I promised. "Let's hope we can time this thing."

"Uh, folks," Aparna said. "Look at the monitor."

I looked. Bella was gaining on us, mouth open, screaming. From inside of her, there was an emerging glow.

"I think we're out of time," I said.

"Almost there," Satie said.

"Almost isn't gonna work right now," I assured him.

We cleared the trees to the site as Bella screamed and released her blast, which shot over the top of Chopper Two.

Satie dived and flew what felt like inches above the ground. Around us, the world turned golden. Behind us the world was dark in the monitor as Bella's blast tore up the ground, flinging earth and soil into the sky.

"Hang on," Satie said. He jerked us up just enough for Bella's breath to skip over the capacitor perimeter. A wide, brilliant wall of light flew aside Chopper Two. It was beautiful, and close enough that I could almost reach out and touch it. It would kill me if I did so.

We passed the other side of the perimeter and the beam shut off. In front of us, large trees were coming up impossibly fast. Aparna and I screamed. Satie pulled up just in time and then hovered over the treetops. He turned Chopper Two around.

Bella and her eggs were gone.

And not just gone.

It was like they had never been there at all.

I stared at the place where Bella wasn't. "It worked," I said. "We did it."

"Look," Aparna said, pointing. Kahurangi and Niamh were running toward the perimeter, awkwardly, packs in tow.

"Nice shooting," I said to them, once they were in Chopper Two, strapped and with headsets on.

"You didn't tell us you were coming in right over the damn treetops," Niamh said. "I barely had time to signal Kahurangi. We almost missed it."

"Yeah, but you didn't."

"How did you get her to follow you?" Kahurangi asked.

"We enraged her," Aparna said.

Kahurangi nodded. "That sounds about right."

"Let's hope kaiju don't have good memories," Satie said. "Otherwise life is going to be very uncomfortable for Chopper Two when we get back."

"Do you think she's safe?" I asked Aparna. "Bella, I mean. There wasn't a lot of time between her intervals."

"I don't know," Aparna said. "I think so. But I don't know. What I do know is that she has a chance now that she's back where she belongs. She didn't have one here."

"We did our job," Kahurangi said. "We preserved a kaiju."

"Maybe," Aparna amended.

"I think *maybe* counts this time."

"What happened to that asshole Sanders?" Niamh asked me.

"The same thing that happened to everyone else here," I said. "Just on the other side of the barrier."

We landed at Canadian Forces Base Goose Bay at five a.m. and with Chopper Two flying on literal fumes. Because we were entirely unscheduled and appeared as if from nowhere, with no itinerary, we were welcomed by an impressive array of Canadian military.

"That's nice," Niamh said, eyeing the layout of military. "How are Canadian military prisons? Asking for a friend."

"You're not going to prison," Satie said.

"What are we going to tell them?" Aparna asked.

Satie looked back at her. "*You* aren't going to tell them anything. None of you are. You're going to leave this to me."

"Happy to," Kahurangi said. "But why are they going to listen to you?"

"Because of who I am," Satie said.

"It matters to them that you're a pilot?"

"He also has a doctorate," I said.

"They won't care that I'm either of those," Satie said. "They *will* care that I'm a colonel in the Royal Canadian Air Force."

"Which means what to them?" I asked.

"Among other things, it means I outrank the base commander here."

"Look at you," Niamh said, admiringly. "Slumming all this time."

"Not slumming," Satie said. "Official Canadian liaison to the KPS. You can ask MacDonald and Danso when you get back."

"So why do you fly Chopper Two?" I asked.

"I fly Chopper Two because being a liaison is *boring,*" Satie said. "This is much more fun. Now, you all stay in here and shut up. Let me do my thing." He got out of the chopper and went to talk to the soldier in charge. He reached into his pocket and pulled out his wallet, took out a card.

He showed it to the soldier.

The soldier saluted Satie.

So did the rest of them.

CHAPTER 28

We did not have to go to Canadian military prison. Or any prison, for that matter.

We didn't go back to Tanaka Base right away, either.

First, because we couldn't; the gateway at Honda Base was still down and would be down for the full length of time. Satie—Colonel Satie, I should say—had relayed the information to the crew of the *Shobijin,* who forwarded it back to base, albeit waiting for him to go through the barrier in Chopper Two before they did so. As soon as he made it through, the *Shobijin* hightailed it out of the area.

This was a good thing, because once Bella came back through, she set fire to most of the surrounding jungle. For a week, it was unclear whether she would be able to restore her internal function and her complement of parasites. Then she settled back in, splashed out a final clutch of eggs, and brooded for several more weeks.

She survived. We had, indeed, preserved her.

The second reason we didn't go back right away was because KPS had to investigate the incident, and we were the star witnesses. After we left CFB Goose Bay, we spent two weeks in a St. John's hotel, having Zoom meetings with KPS higher-ups and various other stakeholders, explaining what Rob Sanders had done and why, and how it related to Tensorial, his family's company, and its predecessors. We were backed up on this by Dave Berg, a.k.a. Dave-barely-above-an-intern, who survived thanks largely to being unconscious and sprayed with kaiju pheromones. All things considered, he forgave Niamh for the zapping.

The new information about the destruction of the first Tanaka Base, it turned out, had not come as a complete surprise to the folks at KPS. There had always been a suspicion that the Sanders family had not been entirely forthcoming. The information, however, appeared to come as a surprise to the representative from the U.S. Department of Energy. It's possible the representative had other things on his mind; the United States election had happened, without a rogue nuclear explosion to derail it, and this fellow would likely be out of a job in a couple of months. He seemed willing to let KPS handle it however they liked.

KPS handled it by doing what it does—by having the event not officially exist.

The mission to bring Bella over stuck with its official cover story of being a group of scientists trying a new method of radio interferometry.

Which went horribly wrong.

And exploded.

As radio interferometry projects sometimes do.

"They do *not*," Niamh had protested, as they were an astrophysicist. But they were overruled.

As for the tech billionaire Rob Sanders, who had funded the project out of his passion for science and knowledge, it was assumed he was killed in the explosion and his body predated before it could be retrieved, possibly by Labrador wolves.

"Labrador wolves?" Kahurangi had asked. "Are those a real thing?"

"Oh, yes," Aparna had assured him.

While Tensorial could not officially be held accountable for Sanders's activities, or the activities of the company involving KPS over the years, at the turn of the U.S. government in January, the Department of Justice announced that Tensorial and its past and current CEOs, all members of the Sanders family, were being investigated for a decades-long pattern of fraud involving the Departments of Energy and Defense, among others. It would be a long and uncomfortable process for the company.

Which, well. Good.

While we were away, Tanaka Base held its memorials for those it had lost from Sanders's taking of Bella. The official cover story given to family and survivors was close enough to the truth: While doing research on the animals they were tasked with protecting, they were ambushed by poachers and killed. KPS's survivor benefits were always generous, and its grief at the loss sincere.

We learned that everyone at Tanaka Base held their breaths until they learned whether Aparna, Kahurangi, Niamh, Martin Satie, and I had survived. When they learned we had, they collectively celebrated, and swore to murder us for making them worry.

They did not murder us when we returned. Instead, they declared a holiday. One whole day of partying and feasting and drinking and karaoke.

Then we went back to work. Aparna to the bio lab, Kahurangi to the chem lab, Niamh to physics, and Satie to—well, in the short term, to doing not a whole lot, because getting a whole helicopter back to Kaiju Earth was an actual project, but then, back to flying.

I went back to lifting things.

MacDonald had offered me Tom's job on a temporary basis, with an eye toward making it permanent. I passed. I didn't feel right slipping into his place, and also, I had already forced Val to do a two-person job by herself for several weeks. And anyway, I liked my job. Lifting things was surprisingly good for my brain.

So I kept doing it, without undue drama, for the rest of the tour.

Which, frankly, felt odd. After such a dramatic start to our tour, everything else after we came back to Tanaka Base felt like an anticlimax. "I keep waiting for the other shoe to drop," Niamh said, and we all agreed with them.

But the shoe stayed up. Until the day, in March, when we stood in aloha shirts, drinks in hand, to welcome Blue Team back to Tanaka Base, and for them to see us off.

As was custom, I left a welcoming gift for whichever member of Blue Team was taking over my room, and a note.

Dear whomever:
  If it's your first time here, welcome. If it's more than your first time here, welcome back. When I arrived six months and forever ago, I was given a gift of a plant. I am giving you the same gift.

It's larger than when I got it, and has been repotted. You may need to repot it again before you gift it onward.

This plant was given to me by someone who was leaving this world behind for good. She said that it was time for her to go back to the real world. I understand what she meant—this world is so strange!—but I think it's just as real as the other one. This plant is real. The people here are real. The bonds and friendships we make here are real, too. It's unreal how real this world is and can be.

This plant is yours, but I will be back. And when I come back, I hope I get to meet you, and have a meal with you, and sing karaoke with you, and talk about plants, and perhaps become friends. I can't wait to meet you.

Until then—be kind to our plant.

Jamie Gray

Aparna, Kahurangi, Niamh, and I said goodbye at BMI, which was not quite as deserted as it had been when we left. Vaccines had started to roll out and people, maybe too optimistically, had started to travel again. Aparna was heading to Los Angeles and to family there. Kahurangi was heading to New Zealand and Niamh to Ireland, where both faced a couple of weeks of isolation before seeing friends and family.

"I'm looking forward to that," Niamh had said. "Two weeks of sleeping, eating room service, and screaming at the news." We all hugged and promised to stay in contact through the KPS Gold Team Discord channel.

The last KPS person I saw before I headed off was Brynn Mac-Donald, who waved to me and told me to keep a lookout for a new assistant for her. "We can't replace Tom," she said. "But I still need someone to do that job." I promised I would.

Then I was back home, in my terrible East Village apartment, which actually wasn't as terrible as I remembered it, with Brent and Laertes.

"We missed you," Brent said.

"I liked the quiet," Laertes yelled, from the other room, where he was playing a video game.

"Have you even moved from that room since I've been gone?" I yelled back.

"It's called *quarantine*, Jamie, maybe you should look into it."

"He has left the room," Brent assured me.

"I poop occasionally," Laertes said.

"I've missed this," I said, sincerely.

Brent grinned. "Well, good," he said. "We've ordered Thai, and it'll be here soon. And in the meantime, I can catch you up on the last six months."

"Do I really want to know?" I asked.

Brent moved his hand in a seesaw fashion.

There was a knock on the door.

"That was quick," Brent said, and started to get up.

I motioned him back down. "I'll get it," I said. "I have money for a cash tip."

"Lord our poverty over us, moneybags," Laertes yelled.

"I love you, too," I said, put my mask back on, and went to answer the door.

"Pad thai, tom kha gai soup, and oh my god it's Jamie Gray," said the delivery person at the door.

I looked more closely. "Qanisha Williams?" I said.

"Oh my god, Jamie," Qanisha said. She set down the food and reached out a hand to me, then remembered that it was still infectious times and drew back. "I'm *so* sorry. Last March. When you were fired. I didn't tell you. I should have warned you. But I didn't. I was afraid. I'm so sorry."

"It's all right," I said. "I know what happened. About what Rob Sanders did. That one-dollar bet he made you take."

"He made me pay him that dollar, too," Qanisha said. "Can you believe it?"

"I can," I assured her.

"Did you hear? About Rob?"

"I did."

"They think he was eaten by *wolves*," Qanisha said. "How weird is that?"

"It could have been weirder," I suggested.

"I don't know how."

"How are you doing anyway, Qanisha?" I asked.

"Well, you know." She motioned up and down. "*This* is how I'm doing. After Rob sold füdmüd, the new owners laid everyone off. They didn't want the company or the people, they just wanted the user list. And then it was a pandemic, and there were no jobs, and this was what there was."

"I get it," I said. "I've been there."

Qanisha smiled, but then looked miserable. "I don't know, maybe this is karmic justice, right? I was so scared of losing my job that I let Rob do something shitty to you and those other people. And then I lost my job anyway, and here I am"—she waved down at the food— "delivering your pad thai."

"It's not karmic justice," I said. "It's just bad people and bad luck. It could have happened to anyone."

"Yes, well, this time it happened to me." Qanisha smiled again. "Anyway. Nice to see you, Jamie." She turned to go.

"Hold on," I said, reaching for my wallet.

"Oh, no tip," Qanisha said. "I couldn't take a tip. Not from you. Not after what I did."

"It's not a tip," I said, and handed her a business card.

She took it and looked at it doubtfully. "What is this?"

"The organization I work for has a job opening," I said. "I think you'd be perfect for it."

AUTHOR'S NOTE AND
ACKNOWLEDGMENTS

I started 2020 with the plan to write a novel beginning in March, after I returned from a vacation with friends. This novel, the one you're reading now, was written in February and March of 2021.

So what happened to that novel I was going to write in March 2020?

Well, perhaps not surprisingly, 2020 happened to it.

I probably don't have to remind you how 2020 was, but in case you've blocked it entirely: pandemic and protests and fires and elections and venality and isolation and awfulness all the way through. Plus in November and December, I was sick with something that I was sure was COVID but all the tests told me it wasn't. Whatever it was, it turned my brain into pudding, and I literally couldn't think a thought more complex than "I like cheese" for about a month.

Through all of this I was supposed to be writing that novel, a novel which was meant to be dark, heavy, complex, and broodingly ambitious—in other words, *not* the perfect novel to be writing when the world is falling apart around you.

I *did* write in that novel, nevertheless: tens of thousands of words that made sense on the sentence and paragraph level, but didn't do particularly well as chapters and certainly not as an overarching story. It was a novel that demanded focus, and focus, it turns out, was hard for me in 2020.

But then 2021 happened! New year! New start! Fresh ambition! After my illness at the end of the year my head finally felt clear enough to connect things together again. I started writing again on January 4, did a few hundred words to rev up, did a few more on January 5, and then January 6 happened, and, well. Insurrections really are focus pullers. I didn't know that before! I didn't *have* to know that before. But I know it now. That was January done, in terms of being able to write.

Finally, two weeks after the inauguration of a new president, and with the old one safely shoved into Florida to yell at clouds, I tried again. I wrote thirty-four hundred words in a day, *good* words, words that actually made sense as sentences and part of a larger, overarching novel structure. It felt good. *I* felt good. I was on my way with this book. I closed up my work and was eager to start again the next day.

The next day, I came back to my computer and couldn't find the pages I'd written the day before.

For the first time in years, my computer ate my work. In a world of autosaving word processors and documents automatically sent to the cloud, I thought it was basically impossible to lose a file, especially one that I manually saved, *fucking twice,* before I closed out the document.

But here I was, and three thousand four hundred words—good words, words I liked—were just gone.

And it was at that moment that I had what you might call an epiphany: I was done writing that novel.

It wasn't those three thousand four hundred words, per se. I could replace those words in a day and move on. It was everything else about this particular novel, and my struggle to write it in what was, on a global scale, the worst year I'd ever encountered in my life. It was the wrong novel in the wrong year, and at that point I hated it, and also I hated how it had been making me feel for a better part of a year, as I tried to piece it together in a world where everything was flying apart, and I felt I had to be witness to all of it.

I needed to stop writing that novel.

Which was a problem because that novel was under contract and was due, uuuhhhhh, like, *right now.* And also a problem because over the years I had developed a reputation for being pretty reliable—if you gave me a deadline, I would hit it. I might turn the manuscript in at seven a.m. on the last possible morning it could get in in order for production to get it out in time, but it would still be there.

This time, I wasn't just missing the deadline, I was blowing it up entirely. The book I was writing was *on the schedule*. Cover art was already being mocked up. Marketing was already making a plan for it. And here I was saying, "Nope, done, bye."

This was, shall we say, a moment of professional existential crisis. Who was I as an author, if I was not reliable?

At that point, I had two thoughts. The first was the concept of the sunk cost fallacy, in which people keep doing things, even when they should stop, because they've already invested so much time and effort in it and they don't want that time and effort "to go to waste." The second was a quote by video game designer Shigeru Miyamoto, in reference to games, but applicable in many fields, including writing: "A delayed game is eventually good. A bad game is bad forever." Meaning, to me, that sometimes it's better to stop and reassess and correct, than it is to just keep plugging ahead out of fear (and deadlines). "Reliable" is not an excuse for "bad."

So I sent my editor, Patrick Nielsen Hayden, an email, explaining why I couldn't write that novel anymore. It was probably the most difficult professional email I've sent (to date anyway). It's up to Patrick to tell his side of that email exchange, but I can say he was sympathetic and understanding. Twenty twenty was a year, y'all. That novel was taken off the schedule, and we would figure out where we would go from there.

Just like that, I didn't have to do that novel anymore. All the mental energy—and angst—that was tied up in it over the course of the better part of a year was suddenly and finally swept off the table.

I felt . . . relief! And I felt happy.

That's when my brain said, *Oh, hey, we're not thinking about that old thing anymore? Because I have this other thing that I was playing with when you weren't looking AND HERE IS THE WHOLE THING kthxbye*

Then the entire plot and concept of *The Kaiju Preservation Society* dropped into my head, all at once.

And thus, literally one day after I sent my editor an email that basically said, "I can't write this novel I am full of angst and pain what even is my career anymore," I sent him another email that was, "Oh, hey, never mind I have this new idea it's really cool and you'll have it in March."

Writers. I mean, seriously.

As a writer I feel grateful to *this* novel, because writing it was restorative. *KPS* is not, and I say this with *absolutely* no slight intended, a brooding symphony of a novel. It's a pop song. It's meant to be light and catchy, with three minutes of hooks and choruses for you to sing along with, and then you're done and you go on with your day, hopefully with a smile on your face. I had *fun* writing this, and I *needed* to have fun writing this. We all need a pop song from time to time, particularly after a stretch of darkness.

What about that other novel? you ask. *Will you ever come back to it?* You know what, I might. The *idea* of it is good, and in the future, if my brain is in the right place, and the world is in the right place, I might come back to it. It deserved my full attention, which I wasn't able to give. When I can give it that, I may try again. I'll let you know.

In the meantime, you have this novel: the right novel at the right time for me. It reminded me that I like writing novels and sharing them with you all. For that alone, I'm glad it exists, and that it's in your hands.

With that as preamble, it's time for acknowledgments:

First and most obviously, thank you to Patrick, my editor, literally without whom this book would not exist. A good editor doesn't merely look at words, he looks at the author as well. I appreciate that Patrick sees me, and gets me, and encouraged me in ways I needed to be encouraged in order to get myself back on track.

Thanks also to the entire team at Tor who helped with this book: Molly McGhee, Rachel Bass, copy editors Sara and Chris with ScriptAcuity Studio, Peter Lutjen, Heather Saunders, and Jeff LaSala.

I want to give an extra shout-out to Alexis Saarela, my publicist at Tor, not for this book (although I'm sure she'll do great with it), but because the last Tor book of mine, *The Last Emperox*, came out just as COVID was getting into full swing and all my tour dates were canceled because the entire world shut down. In the space of what felt like days, Alexis and the rest of the PR folks at Tor retooled the entire tour to be online and virtual. It was a huge effort, and it worked—the audiences for the events were great, and the book became a bestseller. I want to be sure she and all the people in Tor's PR department know that I appreciate the work they did for me, and for all of Tor's other authors, in a really difficult time.

Thanks also to Steve Feldberg and his team at Audible for the work they do on the audio versions of my books. In the UK, much respect and thanks to Bella Pagan and Georgia Summers, and the whole team at Tor UK.

And of course, thanks to my agents Ethan Ellenberg, Bibi Lewis, and Ezra Ellenberg, who sell me in the U.S. and overseas. Thanks also to Matthew Sugarman and Joel Gotler for their work on the film/TV side of things.

During 2020, I found it difficult to write for reasons I've already noted above, and in December, I thought maybe if I came at creative things sideways, I might restart my engines. So I wrote out an idea for a holiday-themed song, called "Another Christmas," and called on my friend, musician Matthew Ryan, to see if he might be interested in collaborating with me on it. He was. The resulting song was a real mood-lifter for me in a dark season, and reminded me that indeed, I could still make things. I thank him, and will cherish our song always.

And as always, thank you to my family—my daughter, Athena, who is becoming a fantastic writer in her own right, and my wife, Kristine. Krissy had to watch me struggle through trying to write that earlier novel in 2020, and I know it was difficult for her to see me not quite make it work, because she was concerned for me and because she knows that this is usually a thing I can do well. It's never great to see your spouse struggle with their work.

But through it all she was terrific and supportive, because she's a great spouse, and also, pretty much the best person I know. And when I chucked the other novel over the side and started writing *KPS,* she was cheering me along and reading the chapters as I went and always asking for the next one, which I was always happy to give her. I've said before that she is the reason you have books from me at all. It's even more the case with this one. I really do owe everything to her.

One more: Thank *you.* I'm happy you're reading me.

Finally, here's a fun fact: I finished writing this book on the day the events in the book come to a close. I didn't plan that. But it's cool that it happened.

—John Scalzi
March 20, 2021